18/25.

The Secret of the Lake

The Secret of the Lake

D. H. Ryden

The Secret of the Lake
D. H. Ryden

Published by Aspect Design, 2019

Designed, printed and bound by Aspect Design
89 Newtown Road, Malvern, Worcs. WR14 1PD
United Kingdom
Tel: 01684 561567
E-mail: allan@aspect-design.net
Website: www.aspect-design.net

All Rights Reserved.

Copyright © 2019 D. H. Ryden

D. H. Ryden has asserted his moral right
to be identified as the author of this work.

The right of D. H. Ryden to be identified as the author
of this work has been asserted in accordance with
Section 77 of the Copyright, Designs and Patents Act 1988.

The characters and events in this publication are fictitious and any
resemblance to real persons, living or dead, is purely coincidental.

This book is sold subject to the condition that it shall not, by
way of trade or otherwise, be lent, resold, hired out or otherwise
circulated without the publisher's prior consent in any form of
binding or cover other than that in which it is published and
without a similar condition including this condition being imposed
on the subsequent purchaser.

A copy of this book has been deposited
with the British Library Board

Cover Design Copyright © 2019 Aspect Design
Original photograph by Orla

ISBN 978-1-912078-82-0

To my wife, Carol,
with many thanks for her encouragement
and literary criticism

PART ONE

PROLOGUE
Évian-les-Bains, France, May 1917

What brings one to the point where each day seems harder to bear than the one before?

I have struggled in my mind to try and understand, but always seem overcome by a feeling of intense dread that evil events have rendered me powerless to overcome – with the resultant effect that my very spirit seems broken in two under these malign influences.

Putting on my coat I silently descend the stairs, the household asleep. The chill of the night air hits me, causing an initial shiver, but I purposefully stride into town, the letter in my pocket. Within a quarter of an hour I reach the Dumont residence, a large villa along a tree-lined drive. I check to see that there are no lights visible, and yet I am still fearing discovery as I make my way to the door and post my letter to Felix then retreat quickly back to the road. What agony will he feel upon opening the letter? My resolve wavers momentarily at the thought, and then returns as I follow the road down to the lake.

I will have to hurry, for already the first signs of that hour before dawn are becoming apparent, despite the mist that still hangs over the lake. Before long the first workmen will be abroad, and I have no desire to be seen.

Thankfully, I finally reach the fishermen's huts, the small

dinghies just visible through the mist, beached on the shore. Although I am no swimmer my final moments may result in a frenzy of self-preservation, so I take the precaution of filling my coat pockets with some of the small rocks that are scattered nearby. They will surely have the desired effect of taking me down below the waves.

Unafraid now, I push one of the small boats down onto the lake, scrambling in as it eases away from the shore. Picking up the oars I strike out, the boat now moving at some speed despite my lack of finesse as an oarsman. The mist clings over the water, enveloping me in its cold caress, but on I row, one thing only now on my mind.

Finally, having travelled what seems some few hundred metres from the shore, I set down my oars. The only sound audible is the ghostly rattling of the rigging on the sailing boats moored somewhere nearby. No other earthly thing can be seen or heard. Whether it is the mist now penetrating, like so many daggers, through my coat that causes me to shiver violently, or the knowledge of what is to come, I am unsure.

Voices of loved ones, in broken fragments, like so many pieces of shattered porcelain, seem to assail me from all sides, as if willing me to return. But my resolve has now strengthened, and I bid them all a silent adieu.

I become aware of Papa's voice beckoning to me as I slide over the side of the boat, to be engulfed by the deep, still, silent waters of the lake. My fear dissipates, replaced by a feeling of calm, as I sink lower, the weight of my now-sodden clothing pulling me down into the lake's cold embrace.

I have finally found release.

CHAPTER ONE
Fulham – Spring 1968

The telephone rang just as I finished a leisurely Sunday evening supper in the kitchen of my mews cottage in Fulham. I had become accustomed to eating alone in this manner on most Sundays since moving into the cottage, and usually accompanied the meal with one of my favourite albums, selected from my collection. The Stones album *Aftermath*, its lyrics promulgating contempt for the status quo and liberally interspersed with misogynistic 'bad boy' themes, clearly audible in the background on my hi-fi, seemed to suit my current mood of mild dissatisfaction with life in general. After yet another weekend spent making up the numbers at the latest dinner party given by well-meaning friends (always, these days it seemed, married couples), hoping that the girl they produced on this occasion might engender a spark of romance. Alas to no avail.

There had been previous romantic interludes in my life, though the initial frisson I felt on that first meeting had generally been short-lived. Currently I was being introduced in this way to various eligible young women, their demeanour indicating at once that they came from 'suitable families'. During initial conversation it often transpired that their fathers were landowners or 'something in the City'. Their days were passed invariably working in an art gallery or one of the major auction houses, a position often made possible through family connections.

Evenings were for partying in the shared flats they occupied in London thanks to a benevolent parent; sometimes visiting the latest exhibition at a friend's gallery, where the works of their most recent discovery would be on show. Here the latest gossip would be avidly exchanged, champagne flutes in hand, the paintings or sculpture forming merely a backdrop to the gathering, and afforded only the occasional cursory glance or comment.

Eventually the majority, on finding a suitable partner, would settle down and join the ranks of their married peers.

Of late, as I approached thirty, I had begun to seriously question the future direction of my life. I had embarked some time ago on my legal career, initially as an articled clerk, and now, my academic qualifications completed and consigned to recent history, I was a young, hard-working solicitor. With an increasing client base, I anticipated that I might soon be offered a junior partnership with the city firm of Davies and Walker, my current employers.

Debating whether to answer the phone, I lingered in the hallway, but finally decided that as my solitude had now been interrupted, I should no longer ignore the insistent ringing. As soon as I picked up the receiver the operator asked me to wait while the connection was made, which indicated that this was a long distance call.

It took me a few seconds to recognise the caller, his voice at first just above a whisper. But then there was no mistaking the Gallic tones of Gaston, the Savoyard fisherman, an old friend of my uncle Felix, no doubt calling from his home town of Evian-les-Bains, France. This famous spa resort, on the southern shores of Lac Leman, always drew a chic clientele to its hotels and casino during the summer months. The majestic Alps, which created a natural backdrop to the town, also attracted many visitors, novice and expert alike, to participate in winter sports in the mountain villages nearby.

'M'sieur Jean, you must come quickly – your uncle is very ill and may not last the week,' he rasped in his strong regional accent, exacerbated by a lifetime's addiction to Gauloises Caporal cigarettes.

Reverting to his native French tongue I questioned him further.

'Gaston, can you tell me what happened?'

'Yes, M'sieur Jean. We were conversing in his garden this afternoon as I was tending to the weeds in the potager. He was sitting on the iron bench nearby, when I suddenly realised that he hadn't replied to my question. Repeating it again I looked towards him and saw something was wrong. Rushing over, I could see at once that he seemed unable to speak, and appeared to have suffered from some form of stroke. Telling him that I would get help I went indoors and phoned the doctor, who was fortunately at home and able to come round at once. He immediately called an ambulance and had Felix admitted to the hospital here in Evian.'

'What did the doctor say about his condition?' I asked, the shock of this news now finally registering in my mind.

'M'sieur Jean, he was clearly concerned that such a stroke may prove too much for him. The next few days will be critical.'

My uncle had always seemed to me rather delicate, perhaps accentuated by his right leg suffering a deformity from birth, a club foot. Despite the best efforts of the medical profession at the turn of the century it had never been successfully cured, leaving him with an awkward gait which had become more pronounced in his declining years.

Gaston's message certainly shocked me, as Felix had not given me any cause for concern on the last two or three occasions we had spoken on the telephone, but being the elder sibling to my mother he must now be in his early seventies.

Thinking over the situation quickly, I replied. 'Gaston, I'll set out tomorrow and hope to arrive in Evian on Tuesday. I'll phone you on my arrival.'

'I'll be here waiting for you, M'sieur Jean.'

'Thank you, Gaston. A bientôt.'

Having finished the call, I climbed the stairs to my living room. With Gaston's words still in my mind, I reached for the packet of Gitanes on the coffee table, and lit one before slumping in an armchair to try and make more sense of the news. Stirring up as it did memories of my late mother's last illness, I certainly could not ignore this call, as Uncle Felix had been a major figure throughout my life and was, leaving aside my father, my nearest living relative. As if to dismiss any doubts about this I glanced up at the framed photograph on the mantelpiece, Felix, my mother and me in happier times, on the promenade by Lac Leman.

My thoughts now returned to Gaston's sense of urgency which had initially struck me as being perhaps excessive. Particularly so when I recalled his myriad stories of travels and adventures he had undertaken whilst a young man. These had been told to me when I had stayed with my uncle as a boy, and even to my young ears at that time had often seemed incredible, almost improbable. But the doctor seemed to confirm the seriousness of the situation and on the basis of this I concluded that I must make the journey to France.

I now had to arrange matters in London then decide how best to make my travel arrangements. I made a call to my firm's senior partner, Gerald Walker, who, apart from being my employer was an old friend of my parents.

'Gerald, it's Jean Dawson. I'm sorry to disturb you at home, but I've just received some bad news. My uncle Felix has been rushed to hospital, having suffered a stroke. As his nearest relation I feel I must go to France at once.'

'Yes, Jean, I understand. I'm sorry to hear this, and hope he recovers soon. Your parents often mentioned him to me, and I can quite see your concern. I suggest that you take a week's leave, which can be extended if necessary, of course. We can cover matters during your absence, I'm sure.'

'Thank you, Gerald. I'll let you know how things are once I've seen my uncle.'

I worked closely with Gerald, who was more formally addressed by junior staff and me, whilst at the office, as Mr Walker. He had effectively been my mentor in the firm since my early days as an articled clerk. He was the person I turned to where clarification was needed on some obscure point of law, or how best to satisfy the particular foibles of an old-established client, to ensure that matters were handled fully in accordance with their wishes. He had a clear picture of my current workload, and with the assistance of Miss Nugent, his secretary, I foresaw no problems at present.

I hesitated before calling Daniel, my father. We had become somewhat estranged since his divorce from my mother some years before, and visits had dwindled over time. The divorce was the result of a number of infidelities on which he had embarked, and finally, with the added complication of a child on the way, matters could not be dismissed. He had gone on to marry Estelle, and start a new young family.

It being a Sunday afternoon I found him at home when I rang.

'Hello, Pa, how are you all? Well, I hope.'

'Yes, thanks for asking. Estelle is amusing the children in the kitchen, helping them with their painting. Jean, it seems an age since we last spoke, all is well, I hope?'

'Actually no. I've just had a call from Gaston in France with some worrying news of Felix. It appears that he's suffered a stroke and been admitted to hospital, so I intend to go over to France tomorrow.'

'Of course, I can understand your wish to see him,' Daniel replied. 'If there is anything I can do, please let me know.'

'I'll call you once I've seen Felix, Pa. At present I've only got the doctor's opinion relayed through Gaston as to his condition, which I must say does not seem to bode well.'

'So let's hope things aren't too serious, Jean. Perhaps you can visit us when you return from France. The family will be pleased to see you, I know.'

'Yes, it has been a while, I suppose. I'll arrange something on my return.'

Experience over the years in my regular visits to Felix in Evian, firstly as an eager schoolboy in the company of my parents, and latterly alone, as his sole nephew, led me to think that whereas flying from London may save some hours, the overall journey would be more comfortable using the boat train to Paris. I could then complete the journey the following day, again by rail, to Evian. This would also give me an opportunity to meet up with Michael, an old friend from my schooldays, who was now resident in Paris. I dismissed any thoughts of taking the MG as it was better suited to a more leisurely drive in the warmer summer months.

So the next morning, Monday, saw me travelling by taxi to Victoria rail terminus where I was to board the Golden Arrow on the morning departure to Dover.

CHAPTER TWO
Paris – Monday Evening

I arrived, greeted by a seasonal April shower, at Paris Gare du Nord, late on Monday afternoon. It had been an uneventful sea crossing during which I had occupied myself reading the newspapers. I had decided to eat a light lunch on board the ferry, afterwards somewhat regretting the meal – its appearance and taste had brought back to me memories of school dinners from a decade or so earlier. I had fortunately washed this down with a glass of strong ale, which served to mask the after-taste so often associated with mass catering.

The shower having now abated, a stroll in the warm sunshine reminded me why this city, always so full of promise at this time of year, had inspired poets and songsmiths through the ages. After ten minutes I had arrived outside my hotel in Rue La Fayette. I was as usual shocked when observing the numerous dents in Parisian cars, the result of an aggressive parking culture, which only served to reinforce the sagacity of my decision to leave my MG at home.

I had telephoned the hotel from the station at Paris Nord, and they confirmed that a room would be available for an overnight stay. The hotel, situated in a busy street, lined predominantly with shops and small offices at street level and apartments on the upper floors, was in a block of typical Parisian buildings: six floors topped with a dark-grey, weathered zinc mansard roof, which housed the attic rooms.

The hotel was of a basic tourist class, where I had stayed occasionally on previous visits to Paris. A few minutes were spent to complete the necessary formalities in the modest reception area; my personal details were entered in the hotel register and passport left with the manager, after which I was given the key to my room.

Having taken the rather antiquated lift up to my room on the fourth floor I busied myself for a while, unpacking and putting the contents of my small suitcase into an ancient armoire, at the same time deciding what to wear for the train journey to Evian the following morning.

I tried Michael's number again from my room, having previously been unable to make contact. He was at home now, and we arranged to meet in a couple of hours at his apartment off Place St Pierre. I agreed with his suggestion that we could go on to visit one of the bistros in the locality, for a drink and a meal, and an opportunity to exchange the latest news.

Having some time to myself before setting out I recalled that it must be four, or maybe five years since I last stayed at this hotel, a time before my mother's illness had become apparent and cast its long shadows over those close to her.

That last visit had been towards the end of my student days, when I was busy preparing for my final law exams, at that time still being articled to Gerald Walker. Thinking back to that last stay in Paris I recalled a conversation with a down-and-out Frenchman I had met as I walked from the Metro at Pont Neuf to cross the bridge to L'Ile de la Cité.

He had presumably singled me out as a tourist, greeting me with 'You are English, M'sieur?' to which I responded in English, and not in French, as I was interested to hear what he had to say – no doubt a request for a cigarette or a franc or two. As I expected he began by asking how well I knew Paris, presumably with a view to offering his service as a guide, but after I told him that I had visited many times, this course was then abandoned.

He then changed the subject, proceeding to tell me about his time in the French army in Algeria during the recent war for independence.

'They were bloody times, M'sieur. There were many executions carried out, and the torture of suspects to obtain information. I have seen terrible atrocities carried out by both sides, the French army as well as the nationalist FLN. Several of my comrades were killed in the fighting. It is not a chapter of my life that I would want to return to. Towards the end of the seven years of war the OAS was formed, with the avowed intention of keeping Algeria part of France, but their campaign of terror, including attempts on the life of the President, was short-lived. So when the end finally came it saw a million or so white settlers, *les pieds-noir*, returning to France; their future options in Algeria seen as either 'the suitcase or the coffin'. No, M'sieur, I would not wish to revisit those times.'

I then rather surprised him by continuing our conversation in French, mentioning how independence for Algeria had finally become a reality following the Evian Accords signed in 1962. I added further, that the mayor of Evian, Camille Blanc, had been killed by an OAS bomb planted outside his hotel in the previous year, after he had accepted to host the negotiations in the town.

He congratulated me on my mastery of the French language and knowledge of French affairs. He showed surprise that a young Englishman should have any interest in such matters, at which point I had to explain that I had family connections. My mother being French, and married to an Englishman, she had encouraged her native tongue to be used at home following my parents' move to London. I then offered my pack of Gitanes to him, from which he took two, thanking me, and adding, 'perhaps one for later.'

He then went on to explain how life had been difficult for him since he had left the army, how he had struggled to find regular employment – no doubt, I thought, made more difficult by his general appearance, coupled with the strong smell of alcohol so apparent as soon as he opened his mouth.

The inevitable request for the price of a coffee was gladly met, despite my student's budget. No doubt life had become a struggle for many ex-soldiers like him, once they had left behind the ordered environment of the military. Now back in the wider world, and perhaps lacking any familial support, some, like him, had turned to cheap alcohol for solace, paid for by begging a few francs from tourists.

Glancing at my watch I realised that I must have been reminiscing for quite some time, and should now be making my way to meet Michael. Encouraged by the warmth of the early evening sun as I left the hotel, I decided a walk would be more pleasant – and probably quicker than the Metro, which I calculated would involve at least two changes of line with the inevitable time spent waiting for the next connection on what was otherwise a short journey.

Within no time I had reached Place St Pierre, which already thronged with tourists and residents alike. The carousel was there, as it had been for decades past, with its gaudily painted horses, adding strains of music to the background of conversations being carried out in so many languages. The Basilica of Sacre Coeur stood above us, dominating the skyline of the heights of Montmartre.

Michael's apartment was approached from a small

courtyard, entered through an ancient timber gateway in one of the narrow streets radiating from the square. The building itself was fiercely managed by an elderly concierge, Ange, who had clearly not turned out in her nature as her name may have suggested. By some miraculous personal form of radar she always seemed to be found seated in the entrance lobby, walking stick in hand, ready to challenge any visitor, and, even on occasion, the residents themselves. But I had come prepared. Having met Ange on previous visits I was aware of her one weakness – a particular brand of chocolate – so had acquired the necessary article at the chocolatier adjacent to my hotel before I made my way to the square.

I found Ange seated in her usual position on my arrival, but she recognised me, and hurriedly pushing off her cat from her lap with a 'Va t'on, Minette', then performing a quick adjustment to her pinafore over her ample, dumpy body before brushing her hair with her hand, she was now ready to exchange greetings.

'Ah, bonjour, Monsieur Dawson, ça va?'

'I'm well, thank you, but I've come to France to visit my uncle, who is in hospital, Madame' I replied to her enquiry.

'Oh, I do hope he can soon return home. Please convey my good wishes.'

She then went into raptures of delight on receiving my small gift, uttering, 'Monsieur Dawson, you are too kind, you should not . . .' and she was happy to confirm that Michael was at home if I would care to go up to his apartment.

'Jean, I'm so pleased to see you!' exclaimed Michael as he opened the door, and shook my hand, adding 'Although I'm sorry to hear that your uncle's ill health is the reason that's brought you to France. I do hope that he'll soon recover sufficiently to return home. But, please, don't stand on the doorstep, do come in.'

'Thanks for your concern, Michael. At present I only have the doctor's opinion passed on by Gaston about my uncle's condition. So it's all rather vague at the moment, until I can see him at the hospital tomorrow.'

'Well, let's hope you see signs of improvement. I still remember those holidays we both spent with your uncle in our schooldays – they were great fun.'

Michael and I had spent a number of years as boarders at the same minor public school, where we found we both shared a common interest in French language and culture. This had finally led him to take up residence in Paris, making his living as a freelance journalist, writing articles for magazines and newspapers across Europe. Certainly we differed greatly in our personalities, yet had always seemed to complement one another. Michael was definitely more gregarious, always at the centre of any gathering with an ever-present fund of ready witticisms. I, on the other hand, was more reflective, perhaps if I think about it, even a little shy in company. But I acquired a reputation at a relatively young age of being dependable, and not given to rushing into anything without giving it due consideration, which has no doubt stood me in good stead latterly in my professional life. This is not to say that I was regarded as dull, for I felt that I was always looked upon as good company, and was popular amongst my peers.

A committed Francophile, with a good command of the French language, Michael's English sartorial style and naturally self-confident nature, honed during his years at school, had resulted in him acquiring the nickname 'Milord' amongst his wide circle of Parisian friends. This, coupled with his boyish good looks, expressed in an open, friendly face topped with blond hair, together with his ready wit, had stood him in good stead for a number of years with intelligent young French women of *bon genre*. The result was that every time we had met there was always a new girlfriend to accompany him.

He clearly enjoyed playing the field, so I was a little surprised to be told now that he had met someone, and things were, in his words, 'serious'. Her name was Yvette, and it was clear by the way his eyes lit up at the mention of her name that this was indeed someone special. They had initially met at a party given by a mutual friend, had spent the evening chatting together almost to the exclusion of everyone else, arranged to meet the following evening, and were by now, after three months, almost inseparable. Unfortunately, a prior family commitment had meant Yvette was unable to join us tonight. I told him how pleased I was to hear his news, and sorry that I would not be able to meet her.

Michael was beginning to make a name for himself as a writer. With his wide circle of friends, and an easy-going nature that always seemed to promote conversation with whoever he met, he had acquired a deep understanding of life in France today, particularly when seen from a young person's perspective. He had recently achieved nationwide prominence as a result of some of the articles he had written. These had convincingly explained the rationale behind rebellious youth in France today, which had manifested itself most recently in student revolt against the authorities on the campus at Nanterre University, Paris. What started initially as student demands to allow members of the opposite sex to stay overnight in their rooms on campus had now widened further to include protest against consumerism, the conservative policies of the

French government, and American involvement in the war in Vietnam.

Michael went on to explain to me that towards the end of March, following months of student unrest, a few hundred students had invaded an administration building at Nanterre, holding a meeting to debate class discrimination and political bureaucracy that controlled academic funding.

France had seen a huge rise in the number of students during the last decade, and by now they numbered in excess of half a million. The economy was booming as the country had enjoyed a period of rapid economic growth since the rebuilding of industry following the end of the Second World War. Despite general prosperity in the country there was currently a feeling of unrest. The demonstrations by the students were expanding to include general workers, who claimed that they had not seen any real benefit from this growth. Many of them were still being paid relatively low wages.

In response to this latest event the administration at Nanterre called in the police, who surrounded the university. The students later left, peacefully, having let their wishes be known. However, the student leaders were later called in to face a disciplinary committee, which only served to fuel further unrest.

Protests against the Establishment were now a widespread occurrence throughout Europe and America. While strong feelings against the war in Vietnam had been a common rallying cry, originating in America, but now widely seen across Europe thanks to the stark images of war being played out on television, it was also clear that there were other issues coming to the fore here. France was certainly lagging behind many other countries in terms of societal change.

The 'Summer of Love' had occurred a year earlier, originating from San Francisco. The hippie movement which had developed at this time promoted a lifestyle of drug experimentation, particularly with LSD, to the accompaniment of psychedelic music, and espoused communal living with its connotation of free love.

Michael and I both agreed that the young in England had already experienced a sexual revolution during the 1960s. The Establishment in Britain had already been regularly lampooned by popular television shows such as *That Was the Week That Was* in the early sixties, and The Beatles had produced the innovative *Sergeant Pepper* album a year earlier to great acclaim with its allusion to drug-taking. There had definitely been a change in the outward appearance of most young people over a few short years, with many young men now adopting long hair styles and colourful clothing, indicating contempt for the established conservative standards of dress and behaviour which had been followed so slavishly by the younger generation only a decade or so earlier.

France, with anti-establishment protests earlier this year, and rumours of strikes and further protests circulating, had not yet embraced this change – and the government and other established bodies, including the trade unions, seemed fixed upon a paternalistic view towards the population at large. It was notable that the students in France still dressed in a relatively formal manner, not unlike their parents: the young men with short hairstyles and sporting jackets and ties, the girls in dresses, unchanged in appearance over many decades.

The government of President Charles de Gaulle was regarded by many now as being out of touch with the majority, and seemed to regard change with suspicion, seemingly insistent that its policies alone were the best for the nation. De Gaulle's star had begun to fade in many French eyes. He was no longer seen by many as the leader who had adopted the mantle of the Free French government while in exile following his country's fall to the Nazis, returning in 1944 as a hero to liberate Paris alongside the Allied armies. Now a weary populace regarded him as out of touch and authoritarian. Mutual dislike between De Gaulle and the British Government, who had provided him with shelter during the war, began in the 1960s when he vetoed Britain's attempts to enter the Common Market. This was clearly to the dismay of the other five member countries, with De Gaulle accusing Britain of a deep-seated hostility towards European construction and general incompatibility with Europe.

'But enough of this for the moment,' said Michael. 'Let's go out and have something to eat. I'm sure you must be hungry, Jean.'

We made our way down a side street to a local bistro, patronised by local residents and workers, who would have scoffed at the tourist prices charged at the cafés in the adjoining brightly lit squares. We continued our discussions over our meal of cassoulet au canard, the owner's speciality, heartily recommended by Michael, and accompanied this with a fruity red house wine, followed by copious cups of coffee and the inevitable Gitanes.

Michael went on to describe some of the other events that had taken place, notably at the University of Paris Nanterre campus, where unrest had started in the previous year. One of the student leaders, Daniel Cohn-Bendit, gained some notoriety when he challenged the Youth and Sport Minister during a dedication ceremony for a new swimming pool, complaining about the sexual frustration felt by students as a result of the existing policy. In response he was told to cool his ardour by jumping into the pool. This dismissive remark had again demonstrated the paternalistic view of the Establishment. The French student population were now regularly voicing their concerns, and it was becoming clear to the authorities, particularly at Nanterre, that the existing order was becoming threatened.

I had been interested to hear Michael's view of events unfolding in France, and was able to add that I had also been caught up on the fringes of the recent Grosvenor Square anti-war demonstration in London. I had just left a meeting with a valued client of our firm, which had been arranged for Sunday 17 March, as he was in town for that weekend only, and was staying at an hotel off Park Lane. Close to the hotel I encountered a group of tourists who had wandered into the area around the square, and were now anxiously trying to put some distance between themselves and what they described as a riot. Mounted police were trying to keep order, faced with a largely hostile crowd protesting about the American involvement in the war in Vietnam. The demonstrators had gathered earlier in Trafalgar Square listening to speakers that included Tariq Ali and Vanessa Redgrave, before they moved on to the American Embassy in Grosvenor Square, where they were met by mounted police.

We both agreed that discontent with the political establishment was becoming widespread, prompting me to wonder aloud, 'Where do you think it may all end?'

'The signs certainly lead me to think that changes will have to be made in the way the authorities act towards the students. Otherwise I can only see the unrest becoming widespread, and then . . . who knows?'

Finally, finishing our last cigarettes and coffee, and after some hours of conversation in which we attempted, in our own way, to put the world to rights, it was time for me to return to my hotel. I was fortunate to be able to hail a cab almost immediately outside the bistro, leaving Michael to his short stroll back home, with a final wish to me that my uncle would soon be restored to health.

CHAPTER THREE
Journey to Evian-les-Bains

I awoke early, and opening the curtains to my room was pleased to see a bright day in prospect, the sun already reflecting off the mansard roofs on the opposite side of the street. The noise of traffic outside was becoming all too apparent through the tall French windows, despite them being shut. The city had already awoken from its slumbers some hours ago. An unseen army of workers had started their day before dawn. Provisions had already been delivered from outlying farms and other suppliers to the food market at Les Halles, a daily necessity that kept the city fed. Cleaners busied themselves in the streets and buildings, while others prepared the public transport systems before they were manned ready for the daily onslaught of workers, tourists and shoppers.

Having dressed, I went downstairs to the ground floor restaurant at the back of the hotel. Here I joined the other early risers, some obviously tourists, studying their guide books in readiness for the day's excursion. Others were more formally dressed, and no doubt in Paris on business. We breakfasted on croissants and pains au raisin, washed down with strong black coffee. Back in my room I gathered together my few belongings, and then made my way down to reception. Having checked out and bid the manager au revoir, I set out towards the Gare de l'Est railway station.

Arriving with some time to spare before my train departed, I purchased a newspaper on the station concourse to help pass the time on my journey. Boarding the train I found a vacant seat, and having stowed my suitcase I was now able to relax before the train pulled out of the station. At the last minute before departure a rather flustered couple entered the carriage, who, it appeared from their voluble conversation, had suffered some delay in their journey to the station. They appeared to me to be a rather mismatched pair. He had the look of the typical middle-aged business type, dressed in a well-cut suit that attempted to disguise his rather overweight, well-fed figure. His companion was young enough to be his daughter, and, judging by the poor quality of her outfit, was clearly not his wife. This impression was confirmed as he seemed at pains to study his travelling companions, concerned, no doubt, that no one amongst us recognised him, while at the same time attempting to curb his companion's attempts to cuddle up to him and show signs of affection as the train moved slowly out of the station.

As we finally left behind the suburbs of the city I turned my attention to my newspaper, interested to see on an inner page an article written by Michael, which sought to analyse what might lie behind the unrest currently demonstrated by students across France. His observations seemed well founded, but I felt would not give much comfort to the Gaullist Establishment. Remembering our conversation at the bistro last night I was minded to agree with his conclusion that what we had seen so far may only be the tip of the iceberg.

As our journey progressed, passengers came and went. New passengers included an elderly French lady sporting a full-length fur coat, carrying a small dog and struggling with her suitcase as she entered our carriage. I got up to assist her, stowing the suitcase for her as she sank into a seat. She thanked me profusely, then addressed her dog: 'Il est tres gentil, le monsieur,' before finding some small titbit in her handbag that she proceeded to feed to the poor overweight animal, who, it appeared, answered to the name Bonaparte.

Eventually the sapphire-blue waters of Lac Leman appeared ahead of us, shimmering under a cloudless sky, the brooding peaks of the Alps as ever, watchful above. Since a small boy I had always felt a sense of excitement on the first sighting of the lake during my visits to Evian, though now it was tinged with concern for my uncle. The train began to slow down, and within a few minutes, after helping the old lady with the dog to disembark, I found myself on the platform, suitcase in hand.

Making a quick call to Gaston from the station I arranged to meet him at the hospital, deciding to leave my suitcase with the station staff, and arranging to pick it up later in the day. There was a taxi parked in the station rank, so I was able to make the short journey across town in minutes. Paying the driver as I got out, I was greeted warmly by Gaston, still a bear of a man despite his age, which, I reflected, must by now be early seventies. His long grizzled hair surrounded a tanned face, the lines and wrinkles engraved thereon evidence of a life lived to the full, and he now stood before me, almost a head taller than my own not-inconsiderable height that approached six foot. He proceeded to hug me so tightly that I could scarcely breathe. It was no surprise to me when I first heard that from his earliest years, given his size and his surname of Petit, he had acquired the nickname le petit géant. Releasing me, he stood back a pace, and it became apparent to me, from his general demeanour and reddened watery eyes, that he was very troubled indeed.

'I am so glad you have arrived, M'sieur Jean. I was afraid you may be too late,' he said. This remark shocked me, and I had to struggle to find words to respond as he led me into the building. Together we walked through the reception area, ignoring the questioning look of the nurse sitting behind the desk. We made our way up the stairs to the second floor, progressing along a wide corridor with walls painted in colours of institutional green and cream. At the end of this corridor Gaston stopped outside a door, where I saw that my uncle's name Dumont was displayed.

'I will leave you, M'sieur Jean, and wait outside while you see your uncle,' he said, standing aside.

Thanking him for his courtesy I pushed open the door, and entered a small room dominated by a large metal-framed bed, in which my uncle was lying. His eyes were closed, and he seemed dwarfed by the bed; he looked so small and frail, his body connected by tubes and wires to equipment that was set up on a table to the side.

Approaching the bed I saw how the skin on his face appeared almost translucent, like parchment, and noted how his physical features seemed so dramatically changed, since I had last seen him. Moving closer I realised that the cause of this was where the left side of his face appeared to have dropped down, most noticeably in the region of his eye and mouth.

I sat down in the chair to the right-hand side of his bed and stretched over to hold his hand, then, leaning close to him, said in a low voice, 'Uncle Felix, it's me, Jean, I'm here.' Though his eyes remained closed, I was sure that his hand twitched in mine at that moment, as if in recognition of my presence.

I sat for some minutes more, continuing to rest my hand on his whilst deep in thought, listening to his shallow breathing, until the door opened and a nurse entered the room. In answer to her query I confirmed that I was Felix's nephew, and asked her about his condition.

'The doctor will be able to discuss the patient with you. He is at present in the lounge down the corridor. I can take you there,' she replied.

We walked a few yards together along the corridor, and, having knocked on the door, it was opened. A distinguished-looking gentleman of middle years sporting a goatee beard, dapperly dressed in a dark suit with a bright red bow tie, introduced himself as Doctor Sullivant. He bid me enter, after thanking the nurse, who then left us. He motioned to me to take a seat at a low table, before seating himself opposite me. Explaining again who I was, and that I had travelled from England on hearing the news from a family friend, I then asked him for the likely prognosis of my uncle's condition.

It was clear from the serious look on his face that this was not going to be an easy discussion. 'Your uncle has suffered a severe stroke, and although it is clear he has some paralysis to the left side of his body, and is as yet unable to speak, we cannot yet be sure of the full extent of damage to the brain. If I may speak frankly, I fear that the signs are not good. Given also his general frailty I am afraid that I do not hold out much hope of a recovery. I am sorry, Monsieur.' He assured me that everything was being done for Felix – a specialist had been called in to see him yesterday, he was being provided with liquids to keep him nourished and had been made as comfortable as possible – but the over the next hours or days . . . it was impossible to say.

I returned to the room, again sitting by the bedside, trying to take in everything that the doctor had explained to me. Was it so certain that recovery was now merely a faint hope? Looking down at my uncle, lying so still, I became slowly resigned to this fact, but at the same time silently offered a short prayer asking that he could be spared and restored to health.

The door opened again some time later, and I looked up to see the careworn face of Gaston. He suggested that we should go back now to Felix's house, as several hours had elapsed since my arrival. I was about to challenge him on this when I glanced down at my watch, and was surprised to see that he was indeed correct. My uncle's housekeeper, Florette, had prepared a meal for us, he went on to say, and he would drive us both back to the house. Realising that I was by now feeling rather faint, due in part to hunger, and probably exacerbated by the shock of finding my uncle in such a poor condition, I agreed, saying that I would return to the hospital later in the evening.

Gaston had his car parked outside the hospital, a small white Renault. An unmistakeable tang of fish, a reminder of his livelihood, hit my senses as soon as I opened the door. This vehicle was employed in a dual role, both as workhorse and personal transport. The little car sank to one side, as if in protest, when Gaston got in, his bulky frame dwarfing the driver's seat, with the effect that I was forced to lean hard against the passenger door. With the engine started, every gear change of the Renault's push and pull dash-mounted lever resulted in a crazy dance-like motion. First his right elbow jutted into my ribs, pushing me even tighter against the door, then, as his arm was lowered again I could move back into my seat. He made a slight detour to the station to pick up my suitcase, after which we shortly arrived at my uncle's house, situated in a wooded garden above the Boulevard Jean Jaures.

Les Cyclamens, the large stone-built villa with echoes of the Belle Epoque architectural style, its tiled roof ornamented by oeil-de-boeuf windows clothed in zinc, was set back well from the road. It commanded a view over the town to the lake beyond, the university town of Lausanne being visible on the Swiss shore opposite. The villa was approached along a shrub-lined driveway which led to the imposing front elevation. Double entrance doors of weathered oak were reached from a short flight of wide, time-worn, stone steps. The drive continued round to the right hand side of the house where a smaller building, the original stables, stood, which for many years since had been used as a garage. The edifice, though not excessively grand, presented to the world a sense of comfortable respectability, very much reflecting my uncle's position in local society in his chosen profession of *notaire*, earning him the title of *Maître* to colleagues and clients alike.

The entrance door was opened by Florette, a small, dark-haired woman in her late forties, who must have heard the arrival of our car. Despite appearing never to eat little more than a sparrow, she always seemed to have boundless energy. But today her eyes, usually so bright, reflected her concern in their obvious sadness, her greeting less voluble than usual. 'I am so sorry about your uncle, Monsieur Jean – is there any change?' I could only reply that he had been made as comfortable as possible; to say anything more proving too difficult for me.

'But of course you must be hungry, Monsieur Jean – I have prepared my bouillabaisse soup for you both. If you would like to take your suitcase up to your bedroom I will call you when the meal is ready.'

My bedroom, on the upper floor, and occupied on so many visits since I was a small boy, was at the front of the house. The decor, now unfashionably dark with ancient, but cared-for furniture, seemed to welcome me like an old friend. The scent of wax polish pervaded the room, as it did throughout the house, clear testament to Florette's labours.

'A table!' Florette called out from below, the vowel elongated with vigour, summoning us both to the dining room, where a tureen of her fish soup, liberally fortified with vegetables – no doubt fresh from the potager, Gaston's domain – stood centre table with a large rustic loaf and bottle of red wine. We both ate in silence, my thoughts dominated by the sad condition in which I had found Felix, and the impending visit to the hospital. As we finished our supper, Florette appeared again with the coffee jug, and cleared away the remnants of the meal from the table.

She had originally been employed when Felix's mother, Josephine, began to find the task of managing the house too much to cope with. At that time they had employed Paulette, a young maid, who they found somewhat lacking in housekeeping experience and thus needed constant supervision. It had been decided that additional help should be sought to assist Josephine in her declining years.

Florette Beaumont had been interviewed at the house in the early 1950s. She brought an excellent reference from her previous employer of many years, he being forced to relocate from Evian to Paris for business reasons. She had been widowed at the young age of twenty. Her husband, Lucien, had been killed in action in the rear-guard defence of Dunkerque in 1940, and she had subsequently chosen not to marry again, despite receiving further proposals of marriage, which she had refused. She had been adamant that no one could possibly replace her beloved Lucien, taken from her so soon.

Florette had immediately made a favourable impression upon her employers, proving to be an excellent cook in addition to managing the house to the high standards that Josephine appreciated. When Paulette, the young maid, finally left the household to marry one of the workers at the Evian Water Company, it was mutually agreed that Florette could take on all the duties required in the house. Josephine's husband, Auguste Dumont, had died in 1940, and the household then comprised of Felix and his mother, with the occasional visitors or dinner guests.

Furthermore, Florette became a companion to Josephine in her final years. Following the old lady's death she had stayed on in the household, which was now reduced to Felix and the occasional guest.

Her time these days was split between her duties in the house and daily attendance at Mass in the local parish church. Gaston, who lived nearby in the town in a small apartment he had owned for many years, had taken on the responsibilities of gardener, general handyman and chauffeur since retiring from his livelihood as a fisherman. This business, which included the fisherman's hut on the lakeshore together with the boat and equipment, he had passed to one of his young nephews, his own marriage having been childless. This arrangement had been agreed on the clear understanding that Gaston could still accompany his nephew from time to time on fishing trips – in fact, whenever he had time to spare from his duties at the house.

Thus, most days saw Gaston at work for a few hours in the garden, tending to the herbs, fruits and vegetables in the potager. He had introduced a few chickens, who roamed in the small orchard behind the house, ensuring there was a ready supply of fresh eggs and other ingredients for the kitchen. This was augmented from time to time by fish from the lake, supplied by the nephew.

Having finished our meal, and after a second cup of coffee

accompanied by the inevitable cigarette, it was time to return to the hospital. This time we took the large Citroën saloon car that Gaston often drove for Felix when he was required to meet a client away from the town. With Florette's assurances that she was praying for the Maître fresh in my mind, we set off again.

CHAPTER FOUR
The Hospital

The reception area was very quiet when we arrived. The nurse on duty behind the desk recognised us, motioning us to carry on up to the second floor. At this time in the evening most patients were sound asleep, visitors had departed, supper long since finished. The lighting in the corridors and side wards had been lowered, in acknowledgement of the change from the bustle of earlier activity. As we walked along the corridors only the night staff in the wards appeared visible. Ensconced in their seats, and illuminated by narrow beams of light from desk lamps, they busied themselves as they checked the notes of patients who would be under their care for the night.

I entered the room again, now also softly lit by a wall sconce, and silent, but for the laboured breathing of the patient.

Taking the seat beside the bed I laid my hand on his in an attempt at some form of contact, at the same time saying, 'Oncle Felix, c'est moi, Jean,' but there was no response this time. His eyes remained closed as he lay comatose in the bed.

Deciding to stay now for some time, I went out and spoke to Gaston, who was waiting in the corridor. Reluctantly, he agreed that he would return to the house, but asked me to telephone if there was any change in Felix, or if I needed a lift back.

I settled down in the bedside chair, continuing my vigil, Doctor Sullivant's earlier words reminding me of the stark reality of the situation – that it was probably only a matter of time before Felix succumbed.

Whether it was the effect of the journey from Paris, a consequence of the meal recently eaten, or simply the late hour, but my eyes eventually closed and I drifted off into a shallow sleep. This was filled with dream-like images that included my younger self, my mother and Felix, all presented as if we were appearing in a home movie, jumping without warning from one scene to another; the faces clearly recognisable, yet somehow set against backgrounds which appeared in a hazy monotone of grey. Times and places vaguely stored in my mind over time were now being recalled.

I don't know how long I had been asleep, but the realisation of what had passed dawned on me as I became aware again of activity in the room. A nurse was standing at the foot of the bed as Doctor Sullivant, at the other side of the bed, first checked the monitor, then for a pulse on the patient. His eyes told me everything. 'I am so sorry, Monsieur Dawson. We will leave you for a few minutes,' he said in a kindly low voice, befitting the situation, as they both left me to spend some time to collect my thoughts and grieve at the bedside of my deceased uncle.

Alone in the room now, I inwardly cursed myself for having fallen asleep at the time of his passing. Yet at the same time I reflected that Felix had seemed to acknowledge my presence earlier, on my initial arrival at the hospital, which gave me some comfort.

For the second time in my life I had been present at the death of a loved one, and, whilst feeling a great sense of loss, I was comforted by the hope that he might now be reunited with his sister Eugenie, my mother, to whom he had always been close.

There was a knock at the door, and at my bidding Doctor Sullivant entered again, suggesting that we go to the lounge. There, I accepted and sipped at a glass of water that was offered. I listened as he explained that, despite the efforts of the hospital staff, my uncle's general frailty had resulted in him being unable to overcome the massive stroke he had suffered. Alas, his earlier prognosis had proved correct.

If I could return later today, (and only now did I realise that we were in the early hours of Wednesday morning), after an opportunity to rest for a while, perhaps the formalities could then be completed. A medical certificate of death could then be issued so I could make arrangements for the funeral.

Having my agreement on this, he left me alone in the lounge, offering me the use of the telephone should I need to speak to anyone.

How my thoughts raced inside my head, no doubt exacerbated by the combination of shock and general tiredness. I had promised Gaston that I would phone, so, almost dreading the conversation about to ensue, I dialled the house number. It was Gaston who answered, almost immediately. Clearly he had stayed close to the phone since his return to the house. In a voice choked with emotion I managed to say only, 'Gaston, my dear friend, my uncle Felix has passed away.' There was silence for a moment, a deep sigh, and then in a hoarse whisper he replied, 'M'sieur Jean, I am so sorry for your loss – he was a true friend and gentleman. If I can help in any way . . .'

'Can you let Florette know for me, please? I have decided to walk back . . . I need some time alone.'

Gaston gave a muttered response indicating that Florette was still in the kitchen, despite the late hour. Clearly no one in the house had felt able to sleep at this time.

So I set off on my journey on foot, in the hope that my mind, now spinning round with the energy of a speeding carousel, filled with thoughts of Felix, and all the arrangements that would have to be made, might experience some calm as I made my way back to the house.

The town was silent as I made my way down to the lakeside esplanade, the waters of the lake dark grey, gently rippling to shore in a soft breeze that snapped at the pennants and rigging of the moored boats. Before long the sun would be rising from behind the Alps above Montreux, on its easternmost shore, and those same waters would hungrily absorb its warmth as the daily metamorphosis to a sparkling blue was realised.

This was the lake that for centuries past had inspired poets and writers who had lingered along its shores, numbering amongst them Byron and the Shelleys. F. Scott Fitzgerald had described the lake as 'the true centre of the Western world' in one of his novels.

Within a few hours the esplanade would be once more alive again as tourists took their daily promenade, seeking fresh air away from the confines of their hotels and guesthouses. Life would continue for them as normal, while I must now begin to accept what had passed.

Some would be making their way to the jetty, ready to board one of the graceful steamers that would ferry them around the lake, before they disembarked at their chosen destinations: Lausanne, Vevey or Montreux. But for now the town was still in relative darkness and the outlines of larger buildings which lined the lakeside, among them the Palais Lumiere, l'hôtel de ville and the large domed cupola of the casino becoming more visible in the strengthening pre-dawn light. In a few hours this route would be alive with traffic passing through to St Gingolph and the Swiss frontier to the east, and Thonon-les-Bains and onwards to Geneva to the west.

The inhabitants of the town still slumbered on, save for the fishermen who would soon be making their way to their huts, preparing their nets in readiness for an early departure in their small boats out onto the lake in search of their daily catch of the fish that dwelled in those waters. The resultant piscine harvest would be displayed later that day on the menus of the hotels and restaurants that lined the lake, tempting both tourists and residents alike.

I turned from the lakeside, crossing the road to the stone edifice of the church of St André, which stood on the corner of Rue du Lac, and where, in the next few days, the funeral service would be held, and continued my way uphill through the town, towards the house.

Letting myself in with my key I was welcomed by the silence of the house; the other occupants had kindly respected my wish to be alone at this time. They had taken themselves to their rooms, and would doubtless be finding their own way of coming to terms with the events of the day, and, albeit with a heavy heart, make some attempt at respite through sleep.

Feeling the need to prepare myself for the day ahead I drew a hot bath, in the hope that this would assist me to find some sleep over the next few hours, thoughts of my uncle uppermost still in my mind.

CHAPTER FIVE
The Arrangements

The bath must have worked its magic, for I awoke mid-morning somewhat refreshed, yet vaguely aware of a feeling of dullness in my head, and, having dressed, went downstairs expecting to face a barrage of questions, and a household in disarray.

However, I was almost surprised at the reception in the hall. Florette, though clearly upset, was putting on a brave face, and offered her condolences, expressing her gratitude for the honour of working for such a fine gentleman, which I found deeply touching.

My response was brief, and no doubt a little inept, by responding that this was a difficult time for us all, and, of course, there was much to be arranged. Hopefully she understood that I was still struggling with the reality of the situation, and, sensing my unease, said she would bring fresh coffee into the dining room, adding that croissants and jam were already on the table.

The coffee and croissants had the desired effect. My head now clearer, I felt ready to take on the challenges of the day. Gaston appeared in the dining room as I finished my late breakfast, no doubt having been alerted by Florette, and as I rose to greet him, came over to embrace me, indicating that words alone were not enough between us both at this time.

Despite the obvious grief showing in his eyes, he had come

in to await my instructions for the day, assuming that I might need a driver, or help in some other way.

I had already roughly planned out my day, starting with a return to the hospital, then an appointment at the mayor's office to register the death, followed by a visit to the funeral home, where the arrangements would be finalised. French law was quite specific as to timescales, and I would also need to consult with Jacques Martin, Felix's lawyer and erstwhile assistant, to check whether there were any specific wishes that were required to be carried out with regards to the funeral.

I explained my plans to Gaston and we agreed that he would drive me to the hospital then return home with the car, and I would continue on foot, as the offices I needed to visit were relatively close by in the town. He said that the Citroën would be at the front door ready for departure, adding that perhaps Florette could in the meantime choose suitable clothing for the funeral home, and arrange for a book of condolences to be displayed in the entrance to the house, as was the custom in France.

I readily agreed to this, being aware that both Gaston and Florette would know far better than me what local customs and practices were expected of the family at this time. I made some phone calls before setting off, to my father, my employer and the lawyer, to pass on the sad news, and we finally set off to the hospital with Gaston again at the wheel.

The formalities having been completed at the hospital I walked through the town, now alive with the bustle of tourists and residents enjoying the spring sunshine, and made my way on foot to l'hôtel de ville.

On entering the mayor's office and enquiring at the desk about registering a death, I was surprised, on giving the name of the deceased, to be ushered into the mayor's private office.

He greeted me in a formal, yet kindly, manner, bidding me sit down, and adding how sorry he had been to hear of Monsieur Dumont's illness, and was saddened by his passing. He impressed on me the part that Felix had played, both professionally and personally, in the life of the town, and that he would be sadly missed.

After a few more minutes a member of staff entered with the document, which was checked again before being presented to me. At his request I confirmed the name of the funeral home, and that I expected that the service would be later in the week. Rising from his chair, thus signalling that our interview was now ended, he formally shook my hand, again offering his condolences.

It was a few minutes' walk to the office of Jacques Martin, the notaire. I had arranged to meet him well before noon, knowing that most offices would be closing at that time for the customary two hours, during which a leisurely lunch would probably be taken.

Jacques occupied an office in a side street off Rue Nationale, close to the Evian Spa building. This was a more modern building than that previously occupied for many years past, when the principal lawyer had been Felix. Presumably the lease of the old office had finally expired, or perhaps Jacques had wanted to put his own stamp on the firm in new premises, now that he alone was responsible for the firm.

As I entered the office Jacques' secretary, Clarisse, a middle-aged woman with an outgoing, friendly disposition, who had worked for many years in the firm, and whom I had met on many occasions in the past, was clearly struggling to cope with the situation. She attempted to put on a brave face, and offered her condolences, before calling the Maître on the intercom to announce my arrival.

Opening the door to his private office, he greeted me, a look of genuine sadness on his features, for he had worked for many years as a junior to Felix. Jacques must now be in his mid-forties, I thought, as I saw him now for the first time after a break of a few years. With a hint of grey now apparent in his well-groomed, though thinning, hair, the well-tailored blue suit and his general demeanour he presented the world with the air of a man in control, a professional to be trusted. There was no doubt in my mind that he would have built up a thriving legal practice by now; he would be an obvious favourite, given his charming, attentive nature, amongst the wealthy widows who chose to retire to the lakeside villas and apartments in the town.

He asked Clarisse for two coffees – I definitely felt the need for one – and we went into his office. Here we both sat around the table, an attempt on his part to shake off the obvious formality that would have ensued had he been seated behind his rather formidable desk. Now that we were alone he said how shocked he had been at the suddenness of events. He had visited Felix at home only a month ago, when he had seemed well and in good spirits, and it was so hard to believe we were here today having this discussion, following his demise.

Jacques had clearly prepared for my visit, having a file on the table which he duly opened. He explained that this contained the most recent will of Felix Dumont, which had been redrafted following the earlier death of my mother.

With regard to specific wishes relating to his funeral there had been no changes made. Felix had requested the funeral service be held at the Parish Church of St André, followed by interment in the family tomb at the cemetery in the Avenue de Bocquies. Being a traditionalist he had also requested to be laid out in an open coffin at the house, with a book of condolences to be provided on a table in the hall.

Jacques concluded by saying, 'If I may, I can arrange for the will to be read in full following the funeral. Perhaps this can be done that evening at the house.' I agreed to this, and assured him that I would confirm the funeral arrangements as soon as they had been finalised.

I then left the office, and made my way back to the house in a reflective mood, thinking that the practical arrangements that had to be attended to, did, in their own way, help to assuage the grief that we were all feeling.

It was clear on my arrival back at the house that Florette had been busy during my absence. A side-table had been placed in the entrance hall, draped with a black cloth, on which had been placed an open book of condolences. A small but tasteful arrangement of chrysanthemums, the flower forever associated in France with funerals, stood in a black pottery vase to the back of the table, the whole ensemble crowned by one of Felix's Montblanc pens resting on the open book.

Florette approached me, rather anxiously, pointing to the pen. 'I hope you do not mind, Monsieur Jean – I thought it the correct thing to do.'

'Absolutely, Florette, I'm sure that my uncle would have approved,' I responded.

Later, suitably restored after a light lunch of chicken salad and freshly home-baked bread, I made my way to my next appointment at the funeral home, which was hopefully to be my last visit of the day. The building, its windows displaying monuments in marble of varying designs, was close to the church, and I entered to be greeted by the proprietor, Monsieur Lucas, who invited me into his office.

Having concluded the initial formalities – his offer of condolences on my loss, followed by my production of the necessary paperwork – we then proceeded to discuss in detail the funeral arrangements. I advised him that it was my uncle's wish to be laid out in his open coffin at home. This would be arranged by this evening, he said, suggesting that a suitable room be provided, adding that the housekeeper had already called and left suitable clothing with him. Being already aware that there was a family tomb, he confirmed that this would be opened and prepared in readiness for Friday. He had already arranged that the church would also be available for the service on that day. We agreed finally the order of service, which would be confirmed with the priest, and at which I would give my eulogy. I left the final notifications and arrangements in his capable hands.

Returning home, and feeling rather drained after the exertions of the day, I found Florette and Gaston both working in the kitchen.

'The funeral director will be calling later with the casket. Which room do you think will be the most suitable to place it in?' I enquired.

Without hesitation they answered in unison, 'The blue salon, Monsieur Jean.'

I thanked them both for their suggestion, for by using this smaller room the main salon would be kept free, in which I would be able to meet those who wished to pay their respects.

'I will arrange the furniture in readiness,' added Gaston.

'Then, perhaps, you can both join me for tea and cakes, if you can bring them through to the dining room, Florette, when you are ready.'

'Certainly, Monsieur Jean,' she replied.

This gave me some time to myself to reflect on the events of the day, and consider the preparation of my eulogy, in the study.

The evening meal was an informal affair, all three of us seated at the large pine kitchen table. The heat from the Lacanche range cooker, combined with the effects of a local red wine brought up from the cellar by Gaston, induced a feeling of drowsiness in me and my companions; an understandable reaction following the events of the last twenty-four hours. Conversation was limited, and if at all, rather stilted. All of us seemed to be lost in our own thoughts.

Following the meal I took the opportunity of spending some time to reflect alone with my late uncle's body, as it lay in the open coffin in the quiet atmosphere of the blue salon. Again my thoughts travelled to those times we had spent together in previous years, of joyful conversations, now no longer to be shared between us in future. My abiding hope was that, through his faith, he would in some way be reunited with his sister.

So it was with some relief that I finally took myself upstairs, suggesting that we should all have an early night as it was likely to be another busy day tomorrow, and we could expect a stream of visitors to the house.

Thursday passed quickly. Having realised earlier that I had only brought casual clothing with me, which would be quite unsuitable for the funeral service, being the principal mourner, I found time to slip away briefly after breakfast, having contacted a gentleman's outfitter in advance.

I had only experienced one French funeral, which had taken place many years ago, and that was of my maternal grandmother, Josephine, when I was aged sixteen. I still remembered being given special leave to be absent from my school in England. Only on the periphery of events at that time, I was struck now by the respect being shown by so many visitors to the house. It seemed to me that half the town had called. My role now consisted of being present to accept their offers of sympathy, making some attempt to briefly discuss with them the varied aspects of my uncle's life that had touched theirs, before finally, cards handed over and the book of condolences signed, they left.

Fortunately, Florette and Gaston were on hand to offer drinks to the visitors, initially greeting them on arrival, then showing them through to view the coffin, if they wished. They added some gravitas to the occasion, both adopting a serious bearing when addressing the callers, and formally dressed in black outfits to denote they were in mourning.

Notable visitors included the mayor and his deputy, the local priest, and various businessmen, together with friends and neighbours, some of whom I knew, others not. It became very clear as the day went on that Felix had been very well known and respected in the town; a picture emerging that aside from his professional life, he had given much of his time to helping others, particularly those less fortunate, and had been involved with many charities in the town.

Florette later discussed the catering arrangements with me, suggesting that Paulette, previously employed as a maid in the house, might assist her, with which I concurred as I expected that there would be a large gathering at the house following the funeral.

Thus, by early evening, my eulogy was finished, having already been amended over several drafts as I learned more about Felix's acts of kindness from the day's visitors. I finally felt that I was prepared for Friday.

CHAPTER SIX
The Funeral

Friday morning found me awake early. I was pleased to see, on opening my curtains, the promise of a fine spring day ahead. The funeral service had been arranged for three o'clock in the afternoon, in order to allow time for the Evian stallholders to pack away after the traditional Friday morning market. This would leave Rue du Lac clear for the cortège when it made its way down from the house, to the church, and finally back up the hill to the cemetery.

Shortly after breakfast Paulette arrived. She was no longer the dark-haired, quiet young girl that I remembered as my grandmother's maid, but a self-assured mother now, with a young family back at home. She was smartly dressed in a white blouse with a black waistcoat and skirt, and our initial greetings over, Florette led her through to the kitchen to assist with the preparations in readiness for those returning after the service.

The morning passed quickly in a flurry of activity as glasses, cutlery and crockery were carefully collected from the large old oak dresser, washed, dried and set out in the dining room by Paulette. Florette meanwhile busied herself in the kitchen, baking a selection of quiches and tarts topped with all manner of cheeses, onions, anchovies or asparagus and preparing salads as an accompaniment. The manageress of the local patisserie arrived with boxes containing a mouth-watering display of pastries and cakes, including two large tarte tatins, and a selection of breads, to be shortly followed by the delivery boy from the charcuterie with an assortment of cooked meats and sausage. All of them were duly placed by Paulette, in readiness for later, on the slate shelves in the cool atmosphere of the tiled walk-in larder that led off the kitchen.

Gaston, meanwhile, had been busy from an early hour collecting the salad ingredients from the potager, bringing them into the kitchen in his large wicker basket, then being admonished in a light-hearted manner by Florette, who told him that more ingredients were required. I considered to myself that this activity, though necessary for strictly practical reasons, was also playing its part in the grieving process, and I, for one, felt some relief at this.

After lunch we assembled again in the salon, having changed from working clothes into our formal attire: Gaston and I both in dark suits, white shirts and black ties, Florette attired in a black dress with a small black hat atop her head. We now awaited the funeral director, ready to form the cortège.

Within a few minutes he had arrived with his assistants, who would be acting as pallbearers. Despite his protestations it had been agreed that Gaston, due to his exceptional size, would be unsuited for this task if they were to maintain the coffin on an even keel.

The lid having been screwed down, the moment had arrived for the three of us to leave the house to follow behind the hearse on foot, down the hill to the church, passers-by stopping and removing their hats in a show of respect as the small procession made its way slowly down Rue du Lac.

Upon entering the church behind the coffin I was gratified to see so many people; barely was there an empty pew. I took my seat at the front of the congregation, with Florette and Gaston both beside me. I must confess that the service passed quickly for me, as I was worrying about the delivery of my eulogy in French to so large a gathering, despite my relative fluency in the language.

At last the moment came, and, at the priest's bidding, I rose to take my place to face the congregation. Despite an initial dryness in my mouth, indicating my nervousness, I managed to get through without any major stumbling over my words, and, on rejoining my seat, received a nod of approval accompanied by a light touch on the arm from my two companions.

As was the usual practice the service ended with those wishing to take communion, and pay their last respects, to come forward and pass around the coffin.

Afterwards, I stationed myself outside the doorway to thank those who had attended, adding an invitation to those who wished to join us at the house for refreshments. It had been agreed previously that the interment would be a private affair.

As the cemetery was uphill from the church, and at some distance, a car had been arranged to take me and my companions, our number which now included the priest, to follow behind the hearse.

Situated near the edge of town, overlooking the lake, the cemetery evoked a tranquil, albeit a formal air, bathed now in the warmth of the afternoon sun. Small lizards skittered from chosen sun-filled vantage points, hiding themselves away from sight at our approach. Cared-for gravel paths bisected the neat rows of marble and granite headstones, their inset framed photographs of the deceased lending an air of macabre watchfulness to the unwary visitor. This contrasted starkly with the overgrown grass, and the lichen-covered headstones, some leaning over at odd angles and intertwined with ivy creepers, found in so many English churchyards.

Amongst the neat rows there stood a number of more substantial monuments, their plots bounded by iron railings, a mark no doubt of family status and importance to those remaining in the living world, but one now left behind by their eternally slumbering occupants.

The priest officiated as the coffin was lowered into the Dumont tomb, Felix now being laid to rest with his parents and ancestors. It remained for us to leave our cards and pots of geraniums, our floral tribute in the French tradition, to a dear friend and uncle. I spent a few minutes in silence, reflecting on a life which was now forever ended.

On the journey back to the house I was congratulated again on my eulogy, with everyone agreeing that I had delivered a fitting tribute indeed.

As expected, the house was full as we arrived back. A disparate group, numbering amongst them the mayor with his deputy again, a number of the town's other notable figures, neighbours and friends. Under the watchful eye of Paulette and her assistant, everyone was offered a glass of wine and availed themselves of the buffet. As so often at such gatherings, they had already split into smaller groups, with shared common interests. Whether discussing business or local gossip, their conversations were interspersed with some show of respect, by uttering oft-repeated personal remembrances of the deceased.

Finding the atmosphere in the house rather stifling, and after a few minutes spent talking to the guests, I went through the kitchen to the rear garden. I was shortly joined by Gaston, who sat down with me on a bench that overlooked the orchard. We both lit our cigarettes, as he commented with a shrug of his shoulders, 'It's always the same small talk at these gatherings, M'sieur Jean, always the same.'

We sat in silence for a few minutes, our quietude only broken by three of Gaston's hens, squabbling over some titbit that had been uncovered as they scratched under the trees in the orchard. 'I could sit here watching the hens for hours,' remarked Gaston, 'but I suppose we must return to perform our duties inside.' I nodded, and we both, a little reluctantly I felt, made our way back into the throng.

We had timed our return well, it seemed, as the gathering was beginning to break up and depart. Amongst the first to leave were the mayor and his associates, followed gradually by the friends and neighbours, all finding time to speak personally to me again before departing, their platitudes no doubt well meant, until finally only the household and Jacques Martin, the notaire, remained.

We sat around the table in the salon, Paulette having brought in tea, while she and her assistant dealt with the business of clearing away the remains of the buffet and washing the crockery and glasses left by our guests.

All of us now feeling more refreshed after the tea, Jacques suggested that we go to the study, when ready, where he would read the will; indicating that Gaston and Florette should also join us there. This last request certainly came as a surprise to them, their questioning looks apparent, both no doubt wondering why they should be present when normally the reading of the will would be restricted to close family members only.

We adjourned to the study. Jacques sat, at my request, behind Felix's large mahogany Empire-style desk, and the three of us in front. Florette appeared to be a little overawed at the formality of the situation, which I attempted to defuse by suggesting that I pour us each a small glass of port before Jacques began. This seemed to have the desired effect and the atmosphere in the room began almost at once to mellow.

Jacques now held centre stage, a role that he was well used to perform in his professional capacity. He explained that he was holding in his hand the last will, (the testament authentique,) of Felix Dumont that had been re-drafted following the death of his sister Eugene, my mother. Jacques also confirmed that he had been appointed as executeur testamentaire, being, in Felix's opinion, best placed to assist with the distribution of the various bequests contained in the will.

As Felix had never married, Jacques continued, and there were no parents or siblings surviving him, and there was no evidence of any children, under the French law of inheritance the bulk of the estate would now pass to me, his nephew Jean Dawson, as the privileged collateral heir. Jacques suggested that at this point he would only make outline reference to the fact that the estate comprised not only the family home, but other real estate and assets that he would discuss with me in detail and in private after the reading.

Jacques went on to say that he had requested Gaston and Florette to be present as they were also beneficiaries under the will, and emphasised that he was using Felix's own words when describing them both as loyal and caring friends over many years. This of course brought tears to their eyes. Again Jacques confirmed that he would discuss these bequests individually and in private, after he had finished. In summary he indicated that there were also a number of smaller bequests to named charities which Felix had supported during his lifetime, and, as executor, he would duly distribute them.

Jacques then asked if he could firstly see Florette alone, followed by Gaston, to which we all agreed.

They came out of the study a little later, following their individual interviews, both somewhat in shock, looking as if their ears had deceived them, hardly daring to comprehend their good fortune; Felix had clearly been most generous to them.

Jacques now asked me back into the study. He confirmed that Felix had made financial provision for Florette on the basis that she may no longer be keeping her position as housekeeper. The family home may in future be sold, and she would then have to find somewhere to live. After her years of service to the family he felt a duty to ensure that she had the means to support herself, if she chose to live alone rather than go into service again. Gaston, of course, had his own small apartment in town, but again Felix had wished his old friend, and sometime protector, to be comfortable in his old age, and had made financial provision for this.

Now he explained to me in more detail the full extent of Felix's estate. Felix had inherited the family home following the death of his parents, various stocks and cash, together with the law practice, and other real estate. But it seemed that Felix had also been a shrewd investor, acquiring other buildings in the town, shops and apartments which had often been in a neglected state, but now much improved, were of quite considerable value.

I appeared to have become a wealthy young man.

CHAPTER SEVEN
A Discovery

The next morning, being Saturday, I had proposed to spend some time going through household accounts and generally checking any paperwork, as had been suggested by Jacques, prior to a meeting he had arranged with the bank manager.

It so happened that a change in the weather, a steady rainfall from early in the morning, served to reinforce my resolve to undertake this task. I had left Florette, still somewhat bemused after the reality of her situation had been fully absorbed, to her household chores, whilst I closeted myself in the study. Gaston had, I understood, gone to visit his nephew at the fisherman's hut for the morning, and was unlikely to return until later in the afternoon.

Seating myself at the large Empire desk I busied myself by initially looking to see where Felix kept his paperwork, and was not surprised to see a number of clearly marked folders and box files behind the glazed doors in the upper section of the secretaire bookcase. A number of unopened letters lay in the tray atop the desk, a small indication of the passage of time since Felix's initial illness.

Deciding to tackle the unopened post first, I found these included a couple of small household bills, which I put to one side. My earlier enquiries of Florette had confirmed that Felix provided her with a set amount of petty cash each week to cover any small purchases. Most household expenses were dealt with by way of accounts sent by the various shopkeepers and other trades in the town, settled by cheque.

A check of the files in the secretaire showed an ordered approach to the paperwork, files and folders clearly labelled under headings relating to household expenditure, utility providers, insurances, bank statements. Other files indicated rental properties, charities and personal correspondence. Felix had even kept a ledger in which items of income and expenditure were entered, making the task of reconciling payments with bank statements a relatively simple task. All in all it was clear that the accounts were relatively up to date, and the monthly outgoings over the last twelve months or so followed a similar pattern.

With some more work I should be able to indicate the likely expenditure for the household for the next few months. This of course set me thinking about the future of the house. Whilst I had always regarded this house as my uncle's home, my life at present being very much based in London, I would before long have to face the fact that some difficult decisions would have to be made. Fortunately there were no pressing financial demands forcing my hand at present, the income derived from the rentals together with funds at the bank indicating a very healthy surplus over current outgoings.

With these thoughts still in my mind I decided to check the drawers in the desk in case there were any other papers that I should be aware of. The contents of the drawers produced nothing of particular interest, but I noticed that the top drawers on either side, which were divided into shallow compartments for pens, pencils and other small items, could only be pulled open about six inches, whereas the lower drawers were a great deal longer, and were also removable. Intrigued, I opened the right hand top drawer again and found that I could not remove it from the desk. Was this normal for such a desk? I tried the left hand top drawer and found that this was the same. Surely drawers would normally be removable, so why weren't these?

I vaguely remembered a story by Edgar Allan Poe that featured his detective character Auguste Dupin, in which the Prefect of Police, searching for a compromising letter, remarked about a certain amount of space that had to be accounted for in every cabinet. This set me wondering whether there was perhaps a secret compartment connected to these shallow drawers, or was my imagination now going into overdrive?

The wooden compartments in the drawer seemed solid enough and appeared to be integral to the drawer, but on closer examination I found that although they fitted tightly within the drawer they did not appear to be fixed. With a little care, and not wishing to damage the drawer, I was able to firmly lift out the shallow compartment. Now, clearly seeing it as a tray that rested on formed wooden shoulders within the drawer, it revealed a hidden space below. This in turn revealed a small lock set into the back of the drawer, indicating that there may be another hidden section behind. The next question was where to find the key? On checking the other top drawer I found the same arrangement, but again no sign of a key.

Where would Felix have kept such a thing? Assuming that anything left in a hidden compartment may be of value, it was unlikely for the key to be in plain sight. Checking the underside of the drawers and the desk itself I found nothing, and was about to consider calling in a locksmith when I looked at the ornate ormolu mounted marble inkstand that stood atop the desk, in which lay Felix's Montblanc pens. There was a classical cast ormolu figure in the centre with inkwells to either side, each containing blue glass containers under hinged lids. On checking I found that the glass inkwells were empty, but on removing them I found a small key underneath the right hand inkwell. Surely this must be the key I was looking for.

With some trepidation I first tried the key in the left hand drawer and, although a little stiff, no doubt due to lack of recent use, it turned, and I was then able to pull the drawer further open to uncover a further compartment . . . empty. But, on trying the right hand drawer, I found that it did contain something: a small wooden cigar box.

Retrieving it from the drawer, I laid it on the desk before opening it. Inside was an envelope which contained a small collection of handwritten notes – clearly not of recent origin judging by the foxed condition of the paper – which appeared to comprise pages torn from a small notebook. Amongst these, wrapped in tissue paper, was a small sepia photograph of a girl, of perhaps seventeen years of age, clearly beautiful, but with a shadowy air of sadness about her. Even in this small photograph it was apparent that there was a smouldering intensity in her eyes as she looked towards the camera, perhaps only intended for the photographer, but now committed to print for all to see. From the style of her costume and the general appearance of the photograph it must have been taken somewhere around the time of the Great War, when Felix would also have been of a similar age.

The notes appeared to be confirming meetings, but were very brief and signed only 'C', which shed little further light as to the identity of the writer. I could only assume that this must have been a chapter in Felix's life that, for whatever reason, had not been openly discussed within the family, and certainly never to my knowledge. Felix had always presented himself as the ageing bachelor, the dutiful lawyer whose professional life had seemed the mainstay of his existence. Now it seemed that this may not always have been the case. But how could I now unravel this mystery some fifty years or so later?

Florette had only joined the household around 1950, and, given the relationship between employer and housekeeper, was unlikely to have been aware of much of Felix's earlier life, so I decided not to raise the subject with her. Gaston, on the other hand, had been a friend and no doubt confidante since early boyhood, having adopted the role as protector to the young, rather frail Felix, when they both began their schooling in Evian. It was some time later that Felix moved on to boarding school, in preparation for university and his chosen profession. But the friendship had lasted, despite the diversity of background, and I felt that if anyone had any knowledge of this interlude in Felix's life that person must be Gaston.

A light knock at the study door announced Florette, who enquired if I would like coffee to be brought in. Realising that a change of scene away from the paperwork would be beneficial I said that I would join her in the kitchen in a few minutes, and proceeded to tidy the notes and photograph back into the envelope before joining her.

Putting my discovery aside for the moment I chatted to Florette, who in a roundabout way asked how the house should be run for the present, without directly asking me what my longer term plans would be. I was able to reassure her that things would continue as before as there were further meetings planned with Jacques Martin, the family lawyer, which would take place over the next few months, as well as meetings with the bank and property agent in connection with the estate.

I told her that I would have to return to London shortly, as my clients could not indefinitely endure my prolonged absence. However, I intended to return to Evian as soon as business permitted, in order to make any decisions regarding the estate. 'So if you are happy to continue looking after the house for me, I should be very glad Florette, as I have no intention of shutting it up while I am away.'

'Of course, Monsieur Jean, I will keep things for you exactly as before,' was the swift response, the look in her eyes showing relief that she did not have to make any hasty personal decisions at this difficult time.

A change for the better in the weather prompted me to let Florette know that I would be going for a walk by the lake and have a light lunch in one of the small restaurants nearby, planning to return mid-afternoon. I asked her if she could prepare something for us all later as I was sure Gaston would be hungry on his return from visiting his nephew.

'If you like, I will cook a Gigot d'Agneau, Monsieur Jean – the butcher called this morning.' Her roasted meats were legendary, and my smile in anticipation of this told her all she needed to know.

So later that evening, Florette having been busy all afternoon in the kitchen performing her magic on the Lacanche range, and Gaston on his return gathering such herbs and vegetables as required. I felt my contribution, merely opening a bottle of a local red wine, was somewhat insignificant, as we sat down in the dining room. Florette had surpassed herself, the lamb joint imbued with the scents of garlic, rosemary and olive oil.

I charged our glasses, whereupon Gaston stood up, proposing a toast to Felix, which we quietly acknowledged, and

I then proposed a toast to my two dear friends, after which I proceeded to carve the meat, and we then helped ourselves from the dishes laid out on the table.

In an effort to lighten our mood I tried to explain how Henry VIII had been so impressed by a joint of beef at a state banquet that he had drawn his sword to knight it, saying, 'Arise, Sir Loin.' This immediately prompted Gaston to jump up, and taking hold of the carving knife place it flat side against the lamb joint, saying, 'Arise, Monsieur Agneau' to the accompaniment of our laughter.

He then went on to tell us about his day spent on the lakeside with his nephew and friends, how the fish were quite plentiful at present, and how he had presented Florette with some fine perch, 'perhaps for our lunch tomorrow', which were now in the icebox.

The meal continued, interspersed, from time to time, with appreciative comments made by Gaston and myself. Florette then produced a crème caramel to further acclaim, after which she suggested she would bring in our coffee while she cleared away in the kitchen.

'Perhaps in the study,' I suggested, 'as I wish to discuss something with Gaston.' Clearly puzzled, he nodded, and we made our way out of the dining room.

Sitting down around the desk I hoped to alleviate any concerns by repeating my earlier conversation with Florette and asking if he was happy to continue helping with the upkeep of the garden. 'Of course,' was the reply 'I thought perhaps you had decided to sell up, and wished to speak to me about that.'

'No, I have made no decision in that respect for the present, and I would like the house to be run as before. I expect that I shall be spending some time in Evian over the coming months.'

Florette knocked on the door before entering, bringing in a pot of coffee, cream and cups on a tray. 'I will be in the kitchen if you require anything else, Monsieur Jean,' she said, as she left us alone in the room.

As we poured out the coffee I suggested that we have a brandy, and went over to the side table, pouring us both a large measure. 'This looks serious, M'sieur Jean,' was Gaston's comment, reaching for his packet of Gauloises, offering me one before lighting up, and waiting for me to continue, his weather-beaten face showing a sense of anxiety behind the cloud of smoke now being generated.

I wasn't sure what to say next but started by explaining that I had spent the morning checking the various files and ledgers to understand the household accounts, but had been mystified on discovering two secret locked compartments in the desk. Having finally found a hidden key I had uncovered a cigar box in one of them containing an envelope with brief notes indicating what I assumed where assignations, together with a photograph of a girl, which appeared to date perhaps from the time of the Great War. 'Perhaps, as an old friend of Felix, Gaston, you may be able to shed some light . . .?'

'You have found the photograph, M'sieur Jean? May I see it?' came his quiet response.

I opened the drawer, removed the tissue paper from the envelope and laid the photograph on the desk.

He reached over the desk, carefully pulling the photograph towards him. 'It is as I thought . . . it is Célestine . . . poor sweet child.' He looked on at the face staring out from the desk, and I could sense from the expression evident in his face that a great sadness had now engulfed him.

'If you are able, can you tell me anything about her? I have never heard the name Célestine mentioned before by the family,' I said, eagerly awaiting his response.

He lifted his glass and emptied it in one gulp. Instinctively I poured him another measure.

'It is a sad tale, M'sieur Jean; Felix and I swore never to tell the true facts as long as we both should live, but now that Felix is also gone . . . as his heir I think you have a right to know.'

CHAPTER EIGHT
Gaston's Tale

M'sieur Jean, as you rightly thought, the photograph was taken during the Great War – in fact, in May 1917. At that time France and her allies had endured three years of horrific warfare, fought on an industrial scale, with huge numbers of casualties on both sides. The Boche had occupied parts of northern France, and on the borderlands with Belgium, the city of Lille being, perhaps, one of the largest and most important to be captured.

I had joined my regiment as a volunteer shortly after the onset of the war, expecting that it would soon be over and I could return to my life here as a fisherman on the lake. Due to my height and physical fitness my age was never questioned. I was in fact one of the many who had volunteered in a fervour of national pride, despite being underage. As France had already mobilised reservists and needed more soldiers, little attention was paid to details such as the checking of ages. I was accepted without question, the doctor who carried out the brief medical examination pronouncing me fit and actually commenting on my physique, which was in those days quite exceptional due to my open-air life on the lake and the hard physical labour of my chosen trade. Looking about me I could well understand his comments; as I could not fail but see the unhealthily pale faces and under-developed bodies of the majority of the other volunteers, no doubt the result of poor diet and lack of exercise.

I wondered to myself how some of these poor specimens of French manhood would cope with the training and the fierce fighting that lay before them.

Following a crushing defeat in the Franco-Prussian War in 1871 the French military leaders had attempted to modernise the army, introducing improved training for both officers and the ordinary soldier, and developing new weapons, but always having regard to Germany as the potential threat on their borders.

I am no expert in these matters, M'sieur Jean, I was simply an ordinary poilu, a common soldier, but as the war continued I had lived through hell as our regiment fought in suicidal offensives to gain perhaps a few hundred metres of ground, only to be pushed back again in a counter-offensive by the Boche. Between times we manned our trenches, constantly aware of the constant risk from sniper fire, artillery barrages and mining activities to lay explosives under our positions.

Our rations and conditions were poor; life in the trenches was extremely hard, and as time progressed many of our comrades became demoralised. But, of course, we were fighting on French soil, and knew that we had to hold our line, and eventually beat back the Boche, otherwise all France may have fallen to this hated enemy.

But for some of our comrades it all proved too much, and they deserted or refused to obey orders. These poor souls were hauled up before a military tribunal, where the sentence for 'abandoning their post in the presence of the enemy' was death by firing squad, and this was often carried out, as an example to others, in front of their comrades.

In April 1917 my regiment was stationed on the sector known as the Chemin des Dames, a long ridge in the Aisne region. I was later to learn that the general staff, under the commander-in-chief General Nivelle, had decided on a major offensive in this sector, with which he had promised a swift end to the war, encouraged no doubt by signs of the Boche withdrawing from their forward positions. What they had failed to realise was the full extent of the 'scorched earth' policy that the enemy had carried out. Buildings, whole villages even, had been demolished, trees and hedgerows cut down, as they pulled back, so there was to be no shelter for our army advancing on this new enemy position. Later this new position was to become known to us as the Hindenburg Line, which, unknown to us at the time, had been heavily fortified and was bristling with machine guns and artillery.

But, of course, I was merely one poilu amongst a million men that the generals would soon be unleashing in a great offensive, and knew nothing of the bigger picture. All we knew at the time was that something 'big' was about to happen.

So on 16 April, after days of continuous artillery fire from our side, intended to break the will of the enemy, we were ordered to advance. It was a total disaster. On that day alone, I believe, there were casualties among my comrades in the tens of thousands, many cut down by the ceaseless rattle of machine gun fire, myself included.

I was one of the lucky ones, only wounded, and saved by falling into a slight depression in the ground that shielded me from further enemy fire. I lay there listening to the screams and moans of brave comrades who had fallen all around me, the sounds gradually quietening over time as they lapsed into unconsciousness, or died of their wounds where they lay.

M'sieur Jean, believe me, from that day Hell held no fear for me, I had seen it with my own eyes!

As I said, I was lucky. My leg had received a wound, but miraculously no major artery had been severed, or I would not have survived. That evening, as daylight fell, parties of stretcher bearers came out from our lines to recover the fallen. I was taken back behind the lines to our dressing station where I was treated, and assessed as unfit for combat until my wounds had healed.

This was perhaps my second stroke of good fortune, for I was granted leave to return home after spending a week or so in a military hospital, to make space for others, for the demand for beds had become so great, the casualty numbers swelling with each day that passed. But before I left the hospital rumours had already begun to circulate that morale had finally reached breaking point. There was such anger amongst the common soldier towards the generals that there was talk of taking action by disobeying orders, refusing to advance on the enemy, open mutiny in fact.

You must remember that by 1917 a million young French men had already lost their lives in this war. No family was left unscathed, either having lost dear ones themselves, or knowing of friends that had lost sons or husbands. Following the disastrous events of this latest offensive, which had been heralded as a quick end to the war, widespread anger became apparent.

We had fought at this time alongside our allies in the Russian First Brigade, who were only too well aware of events unfolding in their homeland. Major unrest was already sweeping through Russia which included demonstrations and strikes, protests about food shortages and the war, which had already resulted in the forced abdication of Tsar Nicholas and the end of Tsarist government. These brave soldiers had become extremely disillusioned, and were already showing signs of open mutiny.

So, why do I say that being granted leave was my second stroke of luck, M'sieur Jean? Well, if I had returned to the Front immediately, I believe that I could have become one of the ringleaders of the mutiny that followed in early May. As you know, I have always been one to speak my mind to anyone, regardless of their position in society. But, of course, I had by then returned to Evian on leave, and so was not involved in the mutiny.

Perhaps you are wondering what Felix was doing at this time, M'sieur Jean?

As you know he has always had the infirmity of his club foot, which was never successfully remedied, despite the best efforts of the surgeons. But as a young child he seemed further cursed, and did not enjoy good health; there was one episode in particular of scarlet fever affecting the heart, leaving him unable to participate in strenuous exercise.

I first met him in the playground of the local primary school, on his first day. I was a few months older, and already had acquired a reputation due to my height and the nickname, *le petit géant*, which took account of my surname Petit and my boyhood strength, so the school bullies always kept their distance. But poor Felix became an immediate target for their attentions, and out of compassion I stepped in to protect him, for which he was grateful.

An unusual friendship quickly developed. His father was a leading lawyer in the town, a much respected figure, while mine was but a poor, barely literate, fisherman. But despite these differences our childhood friendship grew; Felix with his quick mind was always ready to help if I struggled with my lessons. I must declare it was due to his encouragement and patient assistance that he laid the foundations of a love of books that has stayed with me throughout my life, much to the initial consternation of my family, who did not regard books as suitable fare for one of their children. I, on the other hand, encouraged him to join me in my interest in nature, so both of us spent as much time as we could outdoors together, which had a beneficial effect on his health.

His parents could see the improvement in Felix, and were wise enough to encourage our friendship. Many others of their class would not be so liberal in their outlook.

But Felix had always been destined for greater things, and the time arrived when he had to leave behind the limitations of the local school and become a boarder at a distant school, in preparation for university. Many would have expected our friendship to diminish, if not to fail completely, but Felix always took the trouble to write to me when he was away, something I rarely seemed to get round to in return, as I was a poor letter writer. Nevertheless, we would meet up again at the end of each term, carrying on our friendship as if we had only been apart for a day or so.

At the outset of the war in 1914 Felix was still away from Evian as a boarder at his school, studying for his Baccalaureate, with a view to eventually continuing his studies in law at university. Due to his infirmity he would not have been considered fit to serve in the army, but he was not yet, at sixteen years of age, old enough to be faced with conscription.

So I returned to Evian in late April 1917, which was, fortunately, situated well away from the fighting and the occupied areas of France. Despite the obvious absence of younger men, life appeared to carry on much as before, although the economic consequences of the war were felt here, as elsewhere – the town suffered from an increase in the cost of living, and significant shortages of grain and fuel.

Having come back home to my family, who joyously welcomed my leave of absence from the fighting, I was treated as a returning hero. Friends and neighbours appeared at our home throughout the day, to be regaled time after time by my mother's tale of my brush with death, how my guardian angel had been looking over me, the story becoming ever more fanciful with each telling.

The next day, having met what seemed to be all the neighbours in our locality, my thoughts returned to my old friend Felix. I decided to call on his family that evening, anxious to hear news of him.

Imagine my surprise, my delight even, to find him at home, whereupon I was immediately invited in to meet his parents again, who greeted me most affectionately. They both marvelled at my lucky escape, wishing me a speedy recovery, but couched it in the hope that I would not be returning too soon to the Front. We all agreed that the war had gone on far too long, its dark tentacles reaching out and touching countless families throughout the land.

I then proposed that Felix and I went out for some air, giving us an opportunity to catch up with events over the preceding years. I did not need to remind Felix that my wound had weakened the right leg, and at his suggestion we ventured into the orchard at the rear of the house where we found a bench to sit upon.

How the hours passed as we first gave our potted history of the last three years – his own mostly concerned with his life at school, his recent success in his examinations, and finally, his resolve to return home. He had decided to help in whatever way he could to assist the work being carried out by the Repatriation Service, and other associated charities, in Evian. These organisations had been set up to assist in the re-settlement of those French citizens who had been allowed to leave the areas of France now occupied by the Boche, and, after passing through Switzerland, finally reaching the southern French shores of Lac Leman. He regarded this as the most important occupation that he could undertake at this time, and had thus deferred commencement of his studies at university.

Felix, having offered his services to a number of organisations, was currently working as a volunteer for one of the charities that had come into existence due to the demands arising from the war, and he assisted them in keeping their records and accounts up to date. His role also brought him face to face with many of the daily arrivals, and he was at first shocked at the pitiful conditions he saw. Signs of malnutrition and general distress were obvious, with many, adults and children alike, suffering from diseases that would necessitate medical treatment.

As there was a risk of contagious diseases being passed to the local population there was established a strict regime of medical examinations for all arrivals. The fear of epidemics was a very real threat to the authorities, who sought to transfer those suffering from diseases, particularly in cases such as tuberculosis, where the need for isolation to designated hospitals was paramount. Some hospitals had even been set up in former hotels due to the demand now present. As a result of the poor living conditions they had endured in the occupied territories, many of the children had arrived suffering from ailments such as diphtheria, whooping cough, scarlet fever and acute tonsillitis, and would also require special medical treatment.

The result was that some families would of necessity be split up for some time, where a child or adult may require treatment for some weeks or months, so arrangements had to be made to provide accommodation in the locality for the remaining family members.

It was then that Felix began to tell me of one case he had been dealing with, the Aubert family. The mother, suffering from suspected tuberculosis, had been sent to the hospital set up in the Hotel des Princes, on the edge of the lake at nearby Amphion-les-Bains. The other family members comprised three daughters (their father having died in the first year of the war in the defence of his country), who had to be found somewhere to stay. Felix, through the good offices of his father, had been fortunate enough to find them lodgings with a kindly widow, who lived in a small house on the western edge of Evian.

I was immediately struck by a change in his demeanour as he proceeded to tell me more about the family, who had originated from Lille. His voice softened as he described the eldest daughter, Célestine. She was a year or so younger than Felix, and was now responsible for the welfare of her two younger sisters until their mother had recovered. It was apparent from the way his face lit up as he described her that Felix had become very fond of her in the short time he had known her. From what he told me it was clear they both shared a common interest in literature and art, and when they were able to meet, with the assistance of the kindly widow, Madame Levell, they discoursed on many topics. No doubt they tried putting the world to rights in their own particular way, as the young have done for centuries past, M'sieur Jean.

I would have always described my friend as a private person who kept his most personal feelings to himself. But I had known him since that first day at school, when I undertook the role as protector, and our friendship had blossomed to the extent that I could almost feel his innermost thoughts, without a word being spoken between us. So, on my return home to convalesce from my wounds I could sense, as he told his story and from the little he confided to me about Célestine, that he had indeed been struck by a coup de foudre.

I was now very much intrigued by all that he told me, and enquired when I might meet Célestine. My last three years' experience in the army had only seemed to bring me in contact with two types of female. The first being the raucous, brassy 'good-time girls' one met in the bars when on leave from the Front, where drinks flowed freely and favours were given, unconstrained, in an alcohol-induced haze, their faces only to become a shadowy recollection the next day. The others being the nurses, those angels of mercy, devoted to the care of the sick, the wounded and the dying. It has been suggested that all men fall in love with their nurses; but for me, despite my undying thanks for their kindly ministrations, this had never come to pass. So I was now feeling, perhaps, a little envious, listening as Felix told me more.

As it was by now becoming late I had to take my leave and return home. Felix promised that I would meet Célestine on the following day, a Sunday, when we could promenade in the afternoon along the lakeside. Her young sisters would remain at their lodgings under the watchful eye of Madame Levell, who, knowing Felix and his parents, did not regard the need for a chaperone a necessity. 'We live in changed times,' was her simple answer if questioned on that subject.

The next day I awoke to a glorious spring morning, the power of the sun already strengthening, removing all signs of the mist that had shrouded the mountains as dawn arose. I spent the morning with my father, dressed in my fisherman's smock, as was the custom, helping as he attended to his nets in readiness for the next fishing expedition. I then returned home to change into my Sunday clothes before setting off towards the esplanade, where I had arranged to meet Felix opposite the casino.

Shortly after arriving I spotted them as they approached our rendezvous, both of them, it seemed, totally entranced in a world of their own, deep in conversation. This spell was only broken when Felix, glancing up, saw me waiting ahead of them, and came over to introduce me to Célestine, who like him was of medium height and was dressed in a dark blue coat that highlighted a rather slight figure, her face framed with lustrous auburn hair, so beautiful that it seemed to set her apart from her peers.

As she offered me her hand in greeting I was immediately struck by an aura of vague sadness about her, one that almost diminished her obvious beauty, and being most noticeably apparent in her eyes. Quelle tristesse! My reaction, however, was to dismiss these thoughts, reminding myself that she had obviously suffered great hardship, like so many others in the occupied territories. And, of course, I was immediately charmed by her kind enquiries after my health and my family, and soon fell into easy conversation with her.

I also became aware of the look of serenity that emanated from my old friend Felix as Célestine continued our conversation, and felt happiness for him, for it was clear that he was indeed smitten.

After a leisurely stroll along the esplanade we found ourselves near one of the small hotels that lined the lakeside. Felix suggested that it would be beneficial to rest my leg, and, despite my protestations, a table was found outside, which we occupied and ordered coffee. The afternoon passed by all too quickly, and it was eventually time for me to take leave of my companions. We parted with promises that we would meet again the following evening, and I set off along the lakeside for home.

I had indeed been charmed by Célestine, and though, like Felix, she was clearly my superior in upbringing and intellect, she seemed to accept me for myself, and gave no hint of awkwardness with my rather rough, unpolished appearance. But still that aura of sadness about her came back to haunt me, and I wondered if I might dare to raise the subject with Felix. Perhaps I had become so aware of suffering in the past months that I was taking such things to heart too easily, for in my earlier carefree youth I doubt that I would have readily recognised such signs.

Felix was at that turning point in life between youth and manhood, and not yet being qualified to pursue his chosen profession, marriage could not be a consideration for some time. But his feelings for Célestine were so clear to me, that I could see their future being together. I suppose you would say that they were sweethearts, an old-fashioned expression, but at the time seemed eminently suitable.

Célestine, however, always seemed to be an enigma. True, there was clear fondness on her part towards Felix, but from that first meeting I could never guess at the cause of the sadness I had detected, other than the assumption that she had suffered under the harsh regime in Lille, being of an age when such trials could have a profound effect on a young girl of only seventeen years of age.

But there was no doubt that their friendship was clearly intense, barely a day passing when they were not together, their feelings for each other apparent to an observer such as myself.

During the next days and weeks a friendship developed between the three of us, and I was always happy to see Célestine in the company of Felix. We met in the early evenings whenever Célestine was able to come, for she was still responsible for the family during her mother's illness. Sometimes her younger sisters, Thérèse and Amélie, were permitted to join us as we promenaded along the lake shoreline, and on these occasions we would stop at one of the cafés, where I would order drinks and confectionery to the obvious delight of the young girls, who thanked me profusely with their 'Merci beaucoup, Oncle Gaston.' It seemed that I was soon being accepted as a member of their extended family.

On several occasions I was able to take our small party out on to the lake in one of my family's boats. From the lake we could look back to the town framed by the mountains above; the younger children, when they joined us, excitedly pointing out those buildings that they recognised. I described to them the fish that lived in the lake, the means of my family's livelihood, and at times enthralled them as I recounted tales that had been passed down through the generations of exotic creatures and monsters that inhabited the darkest depths below us.

It was an enchanting time, poles apart from the horrors of war that we had until recently endured. It was on one of these occasions that Felix brought along his pocket camera, and, as I remember, took the photograph of Celestine that you found in his desk. I can sometimes recall that day as if it were only yesterday. The notes you found in the drawer were left by Célestine for him at his home, and, as you rightly surmised, they were arranging times when she could meet him. His parents were aware of this burgeoning friendship, and, as previously with my own friendship with Felix, they had raised no objections to these meetings.

At other times when Felix and I were able to meet alone

together, he would ensure that the conversation invariably included mention of Célestine, initially it seemed as if he were seeking my approbation of their friendship, which I was glad to give. But I still found difficulty in expressing my concerns to him about Célestine, so I decided to let the matter drop. Felix involved himself most days with his voluntary duties, for the numbers of repatriés arriving daily showed no sign of abating, while I made myself busy helping my family with the fishing business.

As the weeks passed and my leg became stronger I knew that before long the time would arrive for me to rejoin my regiment. Rumours were still spreading in the town about talk of mutiny within the army, but were dismissed by many as simply that, rumours, with no basis in fact.

But of course I was later to see for myself what had happened during my absence from the Front. That month of May saw a widespread refusal on the part of the common soldier, in some units, to obey orders and make yet another suicidal attack on heavily fortified enemy lines. The army was exhausted, morale at an all-time low, but I thank God that there was finally a realisation by our leaders of a need for change. General Nivelle, responsible for the disastrous attack along the Chemin des Dames, was replaced by General Petain in mid-May, a general widely revered by the men for his leadership in the battle of Verdun, and regarded by them as a soldier's soldier. He set about restoring morale with promises of no more suicidal attacks, a moderation of discipline, and exhausted units being allowed rest away from the Front. A rotation system was introduced that gave some respite from the continuous artillery bombardment that could finally grind down the stamina of even the bravest of men.

The mutiny could not be ignored, however, and I understood that courts martial were held in their thousands with hundreds sentenced to death, but I thank God that in the vast majority of cases, I believe, this sentence was finally commuted to a lesser one.

As the month of May neared its end we heard that Célestine's mother was soon to be released from hospital. The combination of a good diet, fresh air and the opportunity to exercise with daily walks, as her strength returned, allowed her health to be restored. The doctors were able to confirm that she had not in fact been consumptive, but her health had become so poor due to the sacrifices she had made by going without food at times in order that her children could eat. It was as a result of this that she had developed the worrying symptoms initially thought to be tuberculosis.

This news was greeted by all with much joy, the widow Levell declaring that of course Madame Aubert could lodge with her, as the family must be re-united, and there would be no argument in the matter. She was not one who regarded those suffering with consumption as 'untouchables'.

The news did not appear to bring the same reaction from all, however, for I observed that Célestine was always guarded in her response when the topic was raised, on occasion, in my company. Little did I realise then that this news was about to prompt an unimaginable tragedy that was to haunt us all for the rest of our lives.

'M'sieur Jean, what happened in the next few days was so unexpected that I felt I had been the unwilling player drawn into a nightmare. It grieves me so to recollect it.'

His sorrowful countenance warned me that he was about to impart some grave information.

CHAPTER NINE
A Tragedy

'Perhaps we should have another brandy, Gaston, before you continue, if you feel able to, that is,' I suggested, becoming concerned at the pain now obvious in the telling of his tale.

'A brandy, yes, but I will continue,' he replied, passing his glass to me, dispatching of the replenished liquid in one simple action.

It was a Wednesday morning and I had gone down very early to help my father prepare the boat, as there was a fishing expedition that morning. When we arrived at our fisherman's hut at the lakeside we immediately noticed that one of the small dinghies, normally beached on the shore, was missing. Perhaps one of the other fishermen had taken it out, we thought. But this seemed unlikely, as at this early hour there was a thick mist over the lake, and it would be another hour before the sun had fully risen and the warmth was enough to disperse it. So we continued our preparations for the day, getting the nets ready and stowing the oars on board.

Slowly the mist began to clear as the sun worked its magic, and it was then that I saw the outline of the missing dinghy, as it appeared a few hundred metres or so out on the lake. Pointing it out to my father, I offered to take our dinghy out to recover it.

Within no time I had reached the small boat, which I found empty, and I was about to tow it back to shore when I caught sight of something glinting in the bilges. Reaching over I plucked it out, to discover that it was a small silver brooch in the design of a cat with inset jade eyes. A feeling of horror came over me, for I knew at once who owned such an unusual brooch. Célestine.

In my mind there could surely be only one reason why she had ventured out on the lake under the cover of darkness, and I frantically looked around to see if there was any sign of her. Seeing nothing on the surface of the lake I knew what I had to do. Kicking off my clogs I plunged over the side of the boat into the depths of the lake.

The waters of the lake held no fear for me. I had swum here since I could barely walk, and furthermore I had been born with a caul, a membrane over my head, which my mother had so often told me was a sign that I would always be protected from death by drowning. In fact, such items had a monetary value. Sailors would often pay handsomely for them, as they considered that the carrying of a caul would prevent the wearer from drowning. But my mother would not entertain selling, despite numerous offers from those within the fishing community, and it was kept for me.

Down I dived, looking about me for any sign of Célestine. I feared that she must have entered the water some time ago and knew in my heart that by now she must already be dead. Her lungs, having been filled with water, would surely have sent her to the bottom of the lake. Three times I dived down, coming up for air each time only at the last possible moment, my chest feeling the intense pain as each time I broke the surface of the water, gasping for air. Finally, on my fourth dive, I saw the outline of her coat enveloping her poor body, lying amongst the weeds on the lake bed.

With a great effort, for, despite her petite frame, her waterlogged clothing added considerably to her weight, I managed to take hold of her and slowly take her to the surface. Managing now to lift her into my boat, I attempted to revive her, but soon realised that my efforts were far too late – her lungs had been filled with water for too long. I was about to hail to the shore for help when I became aware that some of the weight that had hampered my attempted rescue must be attributed to several small rocks that had been placed in her coat pockets. Realising the implications of this discovery, and the problems that would arise when it came to burial – for France has always been a strongly Catholic country – I determined to lose the rocks over the side, taking care to avoid any onlookers from the shore seeing my actions.

In order to present a credible scene, should an investigation ensue, I then removed one of the oars from the dinghy, carefully putting it over the side to float away from us. Thus having presented my tableau, I called out to the shore for assistance.

My father and one of my cousins rowed out to me, and seemed satisfied by my explanation of the scene that greeted them. The girl must have decided to row out in one of the boats early in the morning, for what reason it was unclear, and, losing one of the oars overboard, had over-reached to recover it, and fallen in, her heavy coat then pulling her under.

We set back to the shore, my father taking the empty dinghy in tow, and on arrival a coat was carefully laid over the poor girl. I went to our hut to find a change of clothes, while one of my cousins set off to alert the local gendarmerie.

Such drowning incidents as this, although unusual, would

not normally lead to a full police investigation, although the early hour was already being commented upon. But I shrugged at this as I gave my statement, saying that boats were regularly 'borrowed' at all times of the day and night. I had, of course, to say that I knew the young girl for I was certain this would come out later, as I had regularly been seen with Felix in her company around the town.

Finally, everyone seemed satisfied and I was allowed to leave, an ambulance by then having arrived to transport the body to the morgue.

My immediate thought then was how to break this terrible news to my friend Felix, and I resolved to make my way at once to his house. But it seemed that he already knew something was wrong, for as I was about to turn from the lakeside into Rue du Lac I saw him approaching from the opposite direction, his face showing clear signs of distress as he came nearer.

'I have been to Célestine's lodgings, but she is not there and appears to have disappeared,' he cried out in an agitated manner. I took my arm to his shoulder and steered him to an empty bench, indicating that we should sit down. Then, as tenderly as I was able, told him of the tragedy. He seemed uncomprehending at first, then, as the full realisation dawned, he muttered, 'So she has carried it out, as she wrote in her letter.'

Mystified, I asked for an explanation, and asking only that I read it and mention it to no one, he handed me the letter, which I carefully read, then re-read. I will repeat it now to you to the best of my recollection. Those words have been burned into my mind for the past fifty years, and before today never imparted to a single soul.

Perhaps I should call it Célestine's story – the letter that she sent to Felix in explanation for her actions, which I will now recollect to you. It began:

Dearest Felix,

I write this with a heavy heart in the expectation that I will be no more when you read it. I cannot further bear the burden of the shame that I would bring on my family should I tarry in this world any longer. I have made my decision despite the knowledge of the pain that it will bring you, my family and other dear friends, but I see no possible alternative, and I leave this letter as my testament.

During the occupation, like so many other households, we had German officers billeted with us at different times that we were charged to feed and attend to. The last to be billeted before we were repatriated was a young officer, who in his demeanour to us was at all times formal, though never cruel, unlike others that we had heard about.

Late one evening, while my mother was away nursing a dying neighbour, and the younger children were lying asleep upstairs in bed, he returned to find me alone in the kitchen. He had clearly been carousing with his fellow officers in one of the local cafés that they frequented, and, being unsteady on his feet, was clearly intoxicated. I was surprised when he then demanded that I bring him one of his bottles of wine that were kept under lock and key in the cellar.

I lit a candle and on asking for the key he said that he would come down with me in order to choose the bottle. As soon as we had descended the stone stairs I put the candle holder down on a shelf to light the store cupboard, and as I turned to ask for the key he seized me by the shoulder and pulled me to him. I struggled, protesting at first, but seemed powerless as he proceeded to violate me in so rough a manner that I fell in and out of consciousness.

Finally, having satisfied himself, he then left me without a word. I sobbed quietly to myself as I tried to re-arrange my, by now, dishevelled clothing, before returning upstairs. No mention of this episode was made by him in the days that followed, and then, to my relief, his unit was recalled to the Front three weeks later, and he never returned to our house.

But of course his deed had consequences that became more apparent to me by the day, and thus I see no other way but that I must depart this world before my condition manifests itself to all.

In the short while that I have known you I have been struck by your kind nature, always striving to help those less fortunate. May I ask of you one final favour – namely, to keep this letter strictly between ourselves, and, if you feel able, to lend whatever succour you can to my family at this time. They of course have no knowledge of the event that has led me to this sad outcome.

I write this in the earnest hope that you will feel able to forgive me, but am in such agony of mind that I see no future for myself.

Believe me

Your loving friend

Célestine

'Souviens-toi de moi'

'So I am correct in thinking that she was pregnant and fearing the shame on her family she took her own life?' I questioned, after taking a few moments to fully digest the contents of the letter as told to me by Gaston.

'That is what she believed, M'sieur Jean, but the truth was even stranger,' replied Gaston. 'Let me continue my story.'

I told Felix everything that had happened at the lake that morning and we were both convinced that she must be with child, although I confess that I had not noticed any recent change in her. So we both agreed that her suicide, for such it must surely have been, was a premeditated action. There seemed no doubt that an inquiry would be held, as the death would no doubt be regarded as suspicious, with an Examining Magistrate put in control of the proceedings.

We were both of one mind, however, that the contents of the letter should not be disclosed, and I was to stick to my story that this was a tragic boating accident, although the circumstances, particularly the hour at which it had occurred, made it appear somewhat bizarre. But surely, we thought, there would be a post-mortem carried out by a médecin légiste, and the truth would be uncovered. Faced with evidence of a pregnancy the magistrate may insist on further inquiries by the gendarmerie, adding further to the grief of her family, and delaying release of the body for burial. Feeling like conspirators, which I suppose we were, we realised that we could do no more to influence any inquiry.

Our thoughts now turned to Célestine's family, no doubt already alarmed by the sudden appearance of Felix earlier this morning. We resolved to go to the widow Levell's house at once, to break the sad news and see what assistance we could give to the family, knowing that the mother would soon be joining them following her stay at the hospital.

Madame Levell was naturally horrified to hear what we had to say, but, being of a stoical nature, took control of the situation, promising that she would look after telling the children and their mother the tragic news, as it would be better coming from her than from two young men that they barely knew. This made good sense to us, for, to be honest, we had not looked forward to this task, and, with promises to return soon, and offering to help in any way needed, we left her to her two small charges.

On our walk back to Felix's house we were both deep in thought, struggling to fully understand why this had come to pass. My thoughts kept returning to the earlier signs of sadness I had noticed that seemed to pervade her, wondering whether an opportunity had been missed for Célestine to talk to someone about her troubles. But why, I reminded myself, would she discuss something so deeply personal with us, when it was clear from the letter that she could not even confide in her mother.

Felix attempted to put on a brave face, but the strain on him was clear. Finally he exclaimed to me, 'In the short time that I knew her I believe I had fallen in love, and my dearest hope was that in time we may have been married. From our first meeting she had seemed the perfect companion, so why was I so blind to her suffering?' What could I say to the poor fellow, he was clearly in the depths of despair, and I began to have serious concerns for his state of mind. I intended to stay with him, supporting him for as long as he needed someone with whom he could speak.

On reaching his home we had to relate again the tragedy to his parents, with no mention of the letter, of course. It was clear from the looks between them that they were both deeply shocked, and, I am sure, already had an understanding of the fondness their son had formed with the poor dead girl. His father, after offering their condolences, insisted that he would offer his help in any way, mentioning that he understood the family had limited financial resources. This was typical of the kindness that he had so often shown in the past to others less fortunate. I was glad to think that having the support of a locally respected lawyer could also be of assistance during the inquiry process, if it was required.

Some hours later I returned home to my family. News

of the tragedy had quickly passed round the local fishing community, and no doubt my mother had been in her element regaling neighbours with my attempt to save the girl, no doubt referring to the protection afforded me by my caul, as I dived countless times below the surface of the lake. But there was a genuine sadness in my home as family members individually came to me expressing their concern for my friend and the poor girl's family.

The next few days passed by with only limited inquiries being followed up after the post-mortem was carried out, and finally, the necessary certificates having being issued, the body was released for burial. It appeared that my story of a tragic accident had been accepted.

But a greater shock was about to be revealed to both of us. The results of the post-mortem had been passed to the Examining Magistrate, and Felix's father, Monsieur Dumont, had been asked to write on behalf of Célestine's mother to ascertain details as to the cause of death. The report confirmed that death was due to drowning, as was expected, but it also stated that although the deceased had been in generally good health, an enlarged ovarian cyst was present in the body. With the mother's consent Monsieur Dumont had provided this information to Felix, who in turn discussed it with me.

Célestine had not been with child! The suicide should never have been entertained!

If only the poor girl had confided in her mother, further medical checks would surely have identified the condition, surgery undertaken, and her torment would finally have been put to rest. Our own knowledge of anatomy was obviously limited, so

I suggested that we would ask my mother, for she was regarded in our local community as something of a medical sage, often being consulted in times of illness and regularly assisting neighbours during childbirth.

Her reaction to our questions confirmed our suspicions. She had seen women with such cysts that had been mistaken for the early stages of pregnancy; the condition manifesting with similar symptoms such as nausea, sickness and abdominal swelling. She was mindful of Felix's presence in the room, and so kept her own counsel as to the likely impact this condition would have had on an unmarried and rather naive young girl.

But, of course, when I was later alone she challenged me directly as to whether I thought this had led her to take her own life. What could I say? Felix and I had already conspired to hide the truth, so, difficult as I found it to lie to my own mother, I was dismissive, and again kept to my story of the lost oar. I could see in her eyes, however, that she had already recognised the truth, but no doubt guessing at the motive behind my lies, the subject was never mentioned again.

This revelation did little to improve Felix's state of mind, for now, the unnecessary waste of a life which had held such promise cast a shadow over him to such an extent that I truly feared for his own life. I was so concerned that I ventured to speak alone to his parents about my fears, for I was now about to rejoin my unit at the Front. They thanked me for my concern, and promised to take the utmost care of their son during this most difficult time.

On my last evening in Evian I visited Felix to say goodbye, and having earlier discovered again the silver brooch in my fisherman's coat pocket, I gave it to him, explaining how I had found it, whilst hoping in my heart that this small object would not stir more painful memories. But I was surprised, for he immediately said that he would give it to Célestine's youngest sister, Amélie, as a keepsake – subject, of course, to her mother's approval.

With promises that I would write, and keep in touch, I departed early the next morning to rejoin my unit, and I was not to return home until the Christmas of the following year. The war, having cost the lives of so many of my comrades, had by then ended, with victory finally for France and her allies.

Unfortunately I had been unable to attend the funeral service for Célestine, as my return to the Front could be no longer delayed. But I received a letter from Felix recounting the event. It was clear that his father, Monsieur Dumont, had been instrumental in making the arrangements for the service, finding a burial plot in the town cemetery and arranging for a headstone to be erected.

'So that is my story, M'sieur Jean. You now know everything.'

The evening was getting late by now and I still had so many questions to ask, but I could see that the memories and secrets of fifty years past had profoundly affected him as he had recollected them to me, and Gaston was by now, clearly, very tired. So I decided that my curiosity would have to wait until the next morning when we arranged to meet again.

CHAPTER TEN
Sunday

I could barely wait to hear more from Gaston. I had spent a restless night turning over in my mind the events of fifty years ago. It was clear that Felix and Gaston had both conspired to hide the evidence of suicide from the authorities, surely a criminal act in itself, but knowing all the facts behind the girl's actions, I could not say that I would have acted otherwise. They had clearly been faced with a moral dilemma of huge proportions, perhaps the more so in the case of Felix as he was initially in possession of the letter and was due to commence his studies to become a lawyer when the war ended. For this reason he had asked Gaston to secrete away the letter, the actual hiding place now seemingly forgotten. Would he have wondered how his father may have acted, if placed in a similar position? Their actions were, of course, to protect the good name of Célestine, as any suggestion of suicide would have serious implications, particularly when it came to the funeral ceremony. The Catholic Church would not permit a service for a 'direct suicide', where the deceased had actively sought to end their life. Such a scandal would be hard to bear for the family, as France was a strongly Catholic country.

I greeted Gaston on his arrival, and suggested we go again into the study. He looked refreshed after a night's sleep, which set me wondering whether he had found some relief in finally being able to tell his story after all these years.

Florette brought us in coffee, but did not linger, for she must have sensed that we had important matters to discuss, and excused herself, intimating that she was attending the morning service at the church.

'Did I explain everything clearly last night?' asked Gaston.

'Very clearly,' I replied. 'There is so much that I have learned about my uncle. But if I may, I have some questions.'

'Of course, M'sieur Jean,' he replied, taking his seat again beside the desk.

'Would you say this was the reason why my uncle never married?' I cautiously asked, for this had always been a mystery to me.

'I am certain of it. Célestine had made such a strong impression on him, and then to lose her in such tragic circumstances deeply affected him for many years. In fact, I don't think he ever fully recovered. He seemed to withdraw into himself for such a long time, throwing himself first into his studies, then his career. It was finally his charitable work, helping those less fortunate, the dispossessed and homeless, that helped him to become again the Felix that we had always known.'

'So he never met anyone else with whom he formed a romantic attachment?' I enquired.

'There were one or two young women that I did wonder about as time went by. One was a teacher, the other the daughter of wealthy parents. Your mother of course encouraged these friendships, hoping they might develop into something more, for she had seen at first-hand his pain after the loss of Célestine, but of course had never fully understood, being unaware of the true story. But these friendships never blossomed, and both women eventually went on to marry elsewhere. Over the years he made and maintained a small circle of friends, and he seemed happy enough with this.'

'Do you know what became of Célestine's family?' I enquired, expecting that they had long ago left Evian and returned to Lille.

'I do, and that again is a small story in itself, which I will be happy to recount to you.'

At my nod in agreement Gaston continued.

The mother, Madame Aubert as you recall, was to rejoin her family at the time of the tragedy, following her stay as a patient at the hospital. This event did little to aid her recovery, but she was a strong character, as evidenced by her bringing up her children alone, following the death of her husband in the fighting of 1915. The widow Levell did what she could to help the family, and I believe Felix and his father ensured that they did not want financially. So they had stayed on in their lodgings with the kindly widow until shortly after the war had ended.

With a gradual return to normality after the War it was clear that the tourist industry would again thrive in Evian, and it was Monsieur Dumont who suggested to Madame Aubert that perhaps she ought to open a small restaurant, for her culinary skills had become known to him. It happened that suitable premises close to the lake, and owned by him, had become available due to the retirement of the current tenants, and he offered her the opportunity to take on a lease at a very low initial rent.

The restaurant soon became a success, and Catherine Aubert was helped initially by her middle daughter Thérèse, until Thérèse's marriage in 1925 to the son of one of their old neighbours in Lille. Thérèse then moved away to join her husband and his family, so the youngest daughter, Amélie, stepped in to help her mother.

I was by that time myself married, having met a girl who was a friend of my cousins who lived in the nearby town of Thonon-les-Bains. My wife Alice and I were happy for many years, until her untimely death in 1958. The pity is that we were never able to have children of our own, so I have had to content myself as uncle to my nephews and nieces.

The restaurant business continued to flourish for some years, and Monsieur Dumont's belief in Catherine's capability was justified. After the first few months she had been able to pay the full rent for the premises, and had then moved the family into the upper floor apartment when that became empty.

The pair of them, Catherine and Amélie, continued to run the restaurant for the next few years, numbering amongst their clients the local townspeople and visitors, all keen to sample their speciality dishes. As a young man I counted them among my customers, as fish dishes were always popular, and I got to know them both well.

Amélie was a pretty girl, much like her sister Célestine, and she was wooed by Vincent Bonnaire, the son of a local farmer, eventually marrying him in 1932. Vincent had been able to acquire a small farm with financial help from his family. This is situated in the heights above Evian close to the village of Saint-Paul-en-Chablais, and they have made their life there since. They have their own family now, of course, and the two boys and elder daughter have married and moved away. This leaves only the youngest daughter, Céleste, who has remained at home with her parents since she returned from university in Lyon.

Shortly after the marriage of Amélie, Catherine Aubert

decided to sell the restaurant. Unfortunately she did not live for much longer after that, for her earlier struggles during the war must have caused a weakening of the heart, to which she finally succumbed, and she was laid to rest with her daughter Célestine in the cemetery in Evian in 1938.

I attended the funeral service as a friend of the family.

CHAPTER ELEVEN
Life under the German Boot

Gaston paused for a few minutes as we both had a second cup of coffee, and he took the opportunity to light another of his Gauloises, before continuing his tale.

'M'sieur Jean it may be appropriate for me to tell a little more now of the family's time in Lille during the German occupation.'

Before she finally sold the restaurant, Catherine Aubert had met with Monsieur Dumont and Felix, during which time she discussed with them the intricacies pertaining to the lease, seeking their advice on various points, and during these conversations she had described to them her life in Lille prior to her arrival in Evian. Felix told me of this much later, saying that he felt that Célestine's mother was attempting to offer her own record, a testament even, of events in the occupied territories during the war.

The German occupation of parts of France during the Great War has been forgotten by many today, perhaps overshadowed as it is by the much larger occupation that took place during the Second World War. It was no less harsh, and some would say more so, given the smaller area that came under the control of the German forces, which enabled them to impose their iron-like grip with all the resources at their command.

We French are only too aware that at the outset of the war the invading German army had imposed their will on the population in the territories they occupied with ruthless efficiency. Overnight the lives of countless numbers of people were changed, as German rules were introduced, these often being laid out in posters displayed on the streets. The penalties for disobeying these edicts were severe: fines, imprisonment or even death in certain cases.

All households were required to post the names, ages and occupations of all the inhabitants, for the Boche have always maintained a reputation for record-keeping. It was customary for regular roll calls to be carried out in town or village squares, often purely as a means of exercising control over the population; but at other times used for other purposes. These included the creation of forced labour gangs, who were then transported into Germany to work on the land or in factories. The Boche were only interested in providing for their own needs, and showed no concern over the separation or breaking up of families.

Requisition, which was the euphemistic term used for the looting carried out by German soldiers of any household goods, livestock or machinery that may be of use to them, was widespread. Provisional receipts of compensation were sometimes issued, but were of little consolation as they were only rarely paid.

Civilian morale was further lowered by the large German presence in Lille, as it was commonplace to see German troops passing through the city as they made their way to and from the front lines. Allied prisoners of war were also regularly forced to march through the streets, in an attempt to further crush the morale of the population.

Food shortages were rife, and malnutrition, coupled with

the oppressive living conditions of many, further exacerbated by harsh winters, led to widespread disease and sickness. Madame Aubert was adamant that Lille, being a city, was particularly hard hit in this respect, as there was a lack of the fresh produce that was more evident in rural areas.

In the countryside it was commonplace for farmers to simply give away produce to their neighbours, to prevent it being requisitioned, so there was at least the opportunity to prepare meals containing fresh foodstuffs.

Poor quality food, which was heavily rationed, included a staple diet of bread made from potato, rye and flour, which was almost inedible. Madame Aubert, like so many mothers, often went without meals herself in a vain attempt to keep her own children fed.

Diseases affected both the young and elderly, and these included diphtheria, scarlet fever and measles. Outbreaks of typhoid were also prevalent due to infected water and food sources. The occupying Germans used the Repatriation Service to their own ends, effectively removing the burden of looking after these sick people, returning them to free France via Switzerland.

Collaboration with the Germans occurred on many different levels. Sometimes it was forced upon the local population, where services or goods were required by the occupying forces. At other times it was freely offered, with the prospect of seeking privileges. There were countless examples of French women willingly sleeping with soldiers, for the promise of certain privileges, often resulting in the birth of unwanted 'Boche babies', giving rise to abortion, even infanticide.

Madame Aubert and her daughters lived in a small terraced house in one of the suburbs of Lille, she being a widow since her husband, Georges, was killed in the fighting during 1915.

Life had become beset with difficulties for the family, as with so many others, not the least of which was the acquisition of sufficient food on which to live. The family no longer had a main breadwinner, in common with so many others – husbands either lost, killed in action, or captured, and otherwise absent, fighting for their country. It then fell upon Madame Aubert to fulfil this role to the best of her ability, the family eking out an existence that at least saw them keeping above actual starvation.

But, changes occurred, and their situation was improved somewhat by the billeting of German officers on their household from time to time. These officers were usually destined to be sent to the Front, so the period of time spent with the family was usually of short duration.

This improvement in their living standards was easily explained. The officers had, it seemed, unlimited access to requisitioned food, and in return for cooked meals, which were always to a high standard (for Madame Aubert was a skilled cook), and for ensuring their uniforms were well laundered, any surplus food could be consumed by the family.

These officers were of course of Teutonic origin, and sometimes appeared somewhat uncouth in their manners towards the family, who had been used to a more civilised environment. However, the officers, being older than the troops they commanded, generally posed no threat to the family, seemingly happy enough to be billeted in a household with a capable cook and housekeeper at hand.

Contact between them was kept to a minimum, and thus their presence had not impinged too greatly on family life. There were rumours abounding of officers billeted with other families in the neighbourhood who had behaved in a cruel manner towards their hosts, but fortunately this had not occurred to the Aubert family. This routine followed by the family and their 'guests' allowed Madame Aubert to spend some time ministering to her sick neighbours, despite being in poor health herself. She had also become accustomed to sharing her bed with the two youngest daughters at night, who, cuddled up together with her, seemed to appreciate this closeness, and the warmth that they produced helped to stave off the cold of the wintry nights.

Célestine, being that much older, slept in the adjoining bedroom.

Distant explosions emanated from the artillery, Boche and Allied alike, situated only a few kilometres distant from the city, playing their percussive symphony as they brought death and destruction, a constant reminder of the war, if further needed, playing out in the background of everyone's lives.

The last officer to be billeted with the family was somewhat younger, and judged to be in his late twenties. He was a Hauptmann in rank, what we would call a Capitaine, named Wilhelm Mayer. He was unmarried, as far as the family was aware, and had prior to the war lived in Berlin, thus regarded himself as Prussian, with all of its militaristic connotations.

Despite his rather arrogant nature, given to ways of always demanding rather than simply asking, his aggressive Teutonic accent at times seeming to fill every corner of the house, he did not treat the family badly. His expectations were relatively simple and extended, as with the previous officers, to receiving well prepared meals when demanded, a finely laundered uniform, of which he seemed inordinately proud, and a high polish to his boots, all of which Madame Aubert's family were more than able to provide. Doubtless the conditions in the house, though rather simple in nature, would be in stark contrast to his experience in the forward trenches, and thus he gave her the impression that he was generally satisfied with his lodgings, though always keeping conversation to a minimum.

On most days he left the house early in the morning, meeting up with his Company for drill and training purposes, whilst they awaited further orders from the Staff officers above. The evenings he seemed to spend carousing with his fellow officers at one of the many bars that catered for them. These bars, from which the locals were normally excluded, were often occupied by women seeking the special treatment and gifts that were always on offer from the soldiers, on the clear understanding that they would be expected to bestow their favours in return. Hunger and hopelessness had forced many young women to adopt this course of action, which was, in effect, collaborating with a reviled enemy.

Spending, as he did, comparatively little time at the house, which he regarded simply as somewhere to lay his head when weary. The Hauptmann barely intruded on the family, and in late March of 1917 they were informed that he would be leaving his billet and returning to the Front, after which time they never heard from him again.

This happily coincided with news that the family were to be finally repatriated to free France. The household now became in some disarray, the normal routine of attending to the needs of the Hauptmann having ended, the family busily spent the next week packing what clothes and other items they could take, making their final preparations for the journey ahead. The task of making arrangements for this journey, with all the underlying excitement and thoughts of freedom, now so soon to be realised, helped her put personal worries about her health to one side. All the years of hardship and sacrifice for the sake of the children had by now taken its toll, as was to be discovered by the medical staff on their arrival at Evian.

'Thus you see, M'sieur Jean, that there was no mention of the episode between Celestine and the Hauptmann, the secret was never divulged to other family members.'

'Are you still in contact with the family?' I asked Gaston.

'Why yes, I still visit them at the farm at times. As I mentioned earlier they are still nearby, on the road up towards the mountains. I got to know Amélie well when she worked at the restaurant.'

'Do you think I could meet them, Gaston, before I return to London?' I asked, assuring him at the same time that I had no intention of divulging his secret. Expecting there to be some hesitation, I was somewhat surprised when Gaston offered to telephone Amélie immediately, after explaining to me that the family were most often to be found at home on a Sunday afternoon, taking the opportunity for some time off from the daily farm chores. I happily agreed with his suggestion, for my time spent in Evian was by now becoming limited. I was expecting to return to my office in London within the next few days, once I had concluded my business with the bank.

Leaving Gaston in the study to make the call I went out to the kitchen, having heard Florette return from church. She asked if Gaston would be lunching with us, as she had prepared a quiche, intending to have a more substantial meal ready for the evening, if that was satisfactory. I could only concur with her, explaining that we would be setting off in the afternoon, if the Bonnaire family were found to be at home.

Returning to the study I could immediately see by Gaston's smile that the visit had been arranged . . . for three o'clock, he confirmed.

CHAPTER TWELVE
A Memorable Meeting

Having finished lunch, we went out to the garage where the Citroën was parked. Gaston would drive us as he knew the route, but I took the opportunity to mention that I would check tomorrow and arrange insurance for myself, as it would be useful to have a car at my disposal at any time. He seemed to accept this, adding only that he would of course be happy to drive for me, as he had always driven for my late uncle, when required. I thanked him for his kind offer, and we set off out of town, taking one of the roads that turned upwards towards the mountains.

As we drove higher up into the mountains we found ourselves entering a truly magical alpine scene, so different from the town we had just left behind us. The lush pasture land that lined the road was awash with swathes of colour created by the wild flowers that bloomed abundantly at this time of year, before the strong summer sun later caused them to shrivel up in its heat. The occasional house that we passed now was in contrasting style to the architecture found in the town below. Here the use of timber, in plentiful supply from the woodlands that adorned the mountainside, was much in evidence, the chalet-style roofs clothed in timber shingles and overflowing log stores lining the stone walled basements.

'Another world, M'sieur Jean,' commented Gaston.

After twenty minutes or so we had reached our destination.

A large timber-framed farmhouse stood well back from the road, approached down a narrow track, and with the winter quarters for the animals, cattle or sheep, to one end of the building. There was a small area of land adjacent to the house that had been cultivated to form a potager, providing vegetables and soft fruit for the household, together with a flower garden with its vibrant display in evidence, and to the rear an orchard inhabited by a flock of chickens, their wheeled timber ark standing centrally on the grass, between the rows of trees.

Hearing the arrival of our car the front door was opened, and an attractive middle-aged woman, whom I took to be Amélie, came out to greet us. As Gaston effected introductions I was momentarily struck by her appearance, for there was a marked similarity to the photograph I had discovered of Célestine. But even this could not prepare me sufficiently as she introduced me to her daughter, Céleste, who had been, until now, standing behind her in the doorway. A beautiful young woman of above average height, her auburn hair cut short in the current fashionable style, her eyes had the same smouldering intensity as those displayed in the photograph. But there was one marked difference that I immediately observed; they showed no hint of sadness.

How I must have appeared to them at this first meeting I can't recollect, but it was some time before I had recovered my composure sufficiently to thank them for inviting us over. Amélie, particularly, was anxious to offer her condolences for the loss of my uncle, being so sorry that she had not heard about the funeral in time, and thus had been unable to attend. She complimented me on my mastery of French – 'So unusual for an Englishman,' she commented – then nodded in understanding as I explained that my mother had insisted we spoke in her native tongue at home, whenever possible. I thanked her for her kind thoughts about my uncle, and being told that her husband Vincent would join us soon, we all went into the house.

There was a warm feeling evident in the old timber building. The sitting room where we eventually settled was comfortably furnished, the oak parquet floor polished to a shine that appeared to glow, bedecked with colourful rugs of indeterminate age. For centuries past the house must have provided shelter to generations of farmers, a refuge for them in harsh winters, when logs harvested from the surrounding woodland blazed in an open hearth. Windows then would have been flung open in late spring to let the ancient timbers be imbued with the sun's warmth. Ever present, the house had overseen so many events, at times of great joy, the birth of a child, perhaps, or a family wedding; and at other times of sadness, the passing of a loved one. The old building must have held so many memories, perhaps even dark secrets.

Gaston seemed very much at home as he chatted with Amélie, recalling times spent at the restaurant, and I felt somewhat left out of the conversation. But Amélie, sensing this, played the perfect hostess, with little asides to me, bringing me in to the discussion, seeking my opinion on this point or that particular piece of news. Céleste's opinion was also sought, and it was immediately clear to me, from the opinions she expressed, that she had a better grasp than most of current events in France. As she had only recently completed her studies at Lyon University, I ventured to ask her for her views on the student unrest so prevalent at present. It surprised me to hear that she felt we were probably about to face great changes in French society, echoing the views of my friend Michael so closely that I wondered aloud whether she knew him. No, she did not, but she had read some of his articles, and seemed impressed to know that he was a friend of mine.

'We were at school together in England,' I explained. 'Both of us studied French, and he sometimes came to stay at my uncle's house with me during our school holidays. Later he moved to Paris to continue his career in journalism, and writes today about politics, and society in general.'

This talk of politics indicated to me that there was an obvious divergence of views between mother and daughter, and the atmosphere became lightened somewhat when Amélie suggested that Céleste could, perhaps, show me around the farm. I was certainly more than happy to take up this offer, so we left Gaston and Amélie to their reminiscences.

Now, being alone with Céleste, I felt more at ease, asking her about her student days, and future plans. She gave her answers casually, giving away a little, but always ending them with a question for me. Having spoken French during our time at the farmhouse, I was a little surprised when she began asking me questions in English about my own life and family. Hearing that I lived in London she remarked that she had stayed with a family in Hampstead, on an exchange visit in her last year at school, which had been enjoyable, despite the 'horrible' English weather.

This small talk continued for a while, as I wondered to myself if I could turn the conversation around to family events back in 1917.

'Is Céleste a family name?' I enquired, hoping this may lead her to mention her late aunt.

'In a way, I suppose. I think my mother named me in memory of her sister Célestine. She died during the Great War.'

And that was that. She clearly seemed to know nothing more.

The family had apparently closed ranks after the event, and the next generation was seemingly unaware of Célestine's story. I had to remind myself, of course, that this tragedy had occurred fifty years ago, and during a time of both great personal and national turmoil. Since then another World War had resulted in the surrender and occupation of France for five long years, bringing with it its own tales of misery and injustice. Evian had not escaped this second time as lightly as before.

So I came back to the present day, explaining to her that I would be staying in Evian for a few more days only, before business commitments required my return to London. Her reply to this puzzled me.

'You may have to stay here longer, Jean. Following the events at the Sorbonne on Friday with the harsh treatment handed out by the police, and the arrests of four hundred students, there are rumours of a General Strike looming and that could affect all services, including transport.' I was greatly surprised at this, having been rather out of touch with the news recently. I explained that my uncle's passing and his funeral had totally overshadowed my life these past days, and commented that I would speak to my journalist friend, Michael, as he would surely be aware of any planned strikes.

'How well do you know him, Jean? He is fast becoming a well-known journalist, and particularly writes his articles from the viewpoint of the young people in France. He reflects the general feeling that the Establishment is out of touch with a majority of the people, who are becoming tired of its paternalistic, somewhat old-fashioned approach. His articles, I believe, are becoming a cause of some consternation to the Government in particular.'

'As I've already told you, we were at school together, and I met up with him again recently, last Monday evening in Paris, on my way to Evian. I understand that he's proposing to drive through France, to ascertain what impact, if any, the actions of the students and workers in Paris is having upon the provinces. I am hoping that he'll have time to come here after he visits Lyon. He has written extensively about the situation in Paris, but, of course, as is often the case with London, events in the capital do not necessarily reflect what is happening elsewhere in the country.'

'But surely the students' viewpoint will be heard wherever there are universities?'

'Yes, perhaps so – but to what extent will their actions mirror Paris? Will we see wide-scale protests, riots even, in cities like Lyon, for example?'

I suddenly realised that we must have been discussing the student unrest to the exclusion of all else for the last half hour, and made some clumsy attempt to indicate my pleasure at walking in such beautiful alpine surroundings with my new-found companion.

'Oh you are so poetic, Jean, a veritable Lord Byron,' she replied with a broad smile lighting her face. But, sensing my discomfort, she quickly began to give me a short résumé of the farm, pointing out the meadows, currently awash with colour from a myriad variety of wild flowers, to be used as pasture later in the year when the cattle were brought down from the heights above us, then indicating the stone-based timber barns where they would be spending the harsh winters.

Climbing over one of the wooden stiles that divided two of the meadows I offered her my hand, which she took, with the response 'You are such an English gentleman, Jean,' and then continued to hold onto my hand as we made our way back to the house. The effect of this on me was quite disconcerting, although pleasurable. Here I was, having met Céleste only an hour or so earlier, now walking beside her, hand in hand.

She must have sensed what sway her actions were having on me, saying, 'You must remember, Jean, you are in France now, so forget your English sangfroid,' and squeezing my hand she released it again.

What was I to do? To my own surprise, and perhaps not a little to hers, I reached out and clasped her hand again, saying, 'If this is the French way I will happily be a French convert.' And so, both of us now laughing, and by now feeling so at ease in her company, we walked down the drive back to the house.

Entering the sitting room again we were greeted by Vincent, Amélie's husband. A tall, powerfully built man of about sixty years of age, his receding dark hair peppered with grey framing a ruddy complexion, evidence of an open-air life but with a serious expression, and strong calloused hands indicative of the manual nature of his livelihood. To me he presented an image of the typical bourgeois farmer, owning his few acres and buildings, so commonly found in rural France. He had finished his chores for the present, though he was still wearing his blue overalls, as there were further tasks to be carried out later. Insisting that they were quite clean, he was now happy to sit with us for a while. Amélie and Céleste went through to the kitchen and prepared a tea, which Amélie assured us 'the occasion merited'.

Vincent and Gaston were clearly old friends, and they both explained that some of our chickens back in the Evian garden were originally from the farm. 'Did you see them, M'sieur Jean, on your walk?' Gaston enquired.

'Of course, they are great specimens, such beautiful colours,'

I replied, not daring to say that during the walk I had eyes for one person only, chickens being furthest from my thoughts. The subject was not pursued by Gaston, who, however, looked at me thoughtfully.

Tea was brought in then with great ceremony, accompanied by a delicious selection of home-baked cakes. The tea had a relaxing effect upon us as Vincent regaled us for a few minutes with his future plans for the farm.

'Further pasture for the cattle would allow me to extend the herd, but, of course, I won't be able to carry on forever, and there seems little interest from the next generation in continuing to farm – but time will tell, I suppose.' This latter comment appeared to be said rather pointedly to Céleste, but she seemed to ignore it and made no response.

My own limited knowledge of French inheritance law set me wondering to myself what might eventually happen to this farm. The law was quite strict in its attempt to pass farms down to the next generation, but unlike English law, where the eldest son often inherited, in France all the children were entitled to a share. I was aware that Céleste had older siblings, but apparently, as I recalled, they were now married and had moved away from the area, and presumably had no wish to become farmers.

Gaston, perhaps in an attempt to offer a solution, remarked on his own situation. 'Having no children of my own, I had to decide which of my nephews was to take over the fishing business. Fortunately there was one in particular who from a young age had accompanied me on fishing trips whenever possible.'

Vincent nodded in understanding at this remark. He then proceeded to exchange with Gaston the latest gossip from their respective communities. But, however pleasantly the afternoon passed, the conversation covering so many topics, the time finally arrived for us to take our leave.

I was now becoming increasingly nervous as to how I could contrive a further meeting with Céleste, when she rescued me by asking if my friend Michael was likely to arrive in Evian soon.

'I can phone you as soon as I hear,' I replied. 'Perhaps we can all meet up for a meal in town, as he may be staying for a couple of days.'

'Yes, I will look forward to that,' came her reply, her eyes meeting mine, overpowering me so much with their intensity that I felt I would have to look away, but, mesmerised, I could only hold her gaze. I must confess that I had never felt so spellbound before in my life.

No sooner had we driven up the drive to the main road when Gaston observed, 'The chickens are only white, M'sieur Jean, I don't think you noticed them at all,' adding with a smile, 'She is a beautiful young woman, wouldn't you agree?'

I coloured a little at this, nodding in agreement, realising that little was missed by my old friend.

Gaston returned to his apartment after we had finished the evening meal, as he had a number of household chores to attend to.

Left alone to my thoughts, try as I might, they constantly returned to the young woman I had met only this afternoon, such was the impression she had made on me, and I almost began to count the hours since we had parted. No one had ever had such an intense effect on me before.

CHAPTER THIRTEEN
A Surprise Encounter

I called at Jacques' office on Monday morning, as previously arranged, and, fortified with a coffee from Clarisse, we looked over the paperwork relating to the portfolio. Jacques explained that the management of these properties was carried out by a local agent, a Monsieur Durand, and suggested that he would telephone him to make an appointment for me to discuss the current arrangements. This seemed most suitable to me, knowing that my time in Evian was now becoming rather limited. He was able, a few minutes later, to arrange a meeting for that very afternoon, writing down the address of the office for me.

Jacques had also prepared a letter for the bank, which he passed to me, having already spoken to the manager, to whom my visit was expected.

'That should take care of any immediate bills due on the estate,' he remarked, adding that he was in the process of preparing the various deeds required setting out my position as principal heir, together with details relating to the other beneficiaries.

'This will all take some time, Jean, as I am sure you will understand. But you will have to make some personal decisions as to the estate – will you retain or sell?'

'That is a decision I don't want to face just yet, but I realise that I now have responsibilities to face in France,' I replied. 'For the present I intend to retain the family home and have asked Florette to stay on as housekeeper, as I shall be making regular visits over the next few months. As I understand it, the estate will be no financial burden to me.'

'Absolutely – the estate is in good health, as you may say, with good reserves at the bank. I will keep in touch with you, Jean, and keep you advised of progress.'

Having thanked Jacques, and promising him that I would let him know how I got on with the agent, I made my way over to the bank.

My business at the bank took no time at all, the manager suggesting that it would be helpful were I to open a personal account there, in his words 'to satisfy the head office', which was duly done. Assuring him that no changes were proposed at present to the existing accounts, and being satisfied with Jacques' letter, he instructed one of the clerks to draw out sufficient funds to cover our present housekeeping needs. Having concluded our business, and once more offering his condolences, he showed me out to the main door.

On leaving the bank I almost bumped into Céleste as I came out into Rue Nationale, the central street in town. Both of us were initially surprised, then, quickly recovering, she quipped, 'Jean, you must think I am maybe following you?'

'Oh, I'm used to young women following me,' I replied, trying to keep a straight face, but, unable to maintain the pretence for more than a second or two, I smiled, at which point we both laughed together.

Telling her that I was still trying to make contact with Michael, I asked whether she would care to join me for lunch as I was staying in the town centre before an afternoon meeting with the rental agent. A quizzical look crossed her face at mention of my meeting so I suggested I could tell her more about it over lunch, adding, 'It's my treat.'

Ten minutes later saw us seated outside one of the small restaurants that overlooked the lake, and having chosen from the lunch menu, and with a carafe of the local red wine shared between us, I proceeded to tell her more about my uncle's estate. I explained that I had been left the bulk of it, which included the family home and a portfolio of investment properties.

'So, can I ask if you are proposing to sell?' was her response.

Admitting that I didn't know what I was going to do yet, I added that it would be some months before probate for the estate was finalised. Until then I had decided that I would maintain the status quo, but as to the future, who could say? I would certainly have to spend some time here in the near future, if only to attend to this business. This seemed to please her, so, emboldened, I mentioned that I was arranging to insure the car today so that I could take the opportunity of exploring the surrounding countryside, adding, with a smile, 'Perhaps you would be my guide?'

'Why Jean, I would be delighted. Perhaps we can also visit Switzerland if you have the time, as I haven't been since finishing university. The border is not so many kilometres away.'

'How strange. I was also planning to visit Montreux and Vevey again, perhaps even taking in the Chateau Chillon, in homage to your Lord Byron. I'm free tomorrow, so perhaps I can call for you after nine o'clock. We can lunch in Montreux if you like.'

'Tomorrow will be fine, but I insist that I will prepare a picnic to take with us.'

Both now aware of the time, Céleste having arranged to meet her mother, who would be driving them home, and with my appointment also looming, we finished our meal. Standing on the pavement we said our goodbyes, laughing again as we both simultaneously said, 'Until tomorrow morning.' I wondered at my good fortune in having met Céleste again so soon.

The rental agency was situated on the ground floor of premises close to the casino, with the typical display of property photographs and particulars displayed both in the windows and on the office walls inside. Monsieur Durand was seated at his desk, studying some papers, as I entered. When I introduced myself, he beckoned me to take a seat at the desk before proceeding to lock the entrance door and pull down the blind. By way of explanation he commented that his secretary was out of the office, carrying out an inspection, and would not be returning today, so, by locking the door, we would not be disturbed.

He was older than I expected, certainly turned sixty, a tanned complexion, and exuding success, his well-tailored suit and the gold Rolex watch on his wrist testament to this. But there was an underlying energy also evident in his demeanour, indicating to me that here was an excellent negotiator should the situation warrant it.

'I have acted on behalf of your late uncle for many years, Monsieur Dawson. I was saddened to hear of his death – it was quite unexpected' he said, in a sombre tone, given the circumstances.

'Thank you, it certainly came as a shock' I replied.

'I must congratulate you on the eulogy you gave at the funeral service, which I felt illustrated his life so well,' he continued. 'I introduced myself to you after the service, but of course it would not have been proper to discuss business matters at that time. Monsieur Martin the notaire arranged this appointment today'.

'Yes, I was in his office when he phoned' I replied.

Turning to the file on his desk he suggested that he might first give me a more detailed appraisal of the portfolio, before we visited some of the apartments, with which I concurred, adding that I was keen to see some of them today if possible, as my time in Evian was, for the present, limited.

From what he explained to me the majority of the properties were in good condition, as Felix had always been a conscientious landlord. Over the years he had added a number of properties, some of them being in need of improvement. Generally he had favoured buildings in the better locations, so there was rarely any problem for the agency in finding good quality tenants. Consequently the apartments, together with a few commercial premises, were readily let if they became vacant, and the rent roll was always steadily maintained. I was also interested to see which of the properties were being let to deserving cases, at lower rents, a result of Felix's connections with local charities. I made it clear to Monsieur Durand that I was not minded to consider any changes to these tenancies, and would welcome the opportunity to meet one or two of the tenants to see for myself where they had been housed.

'This is easily done, Monsieur Dawson. I had anticipated this and have made arrangements for us to inspect this afternoon, if that is your wish.' Confirming that this was the case we left the office a few minutes later, walking a couple of blocks away to a small building where Felix had found tenants through his charitable contacts. These currently included a widow with a young family whose husband had been tragically killed in a road traffic accident, and an ex-soldier who, on returning to the locality had found himself homeless, his parents having passed away while he had been stationed in Algeria.

This latter tenant reminded me again of my encounter by the

Pont Neuf in Paris, with the ex-soldier some years previously, and I began to understand more how my late uncle's caring nature would have had a profound effect on the quality of life of these people. How many others in his position would only be interested in maximising the return on their investment?

Monsieur Durand must have been reading my thoughts, as he commented, 'There are not many like your uncle – for most, profit is the only goal.' I nodded in agreement, thinking for the moment back to some of the clients I had left behind in London. How many of them would be prepared to offer their apartment portfolios at reduced rents to deserving cases? Probably none of them, I considered.

Madame Mercier, the widow, greeted us both warmly and invited us in to her apartment. Understanding who I was, she paid her respects to my late uncle, saying that he had helped many people in the town. She was obviously very house-proud, and everything in the apartment seemed to sparkle. She seemed pleased to show us the neat kitchen that led from the living room, commenting to Monsieur Durand that the plumber had already been and dealt with the dripping tap. From their conversation it was clear that the agency was maintaining the properties to a good standard, as was also evidenced by the clean and welcoming communal stairway area. It turned out that Madame Mercier had been offered, and had accepted, the task of cleaning the communal areas of this building and several others in the vicinity, thus providing her with an income and the flexibility in her working hours to accommodate the needs of her young family.

Next Monsieur Durand took me to the top floor and opened the apartment door. 'The tenant is out at work, but has given us permission to inspect the flat,' he said, adding before I could ask, 'he now works as a delivery driver for one of the local businesses. He is the ex-soldier I mentioned earlier.' The flat, situated within the roof of the building with sloping ceilings and dormer windows, though small, provided its occupant with adequate living space, a small kitchen and one single bedroom. It was again in a good state of repair. Certainly it was more basically furnished, and lacked the sparkle we had seen previously. It provided, nevertheless, a comfortable home for this working man. What a life-changing difference this apartment must have made to a homeless man I thought, remembering again the ex-soldier in Paris.

Having completed the viewings for the day we returned to the agency, where I was shown various plans and photographs of other buildings, some of which were clearly of a different class altogether, many having views over the lake. The rents from these helped to subsidise the charitable housing, he explained, and by buying shrewdly over the years, and improving the stock, the portfolio was now in good shape. He produced from his file a document which he handed to me, saying, 'This gives the full picture, the rent rolls, and current valuations should you be thinking of selling, Monsieur Dawson.'

Assuring him that this would not be the case at present, I asked him to continue the management on my behalf, and added, 'Jacques Martin, the notaire, will confirm all this in writing to you, and any monies received for the present should be paid into the bank account as before. As I am sure you know it will take some time to finalise probate, after which I will make any decisions necessary.'

'Very good, Monsieur Dawson, I trust I can be of service to you in the same way that I was to your uncle,' he remarked as he opened the office door for me, before bidding me a good evening.

I had as yet only glanced quickly at the document, but the

figures seemed astronomical to me, even allowing for likely reductions after death duties. There seemed more income here than I had ever previously dreamed of attaining, even were I to become a partner in the London law firm. I would certainly need to take further advice from Jacques, who I was sure could arrange an introduction to a trustworthy accountant, who would be able to advise me further on the tax situation. Judging by his previous comments, advice had already been sought in the past to minimise the tax burden on the estate.

Fortunately there was no pressing need to make any hasty decision, the tax and probate situation would be dealt with over the next few months, and with the benefit of sound advice I would be able to make plans for my future, now beginning to wonder where that may lead me. Only two short weeks ago I had thought my future lay in London, but now other possibilities seemed to beckon on the horizon.

My thoughts were certainly pre-occupied with property matters following the afternoon spent with Monsieur Durand, but as I made my way back towards the house they drifted again to my lunch with Céleste. What would she think of my situation? True, I had made some reference to my uncle's estate, but the reality of my position now began to sink in. I was no longer just a hard-working young lawyer, surely I would be perceived as a fully paid-up member of the bourgeoisie, a capitalist even. Would this affect my friendship with her, being aware of her obvious mistrust of the establishment and her expressed feelings of solidarity with the students?

Tomorrow, I felt, would be an opportunity to talk openly about my business affairs and hoped that they would not cast a cloud over our fledgling friendship.

CHAPTER FOURTEEN
A Trip to Switzerland

The next morning I awoke to a cloudless sky, which I took to be a good omen for the day ahead. I had told Florette that I would be driving into Switzerland for the day, and was unlikely to return until late evening. Gaston had been busy with his nephew on Monday, carrying out some repairs to the fishing boat, so we had not spoken since our visit to the farm.

I had arranged the car insurance in town yesterday, so was now ready to drive the Citroën up to the farm, ensuring that I had my passport with me, if required at the border. Gaston always kept the petrol tank full – a habit of many years, as he had often driven Felix to Lyon or Annecy at short notice, when clients had requested his presence.

As the Citroën was much larger than my MG, it took a little time to become used to handling the large saloon, but I was impressed with the smooth ride as I headed up the rural roads towards the farm. The futuristic styling of the large black Citroën DS, with its hydro-pneumatic suspension, was also the favoured car of the President of France, General de Gaulle. His life was saved when, as a passenger with his wife, they survived an assassination attempt by members of the OAS, because the car was still being capable of being driven off at speed despite tyres having been punctured by machine-gunfire. The car certainly left its passengers oblivious to the ruts and potholes found so frequently on roads in rural France. The short journey passed with little other traffic in evidence, save for the occasional tractor and a yellow La Poste van, slowly making its progress up the mountain, with deliveries of letters and parcels for the inhabitants of the small villages and isolated farmsteads in this region. As I climbed higher two eagles came into view, wheeling effortlessly high above the car on thermal currents of air, eyes searching the ground below for the next meal – a young rabbit or vole perhaps, a catch to feed the voracious appetites of their young eaglets back at the eyrie.

I was greeted by Amélie as I arrived outside the house. She had been picking some bearded iris blooms from the flower garden, and was on her way to the back door, but turned round on hearing the car as I came down the drive.

'Bonjour, Jean, how nice to see you again, Céleste is almost ready,' she called out, inviting me to come in and wait. She stood the flowers in a large jug on an enamel draining board next to the stone kitchen sink, commenting on their colour in an attempt to make conversation. 'I try to bring them into the house as they seem to bloom for such a short time, and I don't like to miss them,' she said, then went on to ask about our planned trip.

She asked whether I was a notaire, and I attempted to explain to her the differences between the legal systems in France and England, which seemed to satisfy her. Being free today, I was looking forward to a drive in the area before my impending return to London, where I practised law 'in the English legal system,' I added with a smile.

Saying she hoped that I would have time to visit them again before leaving France, Amélie then called out to Céleste, who appeared some moments later, a large wicker basket in her hand containing the picnic. With a smile on her face she greeted me as her chauffeur.

'Céleste!' her mother chided her, 'Whatever will Jean think of you!'

'Oh, I think he knows my sense of humour,' came back the swift reply, and her mother nodded a little apprehensively.

Taking the basket I decided to act the chauffeur, saying, 'If Mademoiselle is ready, the car awaits,' to the obvious delight of them both. So we took our leave of her mother, who reminded me to visit again at any time, and after stowing the basket in the boot of the car, and each of us checking that the other had their passport, we set off, down towards the lakeside road that would take us to the Swiss border in the nearby lakeside town of St Gingolph.

Céleste made a comment about how smart the car was, and I explained it had belonged to my uncle, but now, like so much else besides, had been passed to me. I found myself recounting events at the agent's meeting, which she knew had followed our lunch yesterday. As I told her everything, including my meeting with Madame Mercier in her apartment, I noticed a more thoughtful look on her face, and she listened intently. Having finished I waited for what seemed some time, before she turned to me and said, 'I think your uncle must have been a very good man, Jean, a true philanthropist. I hope you will allow things to continue for these people. It must make such a difference to their lives.'

I assured her that this was my intention, and she surprised me by saying, 'That pleases me, Jean. Inheriting so much would turn many people's heads, but I don't think you will become a playboy overnight, c'est vrai, n'est-ce pas?' Agreeing with her again, I outlined the dilemma that I now faced. The wealth vested in the estate now threatened to overturn my previous carefully laid plans of a legal career in London, and left me very uncertain as to my future.

'How many others would wish to have your problems, Jean,' came her reply, putting things in context. 'You are a very lucky young man, if you look at your present position, and see the wonderful choices that are now before you.'

'So . . . this doesn't affect the way you see me?' I asked, hesitantly.

'Why should it? Though I hardly know you, I feel certain that your character won't change because of this good fortune. So shall we leave this subject behind and enjoy our day together, my chauffeur?' She smiled.

'Yes, Switzerland beckons,' I happily replied, relieved that my sudden change in circumstances did not appear, outwardly at least, to have an effect on our relationship.

We soon approached the town of St Gingolph and I wound the car through the narrow street towards the Customs control point, waiting for a few minutes in the queue that had formed as officials checked the paperwork of a truck at the front. Easing our way forward, passports at the ready, we were waved through without having to stop, and now, on Swiss soil, carried on with our journey towards Montreux, which I had planned to be our first stopping point. After a few kilometres, having passed through Port Valais, I took a left hand turn at the Chateau de la Porte du Scex, crossing over the River Rhone on a narrow metal-framed bridge, the road ahead now flanked by fields of diverse crops, the Swiss Alps looming above us on our right-hand side, still showing signs of snow on the upper peaks, despite being bathed in sunlight.

Our conversation was of a much lighter tone now, as we

pointed out to each other alpine-style farmhouses set amongst the fields along the way, me reading out loud the signs of produce for sale in a parody of 'typical English tourist' accents, marvelling as if I had never seen such things before. We were both enjoying our day out, happy in each other's company.

We reached the village of Noville, its sleepy narrow streets lined with ancient stone buildings, and seemingly deserted, save for the occasional cat looking down from wrought iron balconies on to the passing car below with an air of aloofness. We followed the road as it swung to the right, before eventually turning left onto the Route du Simplon, as we continued towards Montreux.

As the road joined the lakeside again I knew that we would soon be reaching the famed Chateau-de-Chillon. I asked Céleste if she would like to visit today, which she dismissed, knowing that we had both been taken by our parents as young children, but suggesting we might on another occasion, if it presented itself. So we drove on, passing the majestic castellated stone structure, its lower dungeons sitting below the waters of the lake, which washed against the outer walls, the upper ramparts glowing in the sunlight; both of us sparing a thought for the hapless prisoner previously incarcerated there, and remembered now for eternity, thanks to Lord Byron's poem some century and a half earlier.

Approaching Montreux town now, the road descended down towards the lake where I was able to find a suitable parking space. I suggested we take a stroll by the lake, along the esplanade which was famed for its magnificent floral displays, constantly tended by a small army of gardeners.

Playing at being the English gentleman again I walked round and held open the passenger door for Céleste, who smilingly thanked me, addressing me again as her personal chauffeur. I proffered my hand as she debarked, which she then kept clasped in hers, as she had done previously on Sunday. This time though I was feeling much more at ease in her company, as we strolled along together admiring the displays surrounding us, pausing from time to time as she pointed out a particularly attractive leaf colour or unusual bloom.

She clearly shared her mother's eye for floral beauty, yet was seemingly unaware of her own, appearing not to notice the admiring glances in her direction – mostly from the men – as we passed by other couples. Her auburn hair, cut in a short stylish bob, currently favoured by many chic young Frenchwomen, appeared to glow in the sunlight. She wore a simple dress in green that showed the soft contours of her body, while matching low-heeled shoes completed the ensemble.

How different was her style from that of my mother, I thought, who only a decade or so earlier would have worn a tailored dress, high heeled shoes, gloves and a hat, her face carefully made up, before venturing out on such a promenade, thus always denoting her position in society.

The Sixties appeared to have changed all that, certainly in the United Kingdom. Today it seemed impossible to differentiate, by appearance alone, between a debutante and a shorthand-typist one might see in the Kings Road, Chelsea. The fashion revolution, led by designers such as Mary Quant, had seen to that. Haute couture, beloved of the wealthy older generation for its ability to denote class as much as style, was still alive to its select market. But populist fashion, with its modern colours and dresses with hemlines indicating a new emboldened attitude to sexuality, was now worn by the young, from whatever social background, designed and marketed by young entrepreneurs who had sprung up to meet this demand. Images produced by a new breed of celebrity photographer showed models promoting this new fashion, personified by Twiggy, and shone out from billboards and magazine covers, ensuring a steady stream of customers heading to London's Carnaby Street, Biba and other temples of fashion.

We continued our stroll along the lakeside, pointing out to each other the sleek steamboats as they approached the shore, resplendent in their white livery. Coming in from the lake, their foghorns alerting everyone of their presence, they disgorged their passengers on to the landing stage, before taking on others to further destinations around the lake. There seemed a magical air present as we strolled on hand in hand in the warm sunshine.

'Ah, Montreux is so romantic, Jean – the lake, the perfume of the flowers, n'est-ce pas?' murmured Céleste, as she laid her head against my shoulder. Emboldened, I released my hand from hers, slipping it round her waist before replying, 'That depends on one's companion, I think,' hoping that my action would not be seen to be too forward. 'And what do you think of your companion, Jean?' came her inquisitive reply, as she turned her face towards mine, smiling.

I was suddenly aware that my mouth had gone dry, and I was very conscious of the beating of my heart, as I stumbled to answer. 'I would not have believed today possible, only a short while ago. I feel lucky indeed to have such a beautiful companion at my side. I have truly never felt this way about anyone before, and I must confess it frightens me a little. I only hope I haven't embarrassed you by saying this.'

As if in answer she turned her head again, slowly planting a kiss on my cheek before saying, 'Oui, Jean, I think it is perhaps the same for me; but, as you say, we have only just met.' I nodded in agreement, adding, 'Of course, I do understand that, Céleste, but having found you I feel already that I don't want to lose you.

The pleasure of your company has shown me that there has been something missing from my life.'

'No, I think I understand you, and it rather surprises me to find an emotional Englishman – a rare thing indeed. But I am also very happy to be your friend.'

Hoping that I hadn't let my feelings allow me to say too much to Céleste so soon after meeting her, I decided to tell her more about myself, and, at the same time, try to find out more about her own life. Uppermost in my mind was the question of whether she had a current boyfriend, for I assumed that such an attractive, outgoing girl must be inundated with offers. I suggested that we turn back towards the town centre, where we could sit down and have a coffee at La Confiserie Zurcher, an old established bakery in the Avenue du Casino. I explained that I always had coffee there when visiting Montreux, and always looked forward to returning.

'Ah, Jean, we are so alike, you see – this is also my favourite coffee shop in Montreux.' So we turned around and made our way back to the centre of the town.

A visit to this coffee house was always regarded as a noteworthy event. The salon imbued with an air of elegance, with its classic decor, attentive, smartly attired waiters, and mouth-watering pastries and fruit-bedecked gateaux, protected from inquisitive fingers in their chic glass display counters.

Half an hour later, seated at a table for two, coffee and cakes having been served by our waiter, whom I felt sure I recognised from a visit many years previously, we sat looking across at each other.

Plucking up the courage to tell Céleste more about myself, I opened the conversation by saying how lucky she must be to have a large family around her.

'I am an only child,' I said. 'My parents divorced about eight years ago, my father re-marrying and starting a new family, now with a young son and daughter. I don't see them very often these days. My mother unfortunately died about three years ago after a short illness, and my uncle Felix was my closest relative, so his death has left me rather alone. I do have a number of friends – acquaintances perhaps would be more correct – old school friends and work colleagues mostly; one close friend being Michael, who I've known for many years. In Evian I suppose Gaston is the person I know best, but he is from a different generation, of course.'

We carried on this conversation for some time, Céleste sometimes asking questions, but also telling me more about herself, how she had always been seen as the baby of the family, her siblings being that much older, all now married and with families of their own. From what she told me it appeared that there was no special boyfriend in her life at present. There had been a couple of romantic interludes at university, both short-lived, and at the moment, although pursued by a farmer's son in the nearby village 'who can only talk about tractors and crop yields', she had no serious entanglements.

Comforted by this I felt able to say that I was also on my own at present, relationships with previous girlfriends hadn't developed into anything meaningful, and I had tended to concentrate on my career, putting this before all else.

'That is, until now.' I remarked. 'Suddenly my life seems to have opened up to all sorts of possibilities. I'm not even sure if I want to return to London anymore. It's so strange. I thought I saw the rest of my life being there, but now, who can say?'

'Jean, I can see you have a lot to think about. Thank you for being so open about your life to me. I think we know each other a little better now. So shall we go on and enjoy the rest of our day?' Saying this, she reached across the table and took my hand again. What could I do, but agree.

Returning to the Citroën we decided to drive on towards Vevey, a few kilometres distant, with a view to finding somewhere to have our picnic lunch. Leaving Montreux behind us, we were soon passing through Clarens, then with the lake shimmering in the sunlight to our left, and terraces of vineyards above us to our right, the road dropped down into Vevey.

Tuesday being market day I avoided the town centre, turning away from the lake, the Citroën now climbing up towards Chatel-Saint-Denis. I found a small track, taking us off the main road, and soon, finding a grassy clearing between the surrounding pine trees, I parked the car. This seemed an ideal spot for a picnic, cooler than the lakeside, but with wide panoramic views taking in both the lake and mountains that surrounded it.

Opening the boot I took out the picnic basket, together with a large tartan blanket that was always stored there for occasions such as this. I looked questioningly at Céleste, and she indicated a suitable spot close to the car, where I laid the blanket. She then took the basket, and, placing it on the ground, she sat down on the blanket, motioning to me to join her.

A baguette and cheeses were then produced from the basket, together with serviettes, cutlery and plates, followed by a bottle of a local red wine and two glasses. One of the larger plates was then adorned most decoratively with various cold meats, quiche and pieces of cooked chicken. 'A veritable feast!' I cried, as I uncorked the bottle, pouring the wine, first for Céleste, then for myself.

Our picnic was a delight; the warm sun in a cloudless sky, the pine trees around us and the lake sparkling in the distance below us. All too soon, when it seemed we had finished, Céleste drew out of the basket two small lemon tarts, which we both ate with great relish before finally emptying the bottle.

'I am sorry there is no tea to finish with,' she laughingly said, my reply being to thank her for the picnic, saying it was, 'the best I ever had.' We soon cleared away the remains, and I placed the basket back in the car.

Being a little unsure what to do now, and bearing in mind my earlier outpouring of words down by the lake, I decided to ask Céleste what she would like to do next. Her reply came as a surprise. 'Jean, it is so pleasant here in the sunshine, shall we stay a little longer?' while at the same time beckoning me to join her again on the blanket.

I needed no further prompting, and sat down close to her. 'Come closer Jean, if you like,' her voice becoming a little huskier, she was now lying down almost beside me, her arm stretched out towards me. I needed no further encouragement as I moved closer, before taking her in my arms and passionately kissing her on the lips. My instincts urged me to continue, but I drew back a little, not wishing her to think that I was pressing myself on her too quickly. Despite our obvious mutual pleasure in the kiss, I was only too aware of the short passage of time since we had first met. Sensing my discomfort, and realising my dilemma, she gently whispered, 'We have all the time ahead of us, Jean, to get to know each other better. At this moment I am enjoying having you beside me, feeling the warmth of the afternoon sun and listening to the sounds of the woodland around us. I am content.'

And so the afternoon passed, both of us, it seemed, at peace in the knowledge that this relationship was set to flourish, both of us content to let it develop over time.

Eventually we had to return to reality, the afternoon sun now beginning to cool, so with some reluctance we got up, stowing the blanket away. Now sitting in the car we kissed again, for clearly we were both smitten, and I softly suggested that we might take the car down to Vevey again, and have a stroll around the town for an hour or so before heading back home.

'Yes Jean, we should return back to the world again,' was her dreamy response.

The market had by now long finished, the stalls packed away, the stallholders left for the day, so finding a parking space was easy. We wandered aimlessly around the town, from time to time admiring the stock displayed in the shop windows, otherwise looking with some interest at the architecture, admiring the ancient buildings, but mostly, I felt, just happy to be in each other's company.

After a final look at the lake we turned back towards the Grande Place, where we had left the car. I had earlier suggested that we dine this evening at Evian, and we both agreed that one of the small restaurants would be most suitable as we were rather informally dressed and did not wish to present ourselves before one of the Maître d's at the larger hotels in town.

'I think they would know what we had been doing this afternoon, looking at these creases in my dress,' joked Céleste, whilst in reply I quickly added, 'But they are only human, after all, despite their formal persona, and I'm sure they would be a little bit jealous of me, to have such a beautiful companion.' This caused her to blush a little, before she said, 'No, Jean, I think they would see a beautiful couple, straight from the pages of a novel by F. Scott Fitzgerald.'

We lingered over dinner, not that either of us seemed particularly hungry, both of us perhaps hoping that the day wouldn't end, but eventually, finding ourselves to be the only customers left in the restaurant, I asked for the bill, paid it, and we made our way back to the car.

The drive back to the farm took place in silence, both of us thinking over the events of the day, wondering, no doubt, where this fledgling relationship was headed, if anywhere at all. Practical reasoning reminded me that we had only met two days ago. Could I really know someone at all after such a short time? Yet it felt to me that we had known each other for an eternity, and for some reason my thoughts turned back fifty years to my uncle as a young man meeting Célestine. Had something passed down the generations that now manifested itself between the pair of us?

Clearly I held a secret that was unknown to Céleste. To share this, I felt, would only cause grief to her family, certainly to her mother, and I had no wish to bear such sad tidings. So I must hold my counsel, as both Felix and Gaston had done for so many years. The secret must remain in our knowledge only.

Arriving in front of the farmhouse, I jumped out to open the car door for Céleste, again playing the chauffeur, and remembering to retrieve the basket for her. We stood, facing each other, not knowing what to say, both lost in a reverie for a moment, finally broken when she said, 'Thank you for a lovely day, Jean. Perhaps you would like to call me tomorrow?' Then she turned her face to me and we kissed, before she turned and went into the house.

Tomorrow would not come soon enough, I thought, as I eased the car out of the drive, down towards the town again.

Having parked the car in the garage I walked over to the house, and, on entering, was greeted by Florette, who enquired if my trip to Switzerland had been enjoyable. 'Very much so,' I replied, then realising I hadn't told her earlier that I would not be travelling alone, added, 'I went with Mademoiselle Bonnaire. I met her on

Sunday while visiting her family with Gaston.' Florette's smile told me that Gaston would soon be informed who I had spent the day with.

'You had a visitor today, Monsieur Jean – a friend of yours, Monsieur Phillips. He stayed here with you one summer many years ago, I remember. He left a note for you.' Saying this she picked up the note from the side table and handed it to me. Thanking her, and politely refusing her offer of a late drink, I said goodnight and made my way upstairs to my room.

Excited at the thought that Michael was now in Evian, I opened his note on reaching my room. He was staying at one of the smaller hotels, and was not alone – Yvette was with him! Realising the late hour I decided that I would call him at the hotel tomorrow morning, and propose we meet here at the house. I was also curious to meet Yvette. For Michael to bring her with him on this road trip she must indeed be very special, which set me wondering what he would think of Céleste when they met, for I was already planning in my mind a dinner for four the following evening. Having met up with me in Paris only a week or so ago, Michael would surely be surprised now to hear about Céleste.

I drifted off to sleep later, jumbled thoughts of the next day turning over in my mind, but the secret shared with Gaston returning yet again in my sub-consciousness to haunt me.

CHAPTER FIFTEEN
Two Friends Reunited

Wednesday morning saw me awake early, and after taking breakfast alone in the dining room, I telephoned Michael's hotel and asked to be put through to him. He sounded pleased to hear my voice, asking how I was, and when I suggested that we meet at the house, confirmed he could be over at ten, and would be bringing Yvette with him to meet me. On hearing that he intended to stay in town for a couple of days at least, as he was treating his trip as part holiday, he suggested we meet up later for dinner. His hotel, he informed me, had an excellent dinner menu and he could book a table for three before setting out this morning.

'If you could make that a table for four, please, I'll explain everything later,' I replied. I could tell by the tone of his answer that he was intrigued, asking if perhaps there was a maiden aunt in Evian that he was not aware of.

'No, nothing like that, Michael,' I quickly replied. 'I look forward to seeing you both at ten.' Knowing me of old, Michael didn't press the point again, pleased to think that we would all be meeting later.

My next call was to Céleste. It was her mother who answered the phone, and I sensed she was pleased to hear my voice. She said she would call her to the phone, as she was out feeding the hens; my cheeks reddened a little, remembering Gaston's comment to me after Sunday's visit.

Hearing her voice again, even after such a short parting, sent a thrill through me, but I recovered my composure sufficiently to ask if she had slept well after our long day out. 'No,' she confided in me, 'sleep did not come easily last night – perhaps there had been too much excitement in the day for a poor little country mouse.' Anxious to let her know that I had also had a troubled night, I almost forgot to tell her that Michael was in town, and that he was with his girlfriend, Yvette.

'So I hope you will be able to join us for dinner tonight at his hotel.'

'Should I wear something special, Jean? I don't want to upset the maître d',' she replied in a coquettish voice, recalling our conversation of yesterday.

'Whatever you think best suits a country mouse. Your chauffeur will pick you up at seven.'

Laughing now for a moment, she then became silent again, before saying that she was missing me, but was looking forward to this evening. Promising that I would not be late, and telling her I would be counting the hours, I finished the call.

It seemed that we were both being held under the same spell.

I went out to the kitchen to let Florette know that Michael would be arriving at ten, asking her to provide us with coffee later. She asked me about the arrangements for meals so I gave this some thought, advising her that I was definitely out for dinner with my friends this evening. Then, seeing Gaston out in the orchard, I suggested that we three might lunch together today, but there might be guests for dinner on Friday. This news pleased Florette greatly, for, being a fine cook, she was always happy to prepare a special meal.

'How many guests do you expect, Monsieur Jean?' she enquired, for she would need to know this in advance.

'There will certainly be four, and quite possibly more, and I will confirm the number later. Would you mind having to serve that number?' I asked, aware that she would be busy in the kitchen.

'If this is a special occasion, Monsieur Jean, perhaps I can call on Paulette to assist?' she asked. This seemed an eminently suitable solution, and I agreed that we would finalise the details later in the day.

Stepping into the garden, I greeted Gaston. It was clear from the broad smile on his face that Florette had already told him about yesterday's trip. He commented that I was a fast worker, although he felt sure I was no Casanova. Then he added in a more serious tone, 'She is a good girl, M'sieur Jean. I have known her since she was a baby.'

I sought to reassure my old friend that my intentions toward Céleste were certainly honourable, and that we had literally bumped into each other in Evian on Monday, and while talking, had both expressed a desire to visit Switzerland.

'And did you see much of Switzerland?' he asked, again the broad smile covering his face, 'Perhaps as well as the white chickens on the farm?' At this last comment we both burst out laughing. Gaston certainly knew me too well, and was not one to keep his thoughts to himself.

A call from Florette alerted me to the fact that my guests had arrived, so I hurried back into the house, asking Gaston if he would be about later as I wished to speak to him.

Standing in the entrance hall, Michael greeted me effusively, then he introduced me to Yvette, who had been standing behind him, deep in conversation with Florette. Immediately I saw the effect she must have made on my friend from that first meeting. A well-fitting red dress clung to her, enhancing an attractive figure, natural blonde hair framing her pleasantly open face. An intelligent look showed in her eyes that appeared to light up as she spoke, as she came over to me. 'Jean, Michael has told me so much about you, I am so happy to finally meet you.' She offered her hand in greeting.

We went straight into the salon, Florette leaving us and saying that she would bring in the coffee shortly. Michael had stayed in the house previously, so he was quite at ease, but I sensed that Yvette seemed a little in awe of my situation. I realised it was unlikely that many friends within her circle lived in such a large house with a resident housekeeper, so I explained that it had belonged to my late uncle, and, for the moment at least, things would continue as before.

This set me wondering what would be Céleste's reaction when she eventually saw the house. I had become accustomed to Florette and Gaston being on hand, they had always seemed to be a part of the house. But how would it look to her? My concerns arose with Yvette's initial reaction, but Céleste had already been prepared to an extent, and had previously said that in her opinion my good fortune shouldn't change my character, which heartened me a little.

My reference to my late uncle prompted them both to offer their condolences, Michael reminiscing about previous holidays that he had spent here with me, in our schooldays, and the kindness always shown by Felix. 'And what about his old friend Gaston, is he still a fisherman?' he asked. He showed total surprise when I told him that he was actually here at the moment, looking after the potager and the orchard, as he had done ever since leaving the fishing business to one of his nephews.

The coffee was now brought in, Florette making a fuss about serving everyone, offering us home-made biscuits, which brought cries of ecstasy from Yvette, who immediately asked if she could have the recipe. Promising to write this out for her, Florette returned to the kitchen, a look of pleasure on her face. She was clearly enjoying having guests in the house again after the recent weeks of sadness.

Michael told me that he had booked our table for tonight, then again asked me who the mystery guest might be. 'A dear friend of mine, who I'm sure you will both welcome,' I replied, an enigmatic smile on my face. Deciding to press me a little further he supposed that she was not 'the maiden aunt from Evian' that he had never heard of before, to which I replied that all would be revealed this evening.

Realising that he would now have to wait to meet my friend, and being unable to elicit anything more from me, Michael changed the subject to his present trip with Yvette. 'I am supposed to be working hard at the moment, as so many things are happening in France and I am almost besieged by the newspapers demanding more articles,' he began, 'But having Yvette with me I seem to be treating our time together more as a holiday, which I must say is hugely enjoyable, so the reporting must wait for the moment. It has been so good to spend some time away from Paris, with the newspaper deadlines always looming in front of me, but it does seem to be the wrong time to be away, with all the unrest at present.' Sitting together on one of the sofas, they took each other's hands, both giving a look of total contentment.

We chatted for a while longer about recent events in Paris as we finished our coffee.

There being a short lull in the conversation I suggested that we go outside to find Gaston. On our way out Florette, seeing us, started talking to Yvette again about recipes, who, clearly interested, told us she would come out later, adding, 'I am sure you have lots to catch up on.'

Given her blessing we went outside, and, having the opportunity to speak alone with Michael, I immediately congratulated him on having the company of such a beautiful young woman. 'Congratulations may well be in order, Jean,' he replied. 'I intend to formally propose marriage to her this very afternoon, and I have the ring in readiness back at the hotel. My plan was to make the announcement of our marriage at our dinner this evening, for Yvette and I have previously discussed the possibility, and I feel confident that she will accept my proposal. My reason for coming to Evian was to ask you to be my best man at the marriage, which should be later this year.'

I was delighted to hear my friend's news, and knowing him of old, felt prompted to ask if he was happy to give up his bachelor days, for he had a fearsome reputation as a ladies' man.

'When you meet the right girl, previous conquests are soon forgotten. Yvette may seem a little provincial with her talk of recipes with Florette, but believe me she has a sharp inquiring mind, with a great interest in the state of the nation. It wouldn't surprise me to see her one day as a leading force in politics.'

'So the attraction is her intelligent mind?' I asked. 'If her looks are of secondary importance, you must be a changed man.'

Smiling at this observation Michael said, 'Of course she is beautiful, and the first time we met, at a party in Paris, and she fixed her eyes on me, I was lost. In no time though I was struck by her insight about our society, which as you know has been the main interest in my journalistic career, and we often talk late into the night discussing the problems of the world.'

'A regular debating society, then. Perhaps as with an artist, she is your muse, giving you inspiration,' I commented, to which he replied, 'But she also knows how to enjoy life – she's fun to be with and makes me feel truly alive.'

Seeing Gaston in the orchard we made our way over to him, Michael being warmly greeted like an old friend. 'It must be fifteen years since you were last here,' he commented. 'I often recall those days when you both stayed here as boys, they were good times.'

We both agreed with this, and Michael, after offering his condolences, went on to explain what he was currently doing, and was somewhat surprised that Gaston seemed very knowledgeable about his career, before realising that his articles were being avidly read by him. In an attempt to change the subject Michael commented on the hens which were roaming free in the orchard. Gaston replied that they had come from some farming friends, and that he and I had recently visited the farm, but noticing my discomfort at this last comment, he said no more, much to my relief.

Yvette then joined us, much to the delight of Gaston who always enjoyed the company of attractive young women. I became aware again of the knack she had of putting people at their ease, expressing interest in the garden, and in particular the vegetables, his pride and joy. He took her over to show her the crops, delighting in explaining the routine he undertook each day to ensure the kitchen was kept well supplied.

This provided me with the opportunity to invite them all to the dinner that Florette was planning for Friday, explaining that, unfortunately, my absence from London was beginning to be felt, and I must return shortly. A look from Gaston confirmed that he was wondering who else might be invited, but again, to my relief, he let the matter lie.

The invitation was gladly accepted by all, and we turned to

go back indoors. Before leaving him, Gaston enquired if we could speak later, as he had some news for me, and it was agreed that we could both spare some time after lunch.

Back in the house Michael and Yvette both thanked Florette again for the coffee, and reminding me once more of their hotel address, they took their leave of us.

Having some time to spare before lunch I decided to call my office, and managing to speak to Gerald Walker, confirmed that I intended to return to the office by the middle of next week, my French business having been almost completed for the present. It was clear from his response that he was clearly looking forward to my return.

Lunch was a simple affair, and it was clear from the comments made by Florette and Gaston that Yvette had made a good impression on them.

Having finished lunch I arranged with Florette that Gaston and I would have coffee in the study as we had some business to attend to. Whilst waiting for the coffee I asked Gaston whether he felt it would be acceptable to invite Céleste's parents to our dinner on Friday, on the basis that I was due to return to London next week and I wished to repay their hospitality of the previous Sunday.

With a mischievous grin he replied, 'And I assume the daughter will be invited as well?' My face reddened a little as I nodded in reply. He continued, 'I think your departure next week would be reason enough for the invitation. As they are a farming family it would not be unusual to dine at the home of a friend, so do go ahead and ask them.'

Coffee was now brought in to the study, and Florette left us to our business.

'Do you believe in serendipity, Monsieur Jean?' asked

Gaston. 'Something, a strong feeling almost, compelled me to check all my old papers yesterday, and amongst them I found Célestine's letter. I now remember that Felix had asked me to hide it away while the inquiries continued. Perhaps you could now put it with the photograph for safekeeping?' Saying this he handed me the letter, which I read, noting how surprisingly accurate was his remembrance of it, when he first recalled it after I had shown him the photograph from the secret drawer. He must have read and re-read that letter so many times until the words had been truly burned on his memory.

'I would be delighted to, Gaston, but all this secrecy worries me, particularly as I have now met the poor girl's family. Do you not think they have a right to know the truth? That was what I wanted to speak to you about earlier today.'

'I understand your concern, M'sieur Jean,' came his grave reply. 'But what do you think would be achieved by letting the family know that she had committed suicide after so long a passage of time? I believe it would only serve to resurrect their pain.'

Reluctantly I felt I had to agree with my old friend – for the present at least.

CHAPTER SIXTEEN
Introducing a New Friend

I left the house in the Citroën at about six-thirty, wishing to have sufficient time to speak to Céleste's parents before we left for the hotel. I was greeted by Amélie, who commented on my frequent visits, but at the same time seemed genuinely pleased to see me again. She invited me in to the salon. Her husband, Vincent, being already seated, got up and greeted me – less warmly, I felt, in a rather stiff, formal manner. Amélie informed me that Céleste would soon be ready, and perhaps I would care to take a seat while I waited for her.

This seemed the ideal opportunity for me to explain that as I was due to return to London, for a short while at least, I wondered if they would all care to join me for dinner on Friday, before I left early next week. I added that Gaston, and my journalist friend Michael, together with his girlfriend, would also be present. Amélie replied immediately that they would be delighted, to which her husband, perhaps rather reluctantly, acquiesced, suggesting to me the authority that was held by female members of this family when it came to matters of a social nature.

Pleased with their acceptance I suggested they arrive at seven o'clock, in the knowledge that it was customary in France to turn up a quarter of an hour late for such events.

As if on cue we were now joined by Céleste, wearing a

stylish two-piece outfit in navy blue with a contrasting silk scarf, projecting that air of bien habillé that French women of a certain class always seem to exude. Greeting us as if this were her normal attire for the evening, she turned to me and said, with a twinkle in her eye, 'I hope the maître d' will be satisfied with this country mouse.' To which I retorted, 'No country mouse here, you look trés chic,' then noticing that she was wearing the silver brooch that had once belonged to her late aunt, I was tempted to make some comment, realising just in time that I ought to be quite unaware of its history.

Amelie then apprised Céleste of the dinner invitation on Friday, to which she replied with a thank-you, and said that it would be interesting to see the house, having heard so much about it.

On entering the car I could not resist asking about the brooch, enquiring whether it was antique, for it certainly appeared to have some age. Her reply was quite dismissive: 'It has been in the family for some time, and is really my mother's, but she allows me to wear it occasionally. Do you like it?'

Clearly the history of the brooch seemed of little consequence to her, so I simply replied in the affirmative, adding only that it seemed an unusual piece.

In no time, it seemed, we had reached the centre of town, the journey spent (certainly in my case) in reminiscences of yesterday's trip to Switzerland. I proceeded to park the car close to the hotel. Céleste laughingly suggested that our appearance today should be more acceptable, with which I concurred, but said that it was the person, not the clothes, that really mattered, of course.

'Ah, a true philosopher,' she quickly replied, and I felt pleased that she seemed to be in such high spirits, as we entered the dining room. Inside we were greeted by the maître d', who guided us to our table. Michael, having seen our entrance, was already on his feet, and I introduced Céleste, who clearly made an immediate impression on him, but felt somewhat relieved that he attempted to make no jokes about maiden aunts.

We followed their seating arrangements, I sitting next to Michael, leaving the two young women side by side, opposite us. There followed a short flurry of questions and answers between us, particularly as Céleste was a newcomer to my friends. However, there seemed a good rapport between them all immediately, as it became clear that they shared similar values and interests in politics, which would have been discussed at greater length, I felt, had Michael not interjected, saying he had an announcement to make.

'I am pleased to announce that Yvette and I have become engaged today, as she has accepted my proposal of marriage, thus making me the happiest of men. I have ordered champagne as an aperitif, by way of celebration,' and, motioning to the sommelier, indicated that our glasses were ready to be charged.

Céleste and I both raised our glasses and warmly congratulated the couple, Yvette proudly showing her ring for us all to see. This prompted Céleste to enquire more of Yvette as to how long they had known each other, and a long conversation ensued between the pair, leaving Michael to quietly comment to me, 'Certainly no maiden aunt, my friend.'

Dinner was a pleasurable affair, interspersed with numerous asides. Following the main course the girls excused themselves, as they wished to 'powder their noses'. I guessed that there was an ulterior motive for this, as no doubt Céleste would be quizzing Yvette about me. Any response would naturally be quite limited, as she had only met me earlier today, and Michael would have previously said little more than we were at school together, and that these days only met infrequently.

While the girls were thus employed Michael turned to me, wondering aloud how long I had known such a divine creature. This made me thankful that he was now happily engaged, knowing his reputation of old. My answer of not quite one week rather shocked him, for he ventured to comment that we appeared to be so at ease in each other's company that we could be mistaken for old friends, a married couple even, adding that he was not the only lucky man in the room.

Our private conversation ended abruptly as the girls now returned, and, embarking on the cheese course, we turned again to discussions about the wedding. Michael reiterated his wish that I would be the best man, which I was happy to accept. The wedding would take place in Paris, as both he and Yvette resided there, his own family in England being limited to his parents and siblings only, and who, he felt sure, would be happy to make the trip over. Somewhat to my surprise it was Yvette who then asked Céleste if she would attend, adding that a formal invitation would be sent in due course. Clearly a bond was already being established between the two girls, which heartened me, particularly when Céleste answered immediately that she would be delighted.

Having exhausted this subject for the present we began again to discuss the current crisis, of which I was now more aware, and I sought Michael's views on the present position. 'Day by day the situation seems to change, involving ever more people, students and workers alike. I fear that the heavy-handed actions taken by General de Gaulle's government have exacerbated things, particularly the use of the CRS (riot police), and there are now widespread rumours spreading of strikes being called, with the unions appearing to be rather out of their depth and lacking in any real leadership on behalf of the workers. I do wonder how matters will finally develop, and I have been made well aware in my road trip that this is not just an outcome that will be isolated to Paris alone. I fear we may be about to see something France has not experienced before, perhaps even on a par with earlier revolutions, but hopefully less bloody.'

This set me wondering if my planned return home next week would be put in jeopardy in any way, as at present I was certainly not aware of any planned strikes, so I resolved to take more of an interest in Press and Radio reports.

Dessert finished we asked for coffees, which we took in the hotel lounge. Again our conversation turned to the forthcoming wedding with promises of the date to be settled shortly, when formal invitations would then be sent out. Yvette, having now ascertained that we had known each other for such a short time, was curious to find out how I had met Céleste. I replied that we had met whilst visiting her parents' farm, which had been arranged only last weekend by an old family friend, Gaston, adding that they would all be joining us for dinner on Friday. This seemed to satisfy her, for she then changed the subject, questioning me instead about my life and career in London.

Curiously, Yvette had spent some time in London, both as a student, while attending a course at the London School of Economics – which had a reputation as a hotbed of student unrest – and most recently in the company of Michael, when visiting his parents. Having experienced life in London I was interested to know how she compared the two cities, for she had lived in Paris for some years.

'For me there is no comparison,' she replied. 'I found London very dull and grey, there seemed to be little joie de vivre in evidence, while in Paris there is a culture that seems to fully embrace life.'

'Perhaps you can understand why we English are always so keen to discuss the weather,' I responded. 'So you intend to stay in Paris?' I then asked.

'Yes, we have both discussed this many times,' interjected Michael. 'And you, Jean, where do you see yourself in the future? Your plans must surely be affected by the events of the past weeks.'

I could only acknowledge that my previous plans had now been put awry, while thinking to myself that some major decisions would have to be made eventually. Céleste remained silent during this exchange, but I sensed that she was deep in thought, the reality of my return to London, if only initially for a short time, now being openly discussed.

Eventually, having finished our coffee, it was time to depart, and after warmly thanking our friends for their hospitality, and reminding them that we would meet again on Friday, if not before, we made our way back to the car.

Céleste seemed in a sombre mood as we walked towards the car, prompting me to ask if she had not enjoyed the evening. 'Oh yes, very much, Jean, I like your friends, they are good company,' she responded.

'But you seem a little unhappy,' I replied; at which her eyes moistened and she took an intake of breath. Turning, she clasped both my hands uttering, 'I will miss you so terribly if you go, Jean, but I know you cannot delay your return.'

Feeling rather wretched at her sadness I attempted to mollify her concern, drawing her to me and kissing her, then asking if she thought I was not also feeling equally unhappy about my return to London.

'Jean, is that really true? You will miss me too?' She asked in such a plaintive voice, that I was deeply moved.

'Why of course,' was my reply. 'Despite the short length of time since we met, I can't imagine my future life without you. I am struggling to make sense of everything, to decide what I must do, which may well mean giving up things that I have worked so hard in the past to achieve. But can't we just carry on enjoying each other's company for the present, as I know I will return to Evian again very shortly.'

This seemed to reassure Céleste, for her demeanour seemed to lighten, and she commented, 'I am glad that you feel the same as me. I have to constantly remind myself that we only met for the first time last Sunday. Poor Jean, I am sorry you have so many things to worry about.'

'I'm sure things will be resolved over time,' I replied, as we walked on, 'Yet I'm so pleased that we've both made clear our feelings for each other.'

By now we had reached the car, and as I opened the door for her I kissed her again, which she reciprocated with a hug. My hope was that she no longer doubted my feelings toward her.

Finally reaching the farm I cut the engine, and we remained seated for a while, enjoying the closeness of each other, whereupon I asked, 'Will we meet again tomorrow, or do you think it's becoming too much of a habit, meeting every day?' It pleased me to hear her laugh once more, clearly now recovered from her melancholia, as she replied, 'If you have time in your busy schedule, perhaps in the afternoon?' We agreed that I would call for her at three, and I walked her to the front door of the house, finally kissing once more before I left to go home.

CHAPTER SEVENTEEN
An Old Friend's Advice

Michael called me early in the morning to let me know that he and Yvette were due to leave on Saturday, but would welcome the chance of seeing me again, before coming to dinner on Friday. Having no immediate plans I suggested they call on me at ten.

Florette brought me in coffee as I entered the dining room and sat down to a light breakfast. I was able to confirm to her that there would be a total of seven for dinner tomorrow, and our guests would be arriving shortly after seven o'clock. This seemed to please her as she clearly enjoyed all the preparations associated with a formal gathering, and recounting that she had already contacted Paulette for her assistance her on the evening. Dinner parties had been infrequent events in recent times at the house, and she took great pride in producing memorable meals. She asked if she could discuss the menu with me, seeking my approval of her suggestions, which was hardly needed, as she had clearly given it great thought. She suggested rack of lamb as the main course, followed by cheese and a dessert of crème caramel or assorted pastries. Gaston had been asked to provide the ingredients for a salad, and to arrange delivery, through his nephew, of fresh fish from the lake.

I congratulated Florette on her choice, confirming that I would select suitable wines to accompany the meal, which would include champagne as an aperitif, as we were to celebrate the engagement of Michael and Yvette. Florette showed her delight at this news, saying that they were a charming young couple, and she would be sure to prepare some suitable aperitif dishes.

She then asked me if she would know the other guests, to which I replied the Bonnaire family, the parents and daughter, friends of Gaston, who I had mentioned earlier in the week. 'Ah yes, Monsieur Jean, the daughter accompanied you to Switzerland on Tuesday, as I remember,' she replied, again with the hint of a knowing smile in her face.

Changing the subject, I told her that my friend Michael and his fiancée would be calling at ten this morning. Their imminent arrival pleased her greatly, prompting her to say that she had already written out the recipes discussed the day before with Yvette. Thinking that this would provide me with another chance to talk alone with Michael, I answered, 'I'm sure you will have plenty to discuss with her when she arrives,' adding that I had some paperwork to attend to in the study.

Ten o'clock soon arrived and Florette answered the door to our guests. She congratulated them on their engagement, going into raptures when Yvette showed her the ring. Then, remembering the recipes, she asked me if Yvette could go with her to the kitchen, which is what I had hoped, leaving me with some time alone with Michael.

We went into the study, and taking a seat began discussing the previous evening. He immediately wanted to know more about Céleste, again showing surprise that we had only met a few days ago. 'I have to say I find it hard to believe that you met so recently,' he said. 'You both have the look of a couple who have been together for some time. You really do seem very relaxed in each other's company, which is rather unusual after such a short acquaintance.'

I went on to explain that her family were old friends of Gaston, who had introduced me to them last weekend. He was quite correct in his observations, and I confided that for me a 'coup de foudre' seemed the only explanation, and she had intimated similar feelings towards me. This of course presented me with a quandary. I must shortly return to London to attend to my business, but had now been placed in a strange position, realising that as a result of Felix's demise the opportunity of a new life for me in France now beckoned.

Knowing me of old, Michael was quick to point out that I was not one for snap decisions, tending to carefully weigh up all the options before arriving at important conclusions. 'Therein lies my problem,' I replied. 'I have invested so much of myself in my career, and now I'm faced with this possibility of a complete change, that at the moment seems so tempting, and now, having met Céleste, I can't at the moment think of my future life without her.'

'Perhaps you have already given yourself an answer,' he replied. 'You have a great opportunity here if you choose it, so must balance this against your previous life. In any event France is no great distance away, and I suppose it will be some months before all matters relating to the Will are resolved. I should think that will give you ample time to make return visits to Evian, and to reflect fully on your future. I'm sure that Céleste will be happy to go along with this, if she's as infatuated with you as you say. A little space between visits may help you both to see things more clearly. The last two weeks must have been like an emotional rollercoaster ride for you, and some time apart will be no bad thing.'

I could only thank my friend for his counsel, and agreeing that coffee in the salon would be welcome, went through to the kitchen to find Florette, still busily discussing recipes with Yvette, who now came back to join us.

Again there was further talk of Céleste, but this time it was more in the nature of inquisitive conversation, Yvette wanting to know where she lived, how large was her family, and other such generalities. I attempted to answer her questions as fully as I could, reminding her that we would all be meeting again for dinner, tomorrow.

Michael then exclaimed that they would have to leave, as he had arranged a visit an old friend who lived in Annecy, some distance away, and with reminders of tomorrow's invitation being given again, they left me to continue with my paperwork.

Lunch was much taken up with further discussion about the dinner arrangements for tomorrow. Florette seemed in high spirits, no doubt as a result of her earlier conversation with Yvette, who she now seemed to regard as an old friend. It set me wondering how much of her life she lived vicariously, through the lives of others around her. Other than the time she spent daily at church I had not become aware of any other regular visits made away from the house, but despite this she appeared to be happy enough with her routine. It set me wondering how she would cope if the house was sold eventually, and she would then have to live alone and find her own apartment, which, thanks to the kindness shown by Felix, would at least be financially possible.

Putting these thoughts aside I went back into the study, where I contacted the ticket desk at Geneva airport. I was able to make a reservation for the flight to London that was leaving next Monday with no difficulty. Gaston would be happy to drive me to the airport, and my return to London, so often discussed recently with others, had now become a reality.

Having settled the arrangements, I now took the car up to the farm for my rendezvous with Céleste. She had obviously warned her parents of my arrival, for her mother, on opening the door to greet me, expressed no surprise at my presence, and invited me in.

'You are quite a regular visitor these days, Jean,' she said. 'Céleste does not have many callers these days. She was one of the few of her contemporaries who went away to University, and since her return has led a rather insular life, so I am pleased that she has made a new friend.' This statement rather pleased me, although I knew that I would be leaving in a matter of days, and was unsure at present how soon I would be returning.

'I have been delighted to meet you all,' I replied. 'The atmosphere at the house was understandably rather sad after my Uncle Felix's sudden demise, so it has been like a breath of fresh air for me to visit you all this last week.'

'I am sure you are always welcome, Jean,' she replied, 'But I think your visits are prompted by the presence of our daughter, rather than her ageing parents?' I could not deny this, and coloured slightly, managing to mumble that the change of scene was welcome.

Céleste then joined us, and after a little further conversation, in which I said that I looked forward to seeing them all tomorrow for dinner, we left the house, and I drove back down to Evian. I found a parking space near to the casino, and suggested that we stroll along the lakeside, for I had yet to let her know that I would now be leaving on Monday, and realised that this would not be an easy conversation.

Walking hand in hand again, yet feeling uncertain of her response, I raised the subject of my leaving. It became clear that she had also been thinking of my departure, but indicated by her response that she fully understood that I must go, as I couldn't indefinitely neglect my business in London.

Becoming a little heartened at her understanding of my present position I went on to say that I should be absent for a short while only, as I still had much to do in Evian, and hoped that we would soon be able to meet up again.

Perhaps my choice of words had an effect on her, for I could see that she was troubled, and again reassured her that I would soon be back.

'Yes Jean,' she replied. 'I know that you will soon return, and I will be here, of course. We have been lucky to see so much of each other over such a short time, and we will both have to be patient. I only hope that the bright lights of London don't make you forget your country mouse.'

'There is no risk of that,' I exclaimed. 'London really means little more to me other than my business interests, and these last few days have shown that to me so clearly.'

With this we walked on a little further, now taking more of an interest in the panorama of the lake and the boats plying their way to their various destinations. I then decided to ask Céleste if she would like to see the house this afternoon, rather than wait until dinner tomorrow, as we were not far away. I also assured her that Florette would like to meet her, as she had become aware that we were spending a lot of time together.

'I am curious, of course, and I would be pleased to meet your housekeeper,' she replied. So we retraced our steps back to the car, and drove on to the house.

Céleste's comment on drawing up in front of the house didn't surprise me, for Yvette had previously shown a similar reaction. 'Such a large house for one person,' she commented, but I quickly pointed out that this had been the Dumont family home for many years, even if now the future of it was as yet unclear.

Arriving in the entrance hall I called out to Florette, who

gasped in surprise on coming out of the kitchen and seeing Céleste unexpectedly. However, she quickly recovered her composure as I introduced them to each other. Florette seemed well informed about the Bonnaire family, clearly through talking with Gaston, so there ensued a conversation for a few minutes, with questions asked about the farm and her family, which seemed to put them both more at ease.

Finally she asked if we would like some refreshment, as it was by now mid-afternoon. Settling on tea, which perhaps she would bring a little later into the salon, we left her to return to her domain in the kitchen.

'I think she has been the housekeeper for some time,' Céleste commented. At this I told the story of Florette's time with Felix and his mother, saying that she was really considered a member of the family.

As I guided Céleste on a tour of the ground floor, it was clear that she was impressed by the grandeur of the rooms, taking an interest in the layout of the house, and asking me questions about individual rooms. It almost began to feel as if she was contemplating living here. I tried to dismiss such thoughts, remembering that we had met only a few days ago.

Our tour of the house now completed, I suggested that she may like to see the garden, adding that it was not on the scale of the farm. On going outside we saw that Gaston was working outside the tool shed, and went over to speak to him.

He showed little surprise at seeing us both, perhaps having already been forewarned of our presence by Florette, and he warmly greeted us both, putting his hoe to one side, whilst commenting on the number of weeds already pushing up through the soil. Céleste congratulated him on the lush appearance of his crops, and then remarked on the number of hens in the orchard, prompting Gaston to look over at me, smilingly, but thankfully without comment. Agreeing that we would all be meeting again tomorrow, we returned to the salon.

Florette entered a few minutes later, bringing us in a tray laden with tea and cakes. After we thanked her, she left us, returning to the kitchen. I proceeded to pour the tea, then took my seat beside Céleste on the sofa. She was full of questions about the house and its occupants, past and present, which I attempted to answer. She also asked me more about my life in London, particularly interested in finding out more about the area where I lived, as she knew London a little from her time spent there a few years previously.

'I live in nothing as grand as this,' I replied, describing how I was still putting the finishing touches to my relatively modest coach house.

This prompted further questions about what I planned to do in the future, to which I could only respond that it was still too soon to make any decisions. I also suggested that she would be welcome to visit me in London at any time, the thought of which, judging by her reply, appealed to her.

We spent the next hour sitting closely together on the sofa, both no doubt subconsciously aware of my impending departure, yet not wishing to raise the painful subject again. Instead both of us attempted to steer the conversation to other topics.

Knowing that Céleste had only recently finished her studies at University, I was interested to know whether a career beckoned, for this topic had not been discussed between us before. 'At present I am helping my parents with the running of the farm,' she explained. 'But yes, this is only a temporary situation, and I am proposing to start work as a translator. A good friend in Lyon, who has a small publishing firm, has asked me to assist her, and

I am due to begin in the next month. This will be a way of best utilising the years spent honing my language skills at University, don't you think, Jean?'

With this I could not disagree, but I was unclear whether it would involve a move away from home. 'No, not at all,' she explained. 'Of course I will have to visit Lyon from time to time to attend meetings, but otherwise I will be staying at home here on the farm. It doesn't involve a fixed place of work, like so many careers, and I think this will suit me well.' I agreed, saying that I assumed there would be some flexibility in her working arrangements, and she would not be tied down to rigid office hours. 'Yes, but I will have to be disciplined, and there will be deadlines to be met' she replied.

We talked on for a while longer, as she explained further how she had met her friend Alice through a short spell of work experience, during her time studying languages at university in Lyon. Their friendship had blossomed, and Alice, seeing her potential, had offered her work as a translator on completion of her studies.

'So fortunately I have been able at present to spend time with you, Jean. But soon I will be involved with my work, having less free time as a result.'

'But you'll still have time to see me, when I come back to Evian?' I enquired.

'Of course, Jean – I will not be working every day, even a country mouse has to rest sometime.'

Satisfied at this we talked for a little longer, before Céleste reminded me that she would have to return home soon, as her presence was expected. Neighbouring farmers were due to visit for the evening, and she had promised to help her mother with the catering.

'Do they include the beau that you mentioned to me at Montreux?' I enquired.

'Yes, that is Guillaume, the farmer's son, his family are great friends of my parents, so I expect he will be coming,' she answered, then in a rather sombre tone added, 'I should tell you that I am due to go with him to a local dance this Saturday evening, something that was arranged before I met you. It would be awkward to cancel at this late date, so I hope you will understand.'

Hoping that the shock of finding that there was currently a competitor for her affections was not too apparent, I answered that she must do as she saw fit, and I could not expect her to spend her time exclusively with me. Recollecting her previous comments about him in my mind, I thought to myself that this farmer's son, Guillaume, surely presented little threat to our blossoming relationship, and was almost prepared to dismiss the loss of her company for one evening.

When we arrived back at the farm some little while later, she thanked me again for the understanding I had shown, and, kissing me tenderly, told me how much she looked forward to seeing me again tomorrow.

Driving back to Evian the thought of Céleste accompanying this young farmer to a dance returned to haunt me, but, putting it to the back of my mind, I concentrated on the preparations for the dinner tomorrow.

CHAPTER EIGHTEEN
The Dinner Party

Friday was a whirl of activity in the house, all of us involved in our relevant chores: Gaston sourcing suitable herbs and vegetables for the kitchen, my own simple tasks being to ensure that I selected sufficient wines from the cellar for our guests, and helping to oversee the table decoration.

Florette was in her element, preparing the ingredients for the meal, while at the same time giving Paulette instructions to use the best silver cutlery kept for such occasions, our finest crockery and crystal glasses, all of which were to be set on the pristine white linen cloth atop the dining room table. Fresh candles were placed in the newly polished silver candlesticks, and Gaston was charged with selecting flowers from the garden, which Paulette then arranged most tastefully as a central table decoration. Finally, Paulette laid out the place-cards on the table, as I had indicated to her, and by late afternoon the table looked immaculate, a fitting centrepiece set off by the deep mahogany of the furniture in the room that emanated a lustrous patina, indicating decades of care and polish.

The preparations completed, Gaston and I had sufficient time to change into suitable clothing, after which an air of expectation pervaded the house for a short while as we awaited our guests' arrival.

'Madame Bonnaire – Amélie – will be pleasant company this evening, I'm sure,' remarked Gaston with a smile.

'Yes, she has always been most friendly when I've called on the family, but I have spoken little to Monsieur Bonnaire, he's always busy on the farm,' came my reply.

'A typical farmer, of course – he has so much to do, and must be beset by worry over what the future holds, when he becomes too old to manage matters on his own. His sons are not interested in farming, and have both married and moved away from the district, as has the older daughter; so unless his youngest child, Céleste, is to help him or she marries a farmer, the future does not bode well.'

Thinking about this last remark, I added, 'Do you think that likely, Gaston? Céleste is well-educated and I would be surprised if she took up farming, although, of course, she is helping with the running of the farm at present. But I was under the impression that this is a temporary measure, and will cease once she embarks on her chosen career.'

'Ah, perhaps you know more than I, in regard to her future plans,' he replied, a twinkle in his eye, 'but you must remember she would be regarded as a great prize to any number of young men in the farming community.'

Shortly after seven Michael and Yvette arrived, after having walked up from the hotel, as it was again a fine evening. Paulette took their coats, prompting Yvette to give a surprised look to Michael, on being confronted by yet another servant in the house, but she kept her thoughts to herself, making no comment. I showed them through to the salon where we all chatted for a few minutes before the arrival of the Bonnaire family.

I effected introductions, and was pleased to see that we made a sociable party, as everyone seemed happy to converse with their new acquaintances. Amélie surprised me somewhat by saying that she had visited the house before, back in the late 1920s, when she had accompanied her mother to discuss some legal issues relating to the lease of their restaurant with Monsieur Dumont senior. As she was still relatively young at the time, it had been agreed that Felix would entertain her whilst the meeting took place, so they had both spent some time together, Amélie still remembering the pleasant, if rather serious, young man who had occasionally joined them on their promenades some ten years earlier.

'Yes, Felix must have been rather older than you,' I remarked, to which she replied, 'He was more a friend of my older sister, Célestine.' Attempting to find out more I asked, 'This was the sister who died in the Great War, I believe? Céleste has mentioned her to me.'

'Yes, she died tragically in a boating accident, a few weeks after we had been repatriated to Evian. It was a sad and difficult time for our family.' That seemed to be all that she knew of the incident, having been a young child, only aged seven at the time.

Not wishing to intrude further I attempted to change the subject, and with Paulette requesting that we should now be seated at the table, I showed the way into the dining room, to murmurings of appreciation from the guests, who admired the effort taken over the table decoration.

Everyone having now been seated, and the champagne being uncorked to cries of mutual pleasure from the assembled party, Paulette charged our glasses, indicating the aperitif pastries already laid out on the table. This was my cue to stand as host, and after thanking everyone for coming I proposed a toast to the newly engaged couple, wishing them much happiness, which was warmly endorsed by all present.

Gaston then arose, proposing thanks on behalf of the guests, adding that it was a pleasure to see the house being used again for happy events, after the sadness of recent times. We were all agreed on this, and conversed together as the aperitifs were consumed.

Paulette then appeared with the fish dish. 'Perch from the lake this morning, caught by my nephew,' added Gaston, beaming with delight. This prompted Amélie, sitting opposite him, to remember how Gaston used to provide the restaurant with fresh fish, which had always been much appreciated by the clientele.

'Ah, but the skill of the cook, and the presentation of the dish, was most important,' was his rejoinder, bringing a blush to Amélie's cheeks, and he added that Florette had also worked her magic on the fish today, with which we all heartily agreed.

Gaston seemed to be in his element, seated between the two young women, Céleste to his left and Yvette to his right, so there was much conversation, liberally interspersed with laughter at his frequent asides. As host I sat at the head of the table, with Céleste to my right and Vincent, her father, to my left, so I was able to converse freely with them both throughout the meal.

I attempted to introduce the subject of the farm's future to Vincent, who I addressed as Monsieur Bonnaire, as he was older, and I sensed more formal towards me than Amélie. 'The farm must take up so much of your time,' I said, by way of conversation. 'We are fortunate that you were able to come this evening.'

'Being a farmer is a way of life,' he responded. 'It can take up all your waking hours, but one must attempt to relax when possible, otherwise the farm can become your sole raison d'être. However, I am fortunate in having my daughter to assist me for a while longer, before she embarks on her career, 'he added looking towards Céleste. 'But as for the future, I'm not so sure.'

'Your other children don't live locally?' I enquired, and received an honest, albeit unwelcome reply.

'All married with their own families, and showing no real interest in farming, so you understand my concern, I hope.' Again a look of worry clouded his face, perhaps intended for his daughter, as he looked in her direction again.

Amélie, sensing this undercurrent to our conversation, tried to make light of things. 'You shouldn't worry so, Vincent, you are not an old man yet.' This brought the hint of a smile to his face, and he lifted his glass, and commented, 'An excellent wine to accompany the fish, Jean.'

It was also apparent that Michael, although seated away from me, was able to add his own witty repartee readily to the conversation, and clearly felt at ease in this gathering.

The rack of lamb was served next, much to everyone's approval. Paulette then charged our glasses with the red wine chosen for the occasion, as we served ourselves from the selection of vegetables. During this, the main course of the meal, Vincent questioned me further about my impending departure, but on seeing Céleste's reaction at hearing this I was quick to point out to him that I would soon be returning again to France.

'Yes, Jean is intending to return soon to Evian, Papa, as he has business to attend to,' was her response, and I noted a thoughtful look on Vincent's face as he nodded at this.

Further courses followed – a selection of cheeses, and finally the dessert, after which Florette made a brief appearance, to the applause of the party, all now comfortably replete. It was agreed that we would take coffee in the salon, so we arranged ourselves into small groups on sofas and chairs, carrying on our conversations that had commenced during the meal.

Amélie then rather surprised me, expressing an interest in seeing the garden, so, there still being some daylight available, we made our excuses to the others and I led her outside, leaving Céleste deep in conversation with Yvette.

Entering the garden Amélie commented, 'It is much as I remember, Jean, but I don't recall the large potager.'

'Ah, that is Gaston's domain,' I explained, 'He probably started it after he retired as a fisherman. He comes up here most days. The chickens, I assume, you recognise?' I asked.

'Yes, I remember when he started his flock and collected a few birds from us. Not so long ago.'

We took a short stroll around the garden, Amélie admiring the flowers and shrubs in the borders. An encyclopaedic knowledge of horticulture enabled her to name all the plants, most of which were familiar to me by sight only, and making me only too aware of my own scant knowledge.

She thanked me again for the invitation to dinner, saying, 'I have enjoyed this evening very much, Jean, and I will be sorry to see you go away so soon after we have met.'

I tried to make light of this, saying 'I will be sure to return soon, and I hope that my frequent visits to the farm since Sunday have not impinged too much on your family.'

'Why no, Jean,' she replied. 'I can see that you and Céleste must have many interests in common, and I am pleased, as her mother, to see her looking so happy with her new friend.'

'We enjoy each other's company, certainly, and share a similar sense of humour,' I confided.

'Yes, I have noticed how she tries to tease, but not in an unkind way, I hope.'

Further emboldened, I asked if it was unusual for Céleste to be out with a friend such as I so frequently, and was somewhat heartened by her reply.

'Yes, she has not been in the habit of going out much since completing her studies, most of her friends now seem absorbed with their own lives, and as a result have tended to distance themselves somewhat from her. Perhaps I shouldn't say this, but since we are already having this conversation you must be aware that a good-looking girl, like my daughter, will always attract "followers". This was the term we used in my day, and one such "follower" in particular, despite no encouragement on her part, I believe, appears very keen to get to know her better.'

It seemed to me that Amélie was attempting to make me fully aware of Céleste's situation, but I felt that she was very much minded to avoid being seen as any form of matchmaker for her daughter, a decision which I respected.

'I think Céleste has mentioned him to me,' I replied rather too dismissively, although reminded of Gaston's earlier comments. Feeling that our discussion had intruded too far already into Céleste's personal life, I strove to change the subject, after thanking Amélie for her kind observations.

'I wouldn't normally speak so openly to someone of so short an acquaintance,' she agreed, 'But I feel that as I already know your family, and being aware how they kindly helped my mother at a time of great need, I have great respect for the Dumonts.'

Despite my obvious desire to find out more about this chapter in her earlier life, I felt that it would be unwise to talk further about Felix's past at this time, deciding that this was a subject for future discussion. So I passed the topic by, instead asking if she had enjoyed looking around the garden. 'Why yes, Jean, it is a fine garden indeed, no doubt lovingly developed over many years.'

'But unfortunately a little neglected at present, for Gaston prefers to tend his vegetables, and look after the hens.'

'Yes, I always think that a flower garden needs a woman's touch, to achieve that combination of colours and shapes that can bring a garden to life.'

'Perhaps that is so, but I'm afraid that things will have to continue as they are for the present. But now I suggest that we should rejoin the others, as we seem to have abandoned them for some time.'

She agreed with me and we made our way back indoors.

Returning to our guests in the salon, and feeling a little guilty over my recent absence as host, I offered drinks to those who wished to imbibe further. Michael declined, explaining that he had to make an early start in the morning, and felt that he would need a clear head, as he would be driving straight back to Paris with Yvette.

He continued. 'As I had expected, the student unrest in Paris has dramatically increased over this last week, following the demonstration at the Sorbonne last Friday in protest at the closure of Nanterre. There were apparently elements of the far right group Occident also present, threatening to attack the demonstration, so the police, assisted by the CRS, who have a fearsome reputation for brutality, scattered the demonstrators, arresting about four hundred people, often in a most violent manner. This has resulted in running battles on the Left Bank, between students, who have now been joined by many workers, and the police. My journalist colleagues in Paris have urged me to return, as this unrest looks set to continue, possibly worsen, and there are many rumours circulating, some talking of actual revolution.'

Both Gaston and Vincent were quick to agree with Michael about the reputation of the CRS, pointing out some of their previous actions when called in to act as a riot control measure.

'They are not at all liked by many of us, and seem to be called in as a blunt instrument by the Establishment,' added Gaston.

I expressed my surprise at all this, confirming that I had been rather caught up with recent events in my life here, but would make a point of following the news bulletins more closely now. This brought a further retort from Gaston that the news did not always report the true facts, and radio bulletins tended to be slanted in favour of the Government.

Sensing that we were about to begin another lengthy political discussion, Michael stood up, followed by Yvette, and told us all, 'I'm sorry but we must leave now, as it will be an early start for us in the morning.' They said their goodbyes, shaking hands or embracing the other guests, before leaving the salon.

As we were leaving the room Michael again thanked me for my hospitality, reminding me that he would be sending full details of the wedding arrangements shortly, and asking 'Shall I send the invitation to the London or Evian address?' I immediately suggested that he send to both, as I may well be back in Evian quite shortly, and I noted that this comment seemed to be well received by Céleste.

Retrieving their coats from the cloakroom, ably assisted by Paulette, they finally wished me goodnight, with more handshakes and embraces, before he and Yvette left, returning on foot to their hotel.

Our party now depleted in numbers, the evening began to draw to a close. I rejoined my seat next to Céleste on the sofa, and was able to arrange to see her on Sunday afternoon, while expressing the hope, jokingly, that she wouldn't enjoy the dance on Saturday evening too much, without my company.

'I will try not to be too-oo sad,' came her quick response. 'We poor country mice must learn to take our pleasure when it is offered.'

This I took as an indicative of the quiet life she was currently leading, and in a light-hearted manner said that I was looking forward to us both taking many more excursions together on my return, emphasising again that this would be very soon.

Vincent then announced that, reluctantly, they must now depart, despite the enjoyable company, as the farm couldn't look after itself in the morning, and his early presence would be needed. Again, with help from Paulette and me, coats were restored to their owners, and with many thanks and good wishes again they prepared to leave. Amélie kissed me warmly, and I had time to briefly kiss Céleste, whispering that Sunday would not come soon enough, before they were all in the car and setting off.

I went through to the kitchen, finding Florette and Paulette still busily clearing away, and thanked them profusely for their efforts, adding that the meal had been a great success and everyone had praised the cook. This caused Florette to blush again, although I had no doubt that she was inwardly very pleased that her efforts had been so well received.

Going back into the salon I joined Gaston who remarked on the pleasant evening spent seated between two such lovely companions. Expressing the hope that I had also enjoyed the company, he added as an aside, 'You seem to have made a good friend of Amélie. It is never a bad thing to have the mother on your side, M'sieur Jean.'

'And the father's opinion?' I asked him pointedly.

'Ah, that is another matter, he has his own agenda,' he replied, which rather worried me, thinking again of our conversation before the party and Amélie's earlier comments about 'followers', which set me wondering if Vincent possibly had a favourite amongst them.

The hour now becoming late, Gaston had agreed to stay the night rather than make the journey back to his lonely apartment, and the household now prepared to retire to bed, thoughts of the evening's conversations still fresh in my mind.

CHAPTER NINETEEN
The Last Weekend

Saturday was spent dealing with more household accounts, interspersed with such instructions as I felt necessary to be given to Gaston and Florette, covering the period of the impending absence on my return to London on Monday.

The morning passed slowly, as I tried to reconcile my thoughts to the forthcoming return home. I would surely be kept busy on my return, which in the past had always energized me, but at this moment I only felt aware of all that I would be leaving behind, and it had the effect of mildly depressing me. I could only marvel at the changes the last two weeks had brought to me, totally unimagined a fortnight ago, but realising that they were now going to present me with some difficult decisions.

In an attempt to leave these thoughts behind I switched on the radio in the salon, determined to catch up with the latest news of the student unrest in Paris. I was shocked to hear that overnight the students had attempted to liberate the Sorbonne, which was surrounded by the CRS, who, in an effort to prevent them from crossing the Seine, and thereby keeping disturbances on the Left Bank, had blocked the bridges. The police had attacked the demonstrators in the early hours, and were fighting the demonstrators who had erected barricades, overturned and burnt vehicles, and, by lifting the cobblestones from the streets, had counter-attacked, despite facing tear gas grenades. There were reports of many injuries on both sides of the battle that had ensued. Michael had clearly been correct in his prediction last night.

In an effort to leave the news of this strife – and concerns of my own impending departure – behind me for a while, I decided to take a walk into town during the afternoon to find a present for Céleste, something in the nature of a small keepsake.

Walking through town I peered in the windows of various shops, examining the goods on display, then, seeing various bracelets displayed in a jewellery shop, I entered. I was immediately drawn to a collection of silver charms displayed inside the shop, and, finding one of a small mouse, I decided that this, with a simple chain bracelet, would be most suitable.

Indicating the mouse charm, I asked if I could be shown a suitable chain.

'Mais bien sûr, Monsieur,' advised the assistant, pulling a card revealing a selection of chains from a drawer under the counter. We spent some time examining these before settling on one that seemed most suitable.

The items were assembled for me by the shop assistant, who then placed them in a small case, my errand now completed.

Pleased with this purchase, and with time to spare, I decided to make my way down to one of the small hotels overlooking the lake, and spent a pleasant half hour enjoying a coffee and a pastry. How peaceful Evian seemed at present, I thought, as I watched passers-by strolling alongside the lake: old women with their small dogs sauntering along, and families with their young children excitedly remarking on the pleasure boats plying their way on the water, under a cloudless sky. We seemed to be a million miles away from the reports coming from Paris.

On my return Gaston and I finalised our plans for the drive to the airport on Monday morning, and he confirmed that we had a full tank of petrol in readiness for the journey.

Sunday morning saw Florette return from her regular attendance at Morning Mass. She was still commenting on Friday's dinner party, remarking on how good it had been to see so many guests. I must confess this rather saddened me, for I realised that she would shortly be alone again, the sole occupant of the house for some time, save for Gaston visiting to attend to the garden.

Following lunch I explained that I was visiting the Bonnaire family this afternoon, and was unsure at what time I would be returning.

'That will not be a problem, Monsieur Jean. I will be happy to prepare a light meal on your return' advised Florette.

'That will be fine, especially after the feast on Friday' I replied, with a twinkle in my eye – which she acknowledged with a smile.

Driving up to the farm it seemed hard to appreciate again that only one week had elapsed since I had first met Céleste and her family; so much had happened in the week since then. I was met at the door by Amélie, who had been made aware of my visit, and greeted me with a kiss.

Being invited in, I followed her into the salon, Céleste joining us shortly after. I decided not to ask her about the dance, her mother still being present, instead suggesting that she may like a change of scene, perhaps, to visit nearby Thonon-les-Bains. Happy with this suggestion she collected her coat, and we set off, after saying our goodbyes to her mother.

On the road down to Thonon I ventured to ask how yesterdays dance had been.

Somewhat reservedly she replied, 'I am still a little in shock.'

When I asked her for an explanation, she continued

'Guillaume, the farmer I mentioned to you, made a proposal of marriage to me last night. That was the last thing I was expecting.'

Rather shocked, and with an increasingly sick feeling in my stomach, I asked her how she had replied to his proposal. In answer she told me that she had been so surprised she had been unable to say anything, but now had misgivings that this delay would offer him encouragement to continue his pursuit of her.

'What did you intend to answer?' I asked, now becoming intensely worried.

'He is not for me. Of that I'm sure. I have a feeling that his parents, who are old friends of my father, have colluded with him in encouraging this. Knowing how important the acquisition of more land is to most farmers, a marriage would have the effect of a merger of our two farms.'

'But surely you don't think your father would involve himself in such a scheme?' I questioned. 'Has he such little concern for his daughter's happiness?'

'I'm afraid you don't understand the important role land has played in rural life and the psyche of the farming community down the centuries, Jean.'

'And the son, Guillaume, is merely being used as a pawn in all this?'

'Well, I don't deny he is probably being used, but I am conceited enough to know that he feels a great fondness for me, although I have never reciprocated this other than as a friend; and of course we have known each other since our childhood.'

'So what do you think will happen now?' I asked.

'I will have to give him my answer to prevent further attempts at wooing, but I don't think his parents will be easily dissuaded.'

By now I had been able to park close to the port of Rives, and had switched off the car engine. Continuing our discussion

I wondered aloud if this was going to affect our fledgling relationship.

'No, Jean, my feelings for you remain the same.'

I leant over and kissed her, whispering that her feelings were not the only ones that were unchanged. She returned my affection, and we enjoyed this closeness for some time further. Eventually, noticing that the car windows were by now becoming steamed up, I suggested a short walk by the port, perhaps followed by a ride on the funicular railway up to the town centre above.

We strolled on, hand in hand for a while, eventually finding an empty bench, where I indicated we might sit down. Taking the jeweller's case out of my pocket I presented it to Céleste, telling her I had bought a small gift in town yesterday.

She looked at me with surprise, asking why, as it was not her birthday.

'Just a small keepsake for you,' I said, 'I hope you like it.'

On opening the case she expressed her delight, exclaiming, 'You have not forgotten your country mouse!'

'No, and I hope it will remind you of me while I'm away.'

At this comment I was aware of a little sadness becoming apparent in her eyes, but, quickly recovering, she added, 'Not for too long, Jean, I hope.'

A few more kisses followed between us, after which we made our way over to purchase tickets for the funicular, which had taken away the need for the steep climb up to the town centre since the end of the nineteenth century. The short journey took us up the slope to the Belvedere, an extravagant look-out point which afforded spectacular views over the lake and to Lausanne in Switzerland on the far shore. We stopped for a few minutes to enjoy this panorama, and walking on, within no time we found ourselves in the town centre.

We slowly strolled through the streets, glancing at the displays of goods in the shop windows, commenting on unusual items, and in my case, only too happy that we were again alone together, albeit the last time for now.

Finding a small café open we went in and sat down, finding ourselves to be the only customers, and ordered two coffees.

'Not quite La Confiserie Zurcher at Montreux,' commented Céleste quietly, not wishing to be overheard by the waitress.

'I agree,' I whispered, thoughts of that emporium causing me to recollect the pleasurable events of that day.

We spent some time over our coffee, eventually returning again to the subject of the proposal. Not wishing to seem intrusive, I ventured to ask about her present relationship with her parents in the context of Guillaume.

'My father is from generations of farmers, so the prospect of an increase of land holdings is of great importance to him.'

'And your mother's position on this?' I asked, reflecting on the conversation with Amélie in the garden only two days ago.

'Ah, she is from a different background, and I hope that she will be able to carry some influence in the matter. The ownership of more land does not figure greatly in her mind. But you must remember that all my siblings have now married and moved away from the farm, to lead their own lives and their chosen careers, so perhaps he sees this as the last opportunity to increase his land holding.'

'But at the expense of his daughter's happiness?' I exclaimed, rather angry at this statement.

'I hope he will begin to realise the situation eventually. He has always been a loving father to me,' she replied.

I was sorely tempted to throw my hat into the ring at this juncture and make my own proposal, but my cautious nature bade me to dismiss this thought for the present, regarding such an act as premature, saying instead, 'Guillaume is not the only one to be fond of you, Céleste.'

Her response was to take my hand, which lay on top of the table, squeezing it to show her sympathy towards me, whilst uttering softly, 'I know, Jean, I know.'

'Let us hope that your father is sufficiently uxorious to listen to his wife's opinion in the matter,' I suggested, feeling that Amelie had already sensed the feelings of her daughter towards me, and may prove to be an ally in the matter.

Thinking to reassure her further I expressed the hope that she would always regard me as a friend she could turn to if her situation became untenable, her eyes expressing the gratitude I sought.

I rose to pay the waitress for our coffees, who, becoming aware of the drama unfolding before her, had kindly busied herself in the kitchen at the rear of the café, in order to afford us some privacy.

Walking back towards the funicular we both agreed that this being my last evening in Evian for the present, we might share a meal together. We discussed this as we descended in the funicular to the port area where we had parked the car, and decided on one of the hotels overlooking the lake in Evian. Both of us were now in agreement to my suggestion that the name Guillaume would not be uttered again to spoil our last evening together. We soon arrived back in town, and parking the car again, found a table available in the same hotel where we had dined earlier in the week with Michael.

The maître d' showed us to our seats, commenting that he was pleased to see us so soon again. We placed our order for an aperitif, which we sipped as we perused the menu.

I was eager to hear more from Céleste about the publishing house in Lyon, and her work as a translator.

'As I told you before it won't involve me working in an office, or to set hours. Our publishing house will acquire the translation rights to produce an English version of a book that is already published in French. These rights are often sold to us, but can also be given freely, but we must always ensure that we are dealing with the copyright owner, who is very often not the author, and quite often in fact is the publisher. My friend Alice, who set up the publishing house, deals with these acquisitions, which she will then pass to me, or another translator. Alice will normally give me a deadline for the translation, so I will have to be disciplined in the hours I allot to the work.'

'You are to start the work soon then?' I enquired.

'Yes, I have a meeting with Alice in a week or so, at her office in Lyon, and I understand she will have a manuscript ready for translation. So I will be kept busy from later this month.'

Céleste now turned the conversation again to my life in London, asking me more about my work, and what I did in my spare time. I attempted to give a picture of my life, realising that, apart from acquiring my house recently, I didn't involve myself with much else outside my legal work. This set me wondering whether this would be all I had to look forward to in the future, had this current interlude not occurred. It was true that I had acquaintances in London, meeting them occasionally for a meal or drinks, at other times to visit the theatre or an exhibition. But these always ended with my return to an empty house. Yes, there had also been romantic attachments in the past, but these had never developed beyond an initial attraction, and had soon faltered.

My thoughts were interrupted by Céleste confiding to me, 'I

really know so little about you, Jean, and yet it seems to me that we have known each other for an eternity. Is that not strange?'

I could only agree with this, for I had similar feelings, which could not be explained rationally, and I returned in my mind again to that previous relationship fifty years earlier which had ended so tragically. I even wondered to myself if there was not some inherited attraction at work between us, something that had also been present between Felix and Célestine. But, of course, I could only keep these thoughts to myself, as, to the outside world I should know nothing of this, a secret I shared with Gaston alone.

Continuing our conversation about London I innocently suggested that Céleste may care to visit me there, and I would naturally be delighted to act as her guide and show her the sights of the city.

This seemed to cause her pause for thought for a few moments before saying, 'I must check my passport, and see when it expires.'

'So you would like to come?' I enquired, hopefully.

'Yes, of course, but where should I stay?' she replied.

'Oh, I have a spare bedroom, so that is not a problem.' I naively pointed out, thinking that this would provide an acceptable solution to her.

'Is the spare bedroom what you would prefer, Jean?' she enigmatically answered, in a coquettish tone, the hint of a smile evident on her face.

'Whatever you desire,' I replied, curious as to whether I had understood her underlying meaning.

As if to confirm this to me she added, 'There will be no housekeeper to interrupt us in London?' It seemed that she had come to a momentous decision, without any pressure from me.

'No, we will be quite alone.' I replied, blushing a little at what was being suggested.

I continued, perhaps rather too animatedly, by describing some of the landmarks that she might find of interest during her stay, whilst at the same time trying unsuccessfully to put visions of intimate relations that now flooded into my mind to one side.

'So, that is settled, Jean. We will arrange a date for my visit soon. I am already looking forward to it.'

By now we had finished our meal, which for my own part I scarcely even recollected, our conversation having dominated everything. We finally drank our coffee, and I settled the bill, then, after bidding the maître d' a good evening, we made our way back to the Citroën.

'We will have to make do with my small MG in London,' I jokingly commented as we arrived at the car, to which Céleste replied, 'But there will only be room for the two of us, which I prefer.'

'Gaston is driving me to the airport in the morning, so please say you'll see me off. He can drive you back home afterwards.' I was anxiously hoping that we might spend some more time together before I left.

'Why, of course, Jean' she replied, 'I would like that.'

We sat for some time in the car, watching the lights of Lausanne on the opposite shore twinkling in the distance, moving closer together in a warm embrace, which we ended far too soon, remembering that we had an early start in the morning.

Arriving finally at the farm we kissed tenderly, and wishing each other a good night's sleep, in readiness for our journey to Geneva in the morning, I left her to make her way indoors.

CHAPTER TWENTY
Returning Home

I awoke early, having spent an uneasy night filled with vivid dreams of Céleste pursued by an apparition that appeared as a vague, unrecognisable human form. These dreams were interspersed with passionate arguments that I, as an unwitting eavesdropper, heard her making against other unseen spectres, although the substance of them could not be recalled on awakening. I could only interpret these dreams as a reminder of my own fears that Guillaume and his family were not going to be dismissed too easily, despite Céleste's earlier assurances that she would be making clear her unwillingness to accept his proposal.

With these thoughts still in my mind I tried to concentrate on current matters in hand, as, having by now dressed, I went down to breakfast. Florette brought in a jug of coffee, and we spent a few minutes discussing household affairs. I was hopeful that all concerns had now been resolved to our mutual satisfaction, as I did not wish my absence to prove to be difficult for her.

Gaston had brought the car round to the front of the house, in readiness for our journey. Echoes of the events of the last two weeks were spinning round in my mind as I made my final exit, for the present, from the house that I felt in so short a time had become my home. Stowing my luggage in the boot, I took my seat alongside Gaston who was already in the driving seat. Then with a final 'Bon voyage, Monsieur Jean!' cried out by Florette, who was trying her best to appear unruffled at my departure. My last sight was her slight figure with a familiar flowery apron atop her sombre-coloured dress, on the time-worn stone steps to the front of the old house, waving, as we set off down the drive.

Arriving at the farm I was only able to speak for a short while with Amélie, who again expressed her sorrow at my leaving. I felt that I was finally able to convince her that I would certainly be returning soon, and it was my fervent hope that I would become a regular visitor to the farm once again. The Guillaume affair, whilst not openly referred to between us, was, I judged from her tone, a subject of no little concern to her. It had obviously already become a major topic of conversation within the family this weekend, and she seemed to take some consolation from the strength of the reply I gave about my return.

Céleste had been deep in conversation with Gaston during this time, Vincent being absent as he was tending to his livestock, so I was unable to judge his feelings about the Guillaume affair, although I wondered if his not being present perhaps indicated his position in the matter.

Being finally ready to depart, Céleste and I took our seats in the back of the Citroën, Gaston, his grizzled face beaming, was clearly enjoying his role as our chauffeur. With exchanges of 'Au revoir' and 'Bon voyage' from Amélie we sped off once more down towards the lake, on our journey to Geneva airport.

Céleste and I had wasted no time in moving closer together in the back of the car, our hands joined, yet both of us remaining silent for much of the journey. She appeared rather distracted, responding initially in monosyllables only to Gaston's occasional comments. I felt satisfied that we were, for the present, together again as a couple. Gaston commented upon the events in Paris over the last days, and in that respect I was happy that I had my flight already booked, for who could say what may happen in the next week or so to disrupt travel arrangements. Gaston, on the other hand, seemed to have adopted a pragmatic attitude to the events now unfolding, merely expressing the view that life would probably continue much as before, with some minor inconveniences to be expected due to a General Strike that had been called today. More reports of the strike were being sent out in the news bulletins on the car radio, and we listened avidly as we drove on towards Geneva.

Céleste had different thoughts, however, suggesting that as many of the workers were now striking, events may take a turn for the worse, as there was so much pent-up anger towards the Establishment, who still did not appear to be listening to the mood of the people.

As we mulled these thoughts in our minds Gaston followed the road that skirted the lake for some kilometres, finally leaving it at Sciez. We then drove on through the small town of Douvaine before passing into more open countryside between fields on either side of us, many containing serried ranks of sunflowers, not as yet in bloom, but all thrusting upwards to the sky, reaching for the warmth and light emanating from the sun above.

The road finally skirted the lake again as we neared the outskirts of the city of Geneva, and we looked towards the famous Jet d'Eau fountain now plainly visible to our right, always a spectacular sight – the water carried some four hundred feet high above the lake, clearly visible even from aircraft passing overhead.

Passing over Pont du Mont Blanc at the western end of

the lake and into the city centre, Gaston demonstrated his knowledge of the route, having no doubt driven Felix to visit clients in the city over many years in the past. I was certainly impressed by the knowledge of our chauffeur today as he drove on through the city, unperturbed, yet clearly mindful of the pedestrians waiting patiently at the many crossings, and the vehicular traffic around us in the multiple lanes ever present in the city.

Within a short time we had arrived at the airport, its brand new terminal now finally awaiting its inauguration within the next month. Gaston was able to pull in temporarily close to the departure lounge, and I got out of the car, and removed my case from the boot. We had agreed that Céleste would come into the terminal with me, as I checked in for my flight, so that we would have some time alone together to say our goodbyes.

Gaston confirmed that he would remain in the car, in the adjacent car park, and would await Céleste's return, as he would then be taking her back to the farm. Having got out from the car he embraced me, saying, 'Nobody could have imagined that your visit would prove to be so momentous. We all hope to see you soon back in Evian, M'sieur Jean, and I will look after everything for you in the meantime. Have a good trip.' Turning to Céleste he told her there was no need to hurry back, indicating again to her where he would be parked.

We entered the terminal building, which was bustling with its usual activity, and Céleste accompanied me as I made my way over to the flight desk to pick up my ticket, and pass over my suitcase for onward transit to London. Having now disposed of these formalities we decided that there would be plenty of time for a coffee before I boarded my flight.

Having ordered I found a corner table vacant, and we took

our seats side by side on the banquette. Our order was brought over to us, and, looking directly at Céleste, who clearly seemed troubled, I returned to our discussion of yesterday.

'Do you intend to let Guillaume have a clear answer to his proposal soon?' I asked, emphasising the word *soon*, knowing that I certainly did not want this matter hanging over us both for too long.

'Yes, of course, Jean. I intend to let him know later today, if at all possible,' she replied softly. 'You know what my answer will be,' at the same time stretching out her hand to squeeze mine.

'I hope you know how happy that will make me, knowing that he will no longer be in the picture,' I replied. 'But this may perhaps create problems with your father,' I added cautiously, knowing the importance he might already be attaching to this proposed union.

This last comment caused her to take a sharp intake of breath, and look down towards the floor as if she was about to break down, but she quickly recovered her composure.

'I'm not his little girl any longer, and can handle the situation, I'm sure,' was her response, in a surprisingly sharp tone, while still holding on to my hand.

There were so many things I wanted to say to her at this moment, but how best to express them? Felix's death, followed by my meeting Céleste a mere week ago, had turned my rather orderly – some might even say boring – life completely upside down. I had fallen into a routine in which my legal career had become the centre, the focus to the exclusion of much else, and the realisation only now struck me that I had been leading a solitary life in London. My thoughts turned back again to my conversation with Michael. Yes, it was true, as he had observed, that I was never one to make snap decisions, but hadn't I already confirmed my innermost feelings to my friend in saying that I couldn't now see my future life without Céleste? If only this Guillaume business was finally settled, I felt that we could continue with the status quo for the present. Both of us, could, hopefully, be satisfied with my return visits to Evian over the next few months. Of course, there was yet Céleste's proposed trip to see me in London, one that appeared to offer such promise of romance.

'You are rather quiet, Jean,' Céleste commented, which had the immediate effect of jolting me from my reverie.

'I'm so sorry,' I apologised, 'but I can't stop thinking about this current situation. I must confess that if I'm honest I really don't want to go away today, and leave you, even if only for a short time.'

'It's the same for me, Jean, but we both have to accept that you have responsibilities in England, certainly for the present. You have to be away, although I will miss you so dreadfully.' And with this she moved closer to me, putting her arm around me, and moving her face forward and offering me her mouth which I kissed passionately.

'You will wait for me, my darling girl?' I whispered softly to her, aware that my flight was now about to be called.

'We country mice keep our word,' she replied, in her coquettish manner, trying outwardly to appear calm, although I could sense that underneath this show of bravado she was troubled by my departure.

Our intimacy was interrupted by the announcement of the imminent departure of my flight over the tannoy. This resulted in further passionate embraces and protestations of our feelings for each other, before we both finally got up from our seat.

Seeing that she was now becoming tearful I held her closely again, kissing her, before our goodbyes were uttered, and with a final wave to her, I turned away, to join the other passengers who were preparing to board the flight.

'I will phone you as soon as I get back to London!' I called out to her.

'Yes, Jean, I look forward to your call,' she replied, attempting a weak smile.

Looking back one final time before turning a corner, and becoming out of sight, I saw her lone figure in the Departure Lounge, now quietly sobbing, her head downcast, impervious to the other bystanders around her. I could only mirror her sadness, and resolved at once to return at the earliest opportunity.

Making my way across the tarmac to the waiting plane my head was filled with so many thoughts. Felix's death which now seemed a distant event, although ever present, offered me the choice of a future life that would have been previously unimaginable. My meeting with Céleste, a result of the accidental discovery of a photograph, hidden away for so many years, I could only equate to serendipity. There could be no denying my intense feelings for her, and the realisation that my life, without her presence, I now felt, seemed impossible to comprehend. Had these strong feelings somehow managed to jump a generation, or had we somehow been intended to meet in this way, thereby completing some predestined circle?

Now I was troubled by thoughts that her father, seeing the promise of another farm offered, would be influenced to try and persuade his daughter to make this marriage to Guillaume, and failing in this, the family could be split apart, causing great sadness. Could there be any solution to this situation? My feelings were clear, but it seemed certain that Céleste was going to be subject to great pressure while I was away. Was our burgeoning romance strong enough to overcome whatever arguments in favour of Guillaume were to be presented in my absence?

This led me to recall that I was now party to the dark secret that had been shared by Gaston and Felix for the last fifty years, the telling of which would surely bring little in the way of joy or happiness to the family.

The final words written by Célestine in the letter to Felix all those years ago came back to me again.

'*Souviens-toi de moi.*' Remember me.

How apt that this phrase could now be referred to me in the present situation.

PART TWO

CHAPTER TWENTY-ONE
A Shared Confidence

Commencing the drive back from the airport Gaston was quick to detect the sadness that seemed to envelop Céleste as she sat beside him. She remained silent but her body language, the head held low, seemed to be an excessive reaction to the recent parting, as they knew that Jean's absence would only be of a short duration.

Despite having no children of his own, Gaston had always enjoyed a good relationship with the younger generation, often being sought out by the children of his nephews and nieces to give advice on matters that they felt could not be discussed freely with their parents.

'You are missing Monsieur Jean already, I can see,' he commented to Céleste, 'but he will return soon, I know,' he suggested, in the hope of engendering a conversation.

Rather than being comforted by this, her response was to sob openly, and in a low, pitiful voice utter, 'That is not the problem. I don't know if I dare confide in you.'

'Céleste,' he said compassionately, 'I am an old friend of your family, particularly of your mother, and if I can help you in any way, please let me know. If there is any problem with Jean I would feel personally involved, particularly as I arranged the introduction to your family. I regard him as I would a son.'

'Oh, Oncle Gaston,' she sighed, for she had from a young age regarded him as such. 'Everything is going wrong for me, and I don't know what to do.'

'Céleste, my dear, don't be afraid to tell me, for your happiness is my concern, and if it helps you to talk about your problem, I promise that I won't share our conversation with others.'

She sat quietly, as if considering the implications of his suggestion, before asking, 'Can we park the car and have a coffee, somewhere here in Geneva?'

'Of course – I know just the place. Felix and I often stopped there on our journeys. We can find a quiet table, I'm sure.'

Within a few minutes they had arrived, and having parked the car, found a quiet corner table. Gaston ordered two coffees.

She sat opposite him, a little more composed now, but he sensed that she was in a vulnerable state of mind, liable to break down at any moment.

'Now, when you are ready, I am always a good listener,' he began.

'It's my father,' she uttered in an anguished tone. 'We have had such a disagreement, and I don't know what to do.'

'And your mother, is she also involved in this?' He asked quietly.

'No. She can only guess at the situation. We had an argument late last night, after she had gone to bed, and I don't think she heard us, as we were at opposite ends of the house. But she is aware of the reason for our disagreement.'

'And may I ask, what is the reason?' enquired Gaston, his voice now softened, the strong regional accent somewhat diminished.

'You know Guillaume Forestier, of course, Oncle. He has been a family friend since early childhood, the son of a neighbouring farmer. We were at school together, but he left before me to help his father with their farm, while I carried on with my education, finally attending university in Lyon. He has always expressed a fondness for me, which I swear to you I have never encouraged. But recently he has seemed more domineering in his approach to me, almost acting as if he owned me at times, to which I have shown my obvious dislike. Despite this, he made a proposal of marriage to me after the dance on Saturday evening. I was too shocked at this to give him an answer, and am fearful that he has taken this to mean a possible acceptance on my part. But I have told Jean of this, and he is anxious that I make it clear that I have no wish to marry Guillaume, for, as you may already have guessed, Jean is the one that I am very fond of.'

Gaston nodded in agreement, noticing that her eyes lit up at the mention of Jean.

She continued, 'I told my parents of the proposal yesterday and was shocked at the reaction of my father. He seems set on this marriage going ahead, and I fear Guillaume's family have colluded in some way with him on this. I am afraid that he has the mindset of the typical farmer. Land ownership and the passing of it down through the generations seem to be so important, and my feelings as his daughter seem to count for little. My mother will support me, and take my side, I feel sure. But as for my father, many hurtful things were said last night by both of us, and I feel that I can't continue to live under the family roof at present. At the same time it would never be my wish to cause a lasting split within the family.'

'This is indeed serious, my dear – I know how these farmers think, but I'm sure a solution can be found. Forgive my prying, please, but have you yet refused Guillaume?' Gaston asked, with a more serious tone now to his voice.

'No, but I intend to speak to him later today, and have promised Jean that I will.'

'And I am not so old as to see that there is a strong feeling, shall we say, between you and Jean?' Gaston commented, a thin smile apparent on his face.

'Yes, we are very fond of each other, perhaps unusually so after such a short time, and I think we both expect this feeling to grow even stronger over the coming months. But now I have this situation with my father, which I am finding quite unbearable, and I couldn't bring myself to tell Jean everything that happened last night, particularly as he was about to embark on his return to London.'

'I can understand that, of course. So will you be speaking to Guillaume today?'

'Yes, but I daren't telephone from home in case my father is there and overhears. I don't feel able to face Guillaume at his farm, particularly as his parents are likely to be there.'

Gaston gave this some thought before replying, in a kindly tone. 'Now, I have a suggestion to make to you. Why not use the phone at Les Cyclamens to speak to Guillaume? Jean won't mind I'm sure. If you like I can speak to him in London and propose that you would benefit from spending some time staying at the house, until this business blows over. He has left me in charge in his absence, and, if you also explain matters to him, I'm sure he will be delighted for you to stay. Florette will welcome a house guest, of that I have no doubt.'

Sensing her surprise at this suggestion, he continued 'So let's carry on with our journey and you can make the call. Later, after we have spoken to Jean, I can drive you to the farm to collect some clothes, that is, if you wish to remain in the town for the present.'

'I don't want to impose on Jean, but I don't have anywhere else to stay. I'm due to see my friend Alice in Lyon, to arrange commencing work as a translator, so Evian would be a very convenient place to stay. But are you sure that he won't mind about this imposition?'

'You must already have seen that Jean has a kindly nature, and, given the particular circumstances, will be delighted to help.'

'Thank you so much for listening to my troubles, Oncle Gaston. I feel a little more settled, but there is still so much to do.'

'Let's get your stay sorted first, and then I'm sure we can look at deciding what can be done about your father. The fact of your moving out, albeit temporarily, will perhaps focus his mind a little more clearly, and of course we can arrange for your mother to visit at any time.'

'I do hope I haven't burdened you with my problems,' she said, now looking less pale.

'Not in the least, my dear – the happiness of you both is my dearest wish; but as you are no longer a young girl please call me Gaston, rather than oncle, as it would sit more comfortably with me.'

She accepted this, and feeling now more composed she agreed that they could now continue their journey.

CHAPTER TWENTY-TWO
A Surprising Explanation

On finally reaching the house they were confronted by a somewhat surprised Florette, as they entered the entrance hall.

'Mademoiselle Céleste needs to make a private call. Could I ask you to arrange a simple meal for us, as we have driven straight from Geneva?' enquired Gaston.

Florette assented to this, knowing that Gaston would give a good account to her later of Jean's departure. She was struck by the pallor evident in Céleste's face – the eyes, normally so bright, beset with an air of worry.

'If Mademoiselle Bonnaire would care to wash first, after the journey?' she enquired, in a formal manner, being unsure of the form of address she should use, as she indicated the cloakroom door to her.

'Thank you Madame,' Céleste replied, taking the opportunity to freshen up.

While she was thus engaged, Florette questioned Gaston further, who murmured, not wishing to be overheard, 'The poor girl has a problem at home, which I will explain to you later. She may be staying here for a few days, but first I have to speak to Monsieur Jean.'

'Oh, for certain she is clearly worried about something – but I won't pry, 'Florette observed, and going to the kitchen added, 'I'll prepare your meal and bring it through to the dining room shortly.'

Céleste rejoined Gaston, now refreshed, and though a relative newcomer to the house already felt imbued with the feeling of calm that seemed to emanate from the very fabric of the building.

'Perhaps if you make your phone call before we eat,' suggested Gaston, 'the study is quite private.'

'Thank you. Guillaume may be at the farm, as it is lunchtime,' she replied.

Going through to the study, Gaston suggested she be seated, indicating the telephone to her standing atop the desk. 'I will close the door as I leave,' he muttered to her in a kindly manner. 'Remember, you have friends here who are ready to help.'

This last remark had the effect of emboldening her resolve, and she dialled the number with no hesitation.

She was fortunate to find that it was Guillaume who answered, clearly pleased, as he recognised her voice at once.

'Guillaume, I must give my answer to your proposal, which I must say I was most surprised to receive. I have always regarded you as a family friend, but nothing more. I am sorry, but I cannot accept your offer of marriage, for this reason. Since my time at university the direction of my life has changed, I don't see being a farmer's wife as my future, and I hope you will understand this.'

There was a momentary silence at the other end of the line as he took this in, before saying in a shocked voice, 'But I thought we were destined to be together. I always thought of us as certainly more than just friends. We have both enjoyed the rural life, having been raised almost side by side in the same commune, and attending school together from our earliest days. My feelings for you have always been the same.'

She pictured the tall, well-built young man, his features tanned, and crowned with hair of the blackest shade, disappointment now only too evident in his Savoyard accent.

'Guillaume, I hear what you say, but I must insist that I will not marry you!' her voice now becoming a little harsh, angered at the assumptions he was making. Then, feeling some sympathy for him, added, 'You are a good man, and I'm sure you will find someone with whom to share your life, but please, let this be the end of this conversation.'

'Can I speak to you again, perhaps at your farm?' he asked, in a vain attempt to keep the situation open.

'No, I am not likely to be at the farm for the next few days, so I must say goodbye now,' was her response, as she replaced the phone, thus ending the call.

Then, realising that he may attempt to contact someone at the farm, she knew that she must warn her mother. She sat back in the chair her head slumped forward, sighing deeply, as she recalled the strain of that last phone conversation. Had she in any way encouraged the young man's ardour? She considered recent meetings, always in the company of family or friends, never alone, and could not recall that she had in any way behaved or spoken other than as a friend to him. Surely he had convinced himself into believing that any feelings he had were being reciprocated, as if in some fantastic daydream.

Recovering her resolve again she made a further call, which was fortunately answered by her mother.

'Maman, I am having lunch in Evian with Gaston, and may call later this afternoon to collect some clothes. I had a serious argument with Papa last night, after you had gone to bed, and don't feel able to stay at home for the present. You should know that I have rejected Guillaume's proposal, and have indicated the matter is now closed, but am fearful that he will not accept my refusal.'

'Oh Céleste, my darling girl, I am so sorry to hear that you have fallen out with your Papa. I could sense that he was troubled this morning. But please, do come home. Surely you have nowhere to stay?'

'Gaston is kindly arranging things for me, and I will let you know more when I see you later. Please try and let Papa know that my mind is set on this, but I would hate the thought that this will come between you both.'

'My dear, your happiness is my concern, of course; but I know your father – he does seem set on Guillaume.'

'But he isn't the one marrying him! He chose you from outside the farming community, so I'm struggling to see why I can't make my own choice in the matter. I know that he must worry about the future of the farm, but should my happiness be sacrificed because of this? I feel that, for the present at least, I must stay away.'

The sorrow was evident in her mother's voice as she confirmed that she would see Céleste later; her father would be absent from the farm until early evening.

Having finished this final conversation, Céleste made her way to the salon, where she found Gaston, a Gauloise in his gnarled hand, enjoying an aperitif.

'I have spoken to Guillaume,' she said, looking somewhat improved, her eyes beginning to regain some of their customary brightness. 'I have also spoken to my mother, so she is aware of the situation.'

'Good,' uttered Gaston, offering her a glass of vermouth, which she gladly accepted. She held up her glass and with a 'Santé', to which Gaston responded, took a sip.

'I think we deserve this, after the tribulations of this morning,' commented Gaston. 'We will eat soon, and then I will contact M'sieur Jean.' He looked over to her, a kindly smile on his lined face, saying, 'Once M'sieur Jean has agreed to your stay here, I think it best that we let Florette know more. She will clearly be curious and concerned for you, and, of course, you will both be living under the same roof. I'm sure she will look upon you kindly, for, like me, she cares for Monsieur Jean's happiness, and if he wants you to stay, she will be delighted.'

'Thank you, Gaston,' she replied, suggesting, 'Perhaps you can tell her as much as you feel she should know at present. I will only become emotional again if I try to explain.'

They were interrupted by Florette at this juncture, who confirmed that the meal was now ready in the dining room. They thanked her, went in, and took their seats. Gaston poured them both a glass of wine, 'To fortify us for this afternoon,' he commented, and they ate.

CHAPTER TWENTY-THREE
A Friend's Concern

The meal finished some time earlier, the effect of the wine, followed by strong coffee, had given back Céleste a feeling of inner calm. Gaston reflected on her improved appearance, and satisfied, suggested that he would try and contact Jean.

'I'll call you when I've finished, so that you can speak to him,' he said.

Going through to the study, Gaston seated himself behind the antique Empire desk, remembering as he did so, the times he had observed Felix at work here. Picking up the phone and dialling for an international call, he waited patiently while the operator made the connection.

Hearing Jean's voice on the line, he asked, in his rasping regional accent induced by decades of strong Gauloises, how the journey had gone.

'Very well, Gaston. A good flight and then a taxi ride to Fulham. Did you take Céleste back home safely?'

'Ah, this is the main reason for my call, M'sieur Jean. Unfortunately she had a serious argument with her father last night, with the result that she feels unable to stay at home for the present. I'm sure you know the subject of all this is the farmer, Guillaume.'

'But she didn't mention any of this to me before my flight!' was my anguished reply.

'No, she didn't want to worry you on your journey, which is understandable. I'm afraid she was very emotional during the drive back, and has confided in me about the situation. The good news is that she has now definitely rejected Guillaume's proposal. As a result of the argument last night she feels that she can't stay under the same roof as her father for the present. I have suggested that she could stay here at Les Cyclamens, provided you agree, of course, Monsieur Jean.'

'Gaston, if only I'd known, I could have cancelled my flight and stayed longer in Evian.' I replied.

'But this matter may take some time to resolve, M'sieur Jean. Her father seems set on this marriage.'

'I was aware that this could happen, and, of course, I would be delighted if she stayed in the house. Florette will look after her, I'm sure. Is Céleste there at the moment? I must speak to her.'

'Yes, certainly M'sieur Jean, I will call her to the phone. She has also spoken to her mother about this business, and I will drive her over to collect some of her clothes later.'

'Thank you, my friend. I'm pleased that she has you to support her, and I would be most happy if you could drive her wherever she needs to go.'

'Monsieur Jean, you know that I will always do what I can to help. Now I will fetch the poor girl to the telephone.'

Having said this, Gaston called to Céleste, and handed her the phone as she came into the study.

'Jean, I am so sorry for this trouble,' she began in a voice clearly full of emotion. 'But I don't know what to do. I didn't want to burden you before your return to London, but after you had left I couldn't keep my feelings in check any longer. I feel that I must be away from my father, certainly for the present, as we had such an argument last night, and many hurtful things were said.'

'My poor darling girl, of course you can stay as long as you like. Florette and Gaston will look after you. Please treat the house as if it were your home. This is the least thing I can do for you. But is it true that that you have now rejected Guillaume's proposal? If so, I can't tell you how pleased this makes me.'

'Yes, Jean, but despite my strong rebuttal I fear that he will not give up so easily. I will discuss this with my mother later today, in the hope that she can help make things better between my father and me.'

'Having reached my London home I realise how much I already miss you,' I said, care evident in my voice.

'Oh, how I wish you could be here,' uttered Céleste plaintively, her voice becoming choked again with emotion.

'I'll return just as soon as I can,' I answered. 'I'm so sorry I can't be there with you at this time, but please be strong, for both of us.'

'Jean, you don't know how just hearing your voice gives me strength,' she replied. 'But I suppose we must say goodbye for the moment.'

'Yes, my darling girl, we will speak again soon. Perhaps I can speak now to Florette, if she is there.'

'Of course, I'll fetch her for you. A bientôt, Jean.' With this she went out to the kitchen, telling Florette that Jean wished to speak to her.

'Monsieur Jean, how pleased I am to hear your voice,' Florette said, adding in an attentive tone, 'Did the journey go well?'

'Certainly Florette, and thank you for asking. But I'm worried about Céleste, of course. She is to stay for a while at the house, and I'm sure you will look after her. You have no doubt seen that she is in a rather emotional state.'

'Why yes, Monsieur Jean, I will do my best to make her stay comfortable, and will treat her as a favoured guest. A bientôt, Monsieur Jean,' finished Florette, feeling pleased to have spoken directly with him in London.

Going through to the salon she now offered to show Céleste her bedroom, confirming that she had only to ask if there was anything that she required.

'Thank you, Madame,' she responded, aware of the warmth in Florette's voice.

'Oh, please call me Florette, Mademoiselle,' she urged. 'Everyone in the house calls me by my given name.'

'Only if you are sure,' commented Céleste, not wishing to cause offence in any way.

Florette then took her upstairs to the bedroom, which, although like much of the house, a little old-fashioned in its decoration and furnishings, was well maintained. The deep reddish-brown colour of the mahogany furniture seemed to glow in the sunlight, as soon as they opened the shutters, the scent of wax polish pervading the air, further evidence of the care taken by Florette in her duties. A bathroom, which led off to one side, was already amply provided with fresh towels and soaps.

'What lovely rooms!' exclaimed Céleste, to the obvious delight of Florette. 'And such a fine view across the lake!' she remarked, as she took in the view from the window at the front of the house.

'Yes, this is a favourite of mine,' commented Florette. 'This was the room that belonged to Monsieur Jean's mother when she lived here, and she always used it when she came to visit Monsieur Felix, in later years.'

'I feel honoured,' remarked Céleste, to which Florette replied,

'Monsieur Jean wants the very best for you, Mademoiselle, so I think this is appropriate.'

Having now agreed that Céleste would be staying for some time, it only remained for Gaston to drive her to the farm, for the purpose of collecting some clothes, and discussing the Guillaume affair in more detail with her mother.

Arriving at the farm Gaston suggested that he would wait in the car until called, not wishing to intrude on this fraught familial reunion.

Céleste thanked him for his thoughtful gesture, and wondered at the reaction she would find as she approached the entrance. The door was opened at once by Amélie, already clearly aware of their arrival in the car, concern for her daughter at once evident in her drawn expression. They embraced warmly, the love between mother and daughter clear for all to see.

'Oh, Maman, this is such a horrible situation I find myself in!' exclaimed Céleste, attempting to keep her emotions under control.

'Céleste, my dear, don't feel that you are in any way to blame, such things happen from time to time in most families; perhaps more so when a beautiful girl is pursued by unwanted admirers,' her mother replied, still holding her in the embrace. 'At least this is all out in the open now, and I am pleased that you have refused Guillaume. I never felt he was the one for you – your horizons have widened far beyond the farm, of that I'm sure.'

'Yes, Maman, I have felt, particularly since meeting Jean, that there could be so many things possible in my life,' she replied, making no secret to her mother of the deep feelings she held for him.

'I could sense that you were both enraptured almost from the moment that you met, and I must confess that I also like him very much. But Papa will have to be convinced that Guillaume can never marry you, and I'm not sure how best to approach this. So we must give it some thought. But, for now, do you intend to stay in Evian?'

'Why yes, Maman. Jean has agreed to this with no hesitation, and Gaston has been a true friend to me, since I confided in him with my problems.'

'Gaston is a good ally to have, and perhaps he will help us find a way to resolve matters with your Papa. I certainly trust his judgement. Now, let's sort out your clothes before your father arrives, as I'm sure you don't want to see him just yet. I wonder if it will be best that I tell your Papa that you have gone early to Lyon, to make arrangements for your translation work. If he knows the truth about where you are staying, it may inflame his anger.'

'No, Maman, he should know that this has come about as the result of our argument, and perhaps he will then reflect on this.'

They mounted the stairs to Céleste's room, where a suitcase was soon filled with clothes and toiletries sufficient for her needs.

Having accomplished this, Céleste went outside, calling to Gaston to join them. He quickly arrived, and embracing his old friend, Amélie, told her not to worry as a solution was surely going to be found.

'We will look after your daughter well,' he insisted, 'and you must feel free to visit us at any time,' he added.

'Thank you, Gaston, Céleste is fortunate to have such good friends,' remarked Amélie. 'Now I think it will be best if you both leave, for the present, as Vincent will be returning home soon.'

CHAPTER TWENTY-FOUR
A Dilemma

The phone call had left me with so many thoughts, that I barely knew where to begin. Certainly I was personally pleased that Guillaume had now been rejected. But at what cost to Céleste in her relationship with her father? This argument must have had a great effect upon her, for it struck me from my first meeting that the Bonnaire family seemed very close-knit. I would have to think about this, and consider what might be done to restore peace, for the thought of her suffering in misery was hateful to me.

At least I could be assured that she had somewhere comfortable to stay, Florette and Gaston would see to that. I resolved to phone her later in the evening to make sure that she was not too despondent with her situation, and offer my help in any way possible.

But the more I thought about the matter the realisation became clear that our romance would now prosper. This business over the proposal had confirmed that her feelings were for me. How I wished that I could now return to her again, and at once, if possible.

But I had returned to London for a reason, and left to my own company for a while I could perhaps dissect my life, and consider carefully what mattered most to me, and what parts could be thought of as unimportant to my future happiness.

True, the thought of Céleste being with me at all times had

seemed to be my ultimate goal during these last few days in Evian. But I had not been leading my normal life there, where a routine, the satisfaction of pursuing my chosen career, had always previously seemed to me to be of prime importance. Now, back in London, I would have to decide. What were the real priorities, the raison d'etre, in my life, and how best was I to achieve them. Certainly Felix's generosity had now made so many more things possible to me.

My cottage felt rather lonely and cheerless at present, I had to admit, after having become accustomed to Les Cyclamens, where I had been always surrounded by the bustle and activities of others. But this, in turn, led me to think back to earlier days, when I had seemed satisfied with my life in London. I had rarely felt loneliness at these times, but perhaps my life had evolved naturally to that stage, and only now could I make comparisons. Could I say that I now felt my old life was found wanting in some way?

Returning from these reveries, I proposed to call my employer – which merely sought to remind me, that, apart from pursuing my career, I did, in fact, lead a rather lonely existence here in London.

The call having been made, to the apparent delight of a clearly over-worked Gerald Walker, I busily prepared myself for a return to the office in the morning. I was acutely aware, however, that the frisson of expectation that usually greeted my return to business activities had seemed almost absent this time.

Returning to my present situation once more, I realised that a shopping expedition to re-stock my depleted larder, and a general tidy of the cottage was called for. I had not yet employed a cleaning lady, feeling that the cottage was not yet suitable, due to the on-going decoration work taking place. These thoughts reminded me how I already missed Florette's ministrations, where, in Evian, she always made such chores seem to happen as if by invisible hands.

The cottage, my first excursion into home ownership, had been purchased with the help of a legacy left to me by my mother, Eugénie. She had died some three years ago, at a relatively young age, being then only in her early sixties. She had suffered over time from an illness that had slowly sapped her strength, but in this respect she was unlike most French women, who tended towards hypochondria, rushing to the doctor with the slightest imagined ailment. She chose to dismiss the loss of vigour initially brought on by the illness, seemingly in denial that she was afflicted in any way. However, she finally reached a stage where the symptoms could no longer be ignored, and a referral by her doctor to a specialist in Harley Street only confirmed the worst – the condition was inoperable. Within a few months she had passed away peacefully in the nursing home that had been found for her when she was finally too frail to be cared for at home.

Memories of this sad chapter in my life returned to me as I now came to the sober realisation that, following Felix's death, I was now the sole remaining descendant of the Dumont dynasty.

Coming back to the present again I prepared a short list for my shopping trip, which would also give me an opportunity to take my MG out for a short spin, after a fortnight being spent off the road.

CHAPTER TWENTY-FIVE
A Developing Friendship

On returning to the house Gaston sought out Florette, enquiring whether she required any vegetables for the evening meal.

'No, I have sufficient for present, but perhaps you can check to see what eggs have been laid today,' she replied.

'Oh, I had almost forgotten, with everything else that has happened today,' muttered Gaston, before hurrying outside to check on his birds.

Turning to Céleste, Florette asked, 'Perhaps Mademoiselle would care to choose some blooms from the garden for her bedroom. We can both see what is available if you like.'

'What a lovely idea,' replied Céleste. 'Maman and I regularly choose the flowers together at home,' then becoming a little saddened, as the realisation that this mutual activity was curtailed for the present.

'Then shall we go out to the garden now,' enthused Florette, attempting to lighten her spirits a little, gathering her secateurs and a small woven basket from the dresser as she spoke.

Florette delighted in showing the variety of blooms in the flower garden, to the obvious pleasure of Céleste. It was clear that they both shared a love of the floral beauty displayed in the beds before them, although, as Florette was quick to point out 'It is still a little early in the season, but there is some choice available.' Together they gathered a selection of white tulips, purple dwarf iris, and a late-blooming hellebore, its muted green leaves and flowers adding some contrast to the vibrant colours of the other blooms.

The pair chatted as they made their choices, both now becoming more at ease with the other, Céleste feeling that she was indeed being made welcome in her new surroundings. The task now accomplished, and, pleased by Gaston's comments that they had gathered a fine bouquet, they returned indoors to find a suitable vase.

Céleste then carefully carried the filled vase upstairs to her bedroom, and found a suitable space for it to stand on the shelf above the fireplace. She then busied herself for the next half-hour, unpacking the suitcase that Gaston had thoughtfully carried upstairs for her, and left outside her room. She finally finished arranging the clothes carefully in the armoire and chest of drawers. Despite the unpleasant event that had led to her stay at the house, she was now feeling some sense of contentment with her new surroundings, and began to ponder what Jean's mother, the original occupier of this room, would have thought of this new arrival. Would she have felt happiness for Jean, now that he had met someone special, and would she in turn measure up to the expectations Eugénie might have had for her son?

These thoughts were interrupted by a soft knocking at the door, which, on opening, presented the figure of Florette before her on the landing outside.

'Mademoiselle, we are proposing to have our meal at eight o'clock, if that is satisfactory to you?' she enquired. To which Céleste replied, 'Thank you, yes. But, please, treat me as a member of the household. I will fit in with your normal routine for meals.'

'Then if you are sure, we would normally dine in the kitchen, as we often do when Monsieur Jean stays,' responded Florette, still a little unsure about how her guest expected to be treated.

'That will be perfect, Florette, and please let me know if I can help in any way,' answered Céleste.

But on this point Florette was clear. She was the housekeeper and the preparations for the meal remained her responsibility alone. 'Gaston is in the salon, when you wish to come downstairs,' she said. Then, commenting on the pretty arrangement in the vase, 'Madame Dawson always made sure that she had flowers on display when she stayed here, you are alike in that respect.'

This comment momentarily caused Céleste to consider how she might enquire further about Jean's late mother, as she was interested to hear more about Jean's family. She only knew the very little that she had gleaned from her own mother's rather hazy recollections, for Amélie had known the family a little when she was a young girl.

She rejoined Gaston downstairs, shortly after this conversation with Florette. He was pleased to see her again, and also keen to continue with their search for a solution to the estrangement from her father.

'I can, of course, understand your father's concerns for the future of the farm, but you are not the only child,' he began. 'Is there definitely no interest in the farm from your other siblings?'

'I have two older brothers and one sister, all married and with children of their own. I expect you know that they have moved away, and have all found their own niche in life, which certainly does not involve farming,' said Céleste, adding as an afterthought, 'The only one who has ever shown any interest is my nephew Lucas, the son of my brother Henri. He has always enjoyed taking his holidays here during the summer, and helping my father with his chores.'

'Ah, that is interesting,' commented Gaston, 'I vaguely remember meeting with him once, but that was some years ago. What age would he be now?'

Céleste thought for a moment before replying, 'Why, he must be about seventeen by now, and, as I recall, has never shown much interest in his schooling.'

'Then perhaps we have found a possible solution!' exclaimed Gaston excitedly. 'Do you think he may be interested in assisting your father with the farm?'

'I hadn't really thought about this,' replied Céleste, wondering again whether this suggestion was likely to prove viable.

'Perhaps Monsieur Jean can find out how this could be arranged if he speaks to Maître Martin, the family lawyer,' proposed Gaston.

Céleste considered this. 'There still remains the question of whether my father and nephew would be prepared to agree to this, anyway. Surely there must also be implications for future inheritance. The farm would normally pass to any children, not one of the grandchildren.'

'That again is something that needs to be explored, certainly,' replied Gaston thoughtfully, 'the Maître could again examine whatever options may be open. But I think that this idea is certainly worth pursuing.'

It was agreed that Céleste could raise this idea with Jean when speaking to him later, and seek her mother's views about Lucas when they next met. These thoughts uppermost in her mind Céleste now followed Gaston into the kitchen, on hearing Florette's call that the meal was now ready.

They sat at the old pine table, with warming plates of Coq au Vin before them, and Gaston proceeded to pour them each a glass of red wine. The cool of the evening in the kitchen was offset by the heat still radiating from the Lacanche range as Gaston proposed a toast to Céleste, to which she responded, and to murmurs of appreciation they began to partake of the meal.

Again, after more praise for Florette on her culinary skills, Céleste asked whether Jean's mother had been a frequent visitor to the house in later years. She felt that she wanted to know as much as possible about the family.

'She used to visit from London with Monsieur Jean, while Monsieur Jean was still at school, often two or three times a year, and on two occasions, I remember, he was accompanied by his friend Monsieur Phillips, whom you met at the dinner here last week. She sometimes came with her husband Monsieur Dawson, until they were divorced, of course. That was in 1959, I believe,' remarked Florette. 'I didn't arrive here myself until 1950, a few years before her elderly mother's passing.'

'Ah, that divorce was a sad time, I remember it well,' interrupted Gaston. 'Of course, she had lived here as a child, later leaving to continue her studies in Paris, but she always made sure to visit Evian. She was very attached to her brother Felix.'

'So had she lived in London for many years?' enquired Céleste, interested to find out more.

'Yes, but at first, after their marriage, they lived in Paris, where Monsieur Jean was born,' continued Gaston. 'But I think his father was aware that war was looming on the horizon, and so he decided to move the family to England for greater security.' Then in a more reflective mood, continued. 'The war was a great trial for so many in France, the Boche occupying even more of France than during the Great War twenty years earlier. Both times that should, of course, be remembered in France, but in many ways are perhaps best forgotten.' He proceeded to charge their glasses again, before continuing. 'Mademoiselle Eugénie, who was later to become Madame Dawson, was a beautiful young girl. Perhaps you have seen the photographs in the salon? No. Then we can show you them later.'

'I imagine that she received a good education, having a father who was a respected notaire in Evian,' commented Céleste.

'Certainly,' replied Gaston, who knew more than Florette about this earlier life. 'Mademoiselle Eugénie completed her studies in Fine Art at one of the leading schools in Paris. She was always groomed immaculately, and accepted in the best circles, but counted amongst her acquaintances a number of artistic and intellectual types as well. But finally she married the English banker, who came from a similar background to her own. Monsieur Dawson was always a most charming gentleman, so I can well understand the attraction.'

This discourse prompted Céleste to wonder if she could possibly measure up to Jean's late mother, for whilst being well-educated, she would never have considered herself to be moving effortlessly in the highest circles of society, certainly not having enjoyed such a gilded upbringing. But, upon considering the matter further, she wondered if her own background had not served her better; for she regarded herself, intellectually at least, the equal of any man, and, had a natural ability to socialise with others, free from the constraints that were so often imposed on the upper echelons of society. She felt, perhaps, that this had been the attraction for Jean, allowing him to feel immediately at ease with her. Would he have been so enamoured if she were a socialite, where more rigid conventions would surely have to be followed?

The meal was now finished; Gaston suggested that it was time for her to call Jean. Excusing herself from the others, Céleste went again into the study to make the call, being eventually put through by the operator.

It seemed to be a happier Céleste who greeted me this time.

'Oh, Jean, I am missing you so, but I am being looked after so well here by Florette,' she said, her voice now much brighter than earlier.

'I'm so pleased,' I replied. 'You certainly sound a little better, my dear girl. Did you manage to visit your mother this afternoon?'

'Yes, and she understands about the argument, and will try her best to smooth things over with my father. I have told her that I have now definitely rejected Guillaume's proposal.'

'I fear that it will not be so simple to satisfy your father. He had clearly pinned his hopes for the future on such a marriage,' I said.

'Gaston and I have discussed this during the afternoon, and we think we may have found a solution.'

'I'm intrigued!' I said avidly. 'What have you discovered?'

'While discussing the fact that none of my siblings showed any interest in the farm, I happened to mention my nephew Lucas, who has always been keen to holiday here, and help my father with his chores. He is seventeen years old, but he is a strong, well-built boy, and as I remember, is not at all academically minded. Of course, he may not be interested in farming as a livelihood, as indeed my father may not also take to this idea. But we feel it's worthy of further investigation. Of course, there will be other issues to consider, not least being the question of future inheritance, for he is only a grandson, and he may eventually end up with nothing.'

'You have been busy!' I exclaimed. 'How are you going to find out more?'

'I will speak to my mother. She will know better if Lucas could be interested, and could speak to her brother Henri, to see what the parents' aspirations are for their son. Having ascertained that he may be keen to make farming his future, she could seek to gain my father's reaction to the suggestion. We wonder if you could look at the question of inheritance with Maître Martin.'

'I am impressed!' I exclaimed. 'You have both given this much thought. There may, of course, be many questions that have yet to be answered. I would be particularly concerned if Lucas does becomes involved with the farm, and after years of hard work, finds that he has no claim to any share of the farm. Perhaps there is some way to overcome this, and I will certainly speak to the Maître. Now, I have been thinking about returning to Evian as soon as I may, but hope that you will be able to visit me in London first.'

'Why certainly. I shall be free early next month, after I commence my translation work for Alice. I can't wait to see you again, Jean,' she lovingly replied.

'Then we must set a date soon and finalise the travel arrangements. I'm already missing you and feeling rather isolated here. But a return to work tomorrow may take my mind a little off my lonely existence. We'll speak again soon, my darling.'

With that last remark still present in her mind, they ended their conversation, both clearly feeling an inner emptiness, but buoyed up by the progress made with Gaston this afternoon.

CHAPTER TWENTY-SIX
An Unexpected Offer

Tuesday saw me awake early to an overcast morning suggesting rain later, and I busied myself getting ready for the day ahead. I had spent the previous evening turning over in my mind the suggestion proposed by Céleste and Gaston.

The longer I considered the matter, the more it seemed to make sense. But, of course, the two main parties, Lucas and Vincent, had yet to be involved, and their views on this may vary considerably. Nonetheless, I felt that the idea did have merit, and resolved to discuss the matter further with Jacques Martin, the notaire, within the next day or so.

Today my time was certain to be taken up by my clients who had been looked after by Gerald Walker in my absence. Also, there were sure to be questions asked about my future plans, of that I was certain. Gerald must already have some knowledge regarding my good fortune, through regular contact with my father.

I had decided to keep my thoughts to myself for the present. If asked, I would merely confirm that the size of the estate had come as something of a surprise to me; it was yet far too early to consider following a new path in my life. However, if this were to prove the case I would certainly give adequate notice of my intentions.

I arrived at the offices early, the London traffic having not yet reached its peak. I found the receptionist Miss Masters already at her desk as I entered the outer office. After a few short exchanges, during which I received her condolences for my loss, followed by the latest office gossip, I made my way to my own office. I stopped to speak to Miss Nugent, the secretary who worked for Gerald and me. She was seated behind her desk in the typing pool, and, after exchanging a few pleasantries, I asked whether there were any urgent matters outstanding, that I should deal with immediately.

'No, I think Mr Walker has most matters well in hand, Mr Dawson,' she replied. 'He is expected in at nine o'clock, and has asked me to remind you that he would like a meeting at nine thirty, to discuss the various files that he will be handing back to you.'

'That will be fine,' I replied, that familiar feeling of pleasurable anticipation of the tasks awaiting me now returning. I had not lost the commitment to my professional life I felt, as I seated myself behind my desk, once again in the familiar surroundings of my own office.

Miss Nugent knocked, and entered my office, bringing me my customary early morning coffee, and asked whether anything needed to be done.

'Not at present, thank you, but I'm sure there'll be enough to do following the meeting,' I replied, with a smile.

The return to work had the effect of temporarily putting the events of the last fortnight to the back of my mind, but I was sure that my thoughts would return soon enough to the vexed question of Céleste's estrangement from her father.

Soon I was greeted by Gerald Walker, as I entered his office. He was seated behind his desk, and had clearly been studying at least one file, which lay open in front of him. He was of a similar age to my father, being in his mid-fifties, grey hair adding a distinguished look to a face set with firm features. A well-cut navy pinstripe suit, adorned with a regimental tie on a crisp white shirt, completed the idealised image of a professional man, the senior partner of a prestigious law firm.

'Let us use first names, Jean, and be a little less formal,' he suggested, for although being my employer, he had for many years been a good friend of my parents, particularly to my father, and had known me from my childhood. 'First, let me say that I was sorry to hear of your uncle's passing.' He paused, before continuing. 'I understand that you have inherited the bulk of what appears to be a substantial estate, and I congratulate you on that.'

I thanked him for his sympathetic words, but added no further comment about the estate.

'We will need to look at the current files that are being passed to you, of course, but that can wait for a while, Jean,' he continued. 'I wonder whether you have made any decisions about your future, for I would think your inheritance must have given you cause to reflect on this.'

'Yes, Gerald, but I'm no position to make any final decision at this time, and intend to continue working for the firm, certainly for the present.' I replied.

'Good, it never does to make snap decisions. They may not always turn out as expected.'

'That's true. I agree with that sentiment. But I will need to visit France again over the next few months, to meet again with my lawyer and accountant. Hopefully this will not pose a problem, as I will ensure my workload here is carefully managed.'

'I'm sure you will, Jean. But I now wish to suggest something to you that might sway your final decision,' Gerald continued. 'As you well know, the firm has a number of wealthy clients who currently feel that the tax burden being imposed on them in this country has become too great. Some have already taken the decision to be domiciled abroad, and others are certainly considering taking this step. The partners have for some time discussed the merit of opening an office in France or Switzerland to be able to support these clients' interests, with the aim of also increasing our client base abroad. No decision has yet been made as to the location of this office.'

He paused for a moment, possibly for effect, before continuing.

'Given your new financial position, and the fact that you hold dual nationality, having been born in France, and you are also fluent in the language, I would like you to consider taking this position. Your legal expertise would be invaluable to many of the potential clients who are considering such a move.'

'I'm well aware of these taxation issues,' I continued. 'Even The Beatles have drawn attention to them in a recent recording. So would this be more in the nature of a consultancy?' I asked.

'It could be regarded as such, perhaps, as it would include both work in connection with property transactions in England, as well as general legal advice, I'm sure,' added Gerald. 'The partners see this as a natural progression of our services. The salary will, of course, be commensurate with the additional responsibilities you would be taking on, and an associate partnership would also be offered.'

'This is an unexpected, yet most interesting, offer, I must say, and I will certainly give it serious consideration, Gerald. Is there any timescale set for this plan?' I asked. 'And would it commence on a full-time basis?'

'I would expect the office to be set up within the next year, and yes, it would initially be set up on a consultancy basis, so could be regarded initially as a part-time post,' continued Gerald.

'Has any decision been made as to location?' I enquired.

'Paris was the obvious first choice discussed among the partners, but in fact few of our clients are based there, most preferring the Mediterranean coast, those areas around Nice and Cannes being most popular, and of course, some have chosen to move to Switzerland.'

'So Paris may not be the best location, particularly as I would see this as more of a personal service, where most clients would expect to be visited at home, rather than make a journey themselves to an office,' I suggested, thinking to myself that serving such a large geographical area could prove difficult from one office.

'Yes, I think you are right. We are dealing here with wealthy clients, many of them elderly, who would value the services of a professional who was available to visit them at any time,' confirmed Gerald.

'Then, yes, I am indeed most interested in this proposal. But may I state my personal preference for being based in Haute-Savoie, France, a locality near to Switzerland, and with access to the Côte d'Azur,' I confirmed.

'Good. I'll report this to the next partner's meeting, and we can then look in more detail at how best to move forward with this project,' summarised Gerald, clearly pleased at the reaction he had received.

Our focus now turned to the current matters that awaited my attention, which, with suitable updates from Gerald, concluded our meeting.

Returning to my office, my head was now full of thoughts about the possibilities that presented themselves. Not only might I be able to live in France, something that I had already considered, but it offered me the opportunity to continue my career with the law firm. The suddenness of this prospect before me seemed almost unreal, something that only a few days ago I would never even have considered a possibility.

I returned home to the cottage, having finished my work for the day, the current files now updated. I had seemed to be involved in a blur of activity, balancing the calls upon my time by speaking to some clients on the telephone, or receiving occasional visits from them at the office. All of them, not surprisingly, were anxious to hear how their transactions were proceeding. The day had passed quickly enough, but my thoughts were mostly underpinned by Gerald's surprising proposal.

With this thought uppermost I sat down in my favourite chair in the living room, a rather decrepit, but much loved, leather tub chair, which had moved with me from my bedsit. Leaning over, I switched on the hi-fi player, and picking out The Beatles' *Revolver* album from the shelving above. I placed it on the turntable, lowering the arm on to the 'Taxman' track, written by George Harrison, to remind myself again of that earlier conversation. I lit a Gitane, inhaling in slow breaths, as I listened to the lyrics. There was no doubting the anger portrayed in those words coming from the speakers, setting out so clearly the current predicament of the super-rich, persuading some into exile abroad.

I might expect a number of them as potential clients in the future. This certainly raised some concerns of an ethical nature in my mind. But then I questioned my own position. Had I not also joined this 'club' thanks to the generosity of my late uncle? Was I not also looking at the question of keeping my tax bill to a minimum by employing an accountant skilled in such matters? It was certainly true that my own inherited portfolio included an element of what could be deemed charitable lettings, thereby helping the less fortunate in society; but this had not come about without the profitable income and reserves afforded by the more commercial enterprises.

I found myself wondering how this latest opportunity might be perceived by Céleste, who clearly showed a social conscience in these matters. I resolved to phone her later in the evening to discuss this unexpected offer with her.

Later, having finished my supper, I made my call to Céleste. On hearing my voice she seemed much improved in spirits from yesterday.

'Oh, Jean,' she exclaimed, 'I'm so pleased to hear you. How was your first day back at the office?'

'It went well, though I have been busy bringing my files up to date. I had a long conversation with my boss, Gerald Walker, this morning. He has offered me the opportunity to work for the firm in France, which I must say, has come as something of a surprise.'

'But does your firm have an office here?' she enquired, somewhat mystified.

'No. This will be a new venture, where it's proposed that I will be acting as a consultant, travelling when necessary to meet clients face to face.' I replied.

'So who will be the clients, Jean?' she asked in a puzzled tone.

'They will probably be businessmen, high earners who are seeking a softer tax regime.'

There was a pause. She was clearly giving the last statement some thought before she responded. 'I didn't realise that many people move abroad for such reasons.'

'It's a situation that has always been with us to an extent, and it's the super-rich, if I can apply that term, who are most likely to make these decisions.'

'And how do you feel about this?' she enquired, somewhat warily.

'Well, I had already considered a move to France an option, but the chance to continue my career with the firm at the same time could be regarded as a bonus. It's likely that some of these clients are already using the firm's services in London anyway, so if I was to have doubts about the ethics of any of this, I should remember that the firm may already act for them in England.'

'Yes. I understand. But you say you had previously considered moving to France. Was there some . . . reason for this?' I could hear the smile in her voice.

'Well, as you know, my uncle's estate has offered me this possibility, but I hope you can guess at the main reason . . .' I answered enigmatically.

'Why, Jean, the thought of you moving here had not really crossed my mind, but I would be pleased, of course,' she replied, coquettishly, as if innocent of such a thought.

'So you would be happy with the idea?'

'Yes, of course. But do you know where the office will be located?'

'No. That has yet to be decided, and anyway, it's not likely to happen very soon.'

'I see. Now I have some news for you. Maman visited me this afternoon and we discussed our ideas about the farm. Papa is still angry that I have refused Guillaume's proposal, though she can see that he is also very upset that I have left home. She feels quite sure that Lucas will be keen to work on the farm, however, and is going to quietly speak to his parents first, to sound out the idea with them. But there still remains the question of the long term future of the farm, inheritance and all that. This is the underlying reason for my father's strong wish that I marry Guillaume. Being an only son he stands to eventually inherit their farm, and Papa assumes that some future agreement could be reached with my other siblings about our farm, thus creating a farm that would be double in size. In France such agreements commonly happen, I believe, when only one of the children wishes to continue farming.'

'Yes,' I continued, 'I can see the problem. As we previously discussed, your nephew Lucas would have no immediate right of inheritance from your parents, and could potentially be left with nothing, after years of hard work. Also, your father would not have had the opportunity to increase the size of the farm, which seems to be the one thing that he most desires in all this, I'm sure. I will be speaking to Jacques Martin, tomorrow if possible, and get his views on this.'

So, after a few more questions of each other, the call ended.

It was clear to me that I would be depending upon all the experience that Jacques could bring to find a solution that would win over Céleste's father.

CHAPTER TWENTY-SEVEN
A Possible Solution

The following morning I was able to reach Jacques at his office before I left for work, the time in France being one hour ahead of London.

He was pleased to hear from me, enquiring how the journey had been. After exchanging a few pleasantries I then admitted that I was calling to obtain some advice for a friend, as I was no expert in French law.

He listened carefully to all I had to say, commenting that he would have to give the situation some careful thought, whilst agreeing that the grandson could not expect anything out of the estate, other than a small bequest, under normal circumstances.

'But I will see how we may find a way to overcome this question of inheritance,' he suggested.

'You can see that, in any event, the farm will still only remain the same size, even if something can be agreed, so this would probably be unsatisfactory to the farmer, who desires to increase the land holding for future generations.' I continued.

'The mind of the French farmer seems to revolve around this issue of land, and has done for centuries, I'm afraid. But let me think a little more about this,' commented Jacques, before we ended the call.

My conversation with Jacques had, for the present, merely

confirmed my own view about the future of the farm, and had not produced any alternative solution.

My thoughts wandered again to the current estrangement between Céleste and her father, both seemingly immovable in their attitude. Was my recent involvement with her construed by her father as the sole reason behind her refusal of Guillaume's proposal? I considered this for a moment. Thinking rationally, it was clear to me that Céleste's horizons had widened far beyond life as a farmer's wife, long before meeting me. University and her embryonic career had surely shown that. But did her father, or indeed Guillaume, see things in the same light? From their perspective I must surely be seen as a threat to their aspirations, based on a rural culture that spanned the centuries. Guillaume, I felt sure, would now remain unsuccessful, and no doubt unhappy, as a result of his failed conquest, and there was nothing in my power to change that. But I had yet to find a way to placate her father in a way that would reunite the family.

My second day back at the office passed soon enough, though overlaid with thoughts of how this predicament could be overcome. Taking a break for lunch I considered the situation again. If Vincent could not accept his daughter's wish alone, then some other way of increasing the size of the farm must be sought. If such a thing could be brought about, would this appease him? Thinking more along these lines I considered how this may also benefit Lucas. He had no money available for such a purchase, of that I was certain. But if he could eventually rent, perhaps even buy with a suitable mortgage, the question of his future would then be secured. Vincent had already intimated that his own children may come to some arrangement whereby a nominal rent could be paid in lieu of inheriting their share, in order to achieve some form of succession with the family farm.

Lucas was at present not legally of an age to take on such responsibilities, but if an additional acreage was offered initially for Vincent to rent, eventually reverting to Lucas, then the farm should certainly be sufficiently profitable to provide two incomes.

Of course there was yet the question of finding suitable land, and in this respect I neither had any knowledge of local land values, or whether such land was available in the vicinity of Vincent's farm. Giving this further thought I remembered Monsieur Durand, the agent who managed Felix's estate on my behalf. Surely he may be able to help in answering these questions for me, so I resolved to call him to discuss the matter, and left my office early.

I made the call on my return to the cottage, and was put through to him immediately.

After exchanging pleasantries I then proceeded to ask him if he could in any way assist me with my query.

'I am looking at this situation on behalf of a friend,' I said, in answer to his obvious questioning of my sudden interest in agriculture. He was able to provide me with an indication of current local agricultural land prices and rents, but had no knowledge of anything being available in the location that I gave him.

'But I will make some discreet enquiries, Monsieur Dawson, whilst ensuring that I have no apparent interest in anything that may be offered. It is never good practice to appear too keen to purchase when dealing with farmers. I know from experience that this only has the effect of raising the price.'

I thanked him for his advice, and said that I would wait to hear from him further.

'Very well, Monsieur, I will contact you again, hopefully, by the end of the week if I am able to find anything suitable,' he added, before ending the call.

This conversation had heartened me greatly, for it now seemed that the various parts of this convoluted jigsaw might now be joined, and provide a suitable outcome for all the parties concerned. For myself I understood that there would be a financial outlay when suitable land was found, but this could be offset to an extent by the charging of an initial nominal rent. Based on the figures suggested by Monsieur Durand, this ought not prove too difficult a sum for me to raise.

As for the other people involved, their agreement would naturally have to be sought, and I felt that I must leave any such negotiation in the hands of Céleste and her mother. The first hurdle to overcome now seemed clear to me, gaining Vincent's acceptance that his daughter had no intention of agreeing to the marriage that had been proposed. In order that this could be achieved the plans that involved his grandson Lucas, and an offer of additional land would have to be discussed. Céleste and I would have to decide when this conversation could begin, and, being aware of the cautionary words of Monsieur Durand in relation to finding suitable land, I felt we should wait a little longer, and hope for some success in his endeavours, before she had this conversation.

With this plan now uppermost in my mind I made my customary evening call to Les Cyclamens, which was answered by Gaston. I brought him up to date, letting him know how things were proceeding.

'So we must wait a little longer, M'sieur Jean. But Mademoiselle Céleste has settled in well, and seems much happier already.'

'That's good to hear. Can I speak to her?'

There was a slight delay as he called her to the phone. I was able to tell her what I had discussed earlier with Jacques Martin and Monsieur Durand. This prompted questions about the additional land; how could it be purchased, and why should I become involved in such a venture? I explained that this could be regarded as a business opportunity, as there would be an agreement to pay rent. She sounded unsure about this, questioning again my motive for becoming involved.

'I'm worried that you won't be reconciled with your father, and end up staying in my house forever,' I replied, trying to bring a little humour into the conversation.

'Would that be so awful for you, Jean?' came back her immediate response, the hint of laughter apparent in her voice unheard these past few days.

I could have carried on with this pretence a little longer, but after some further playful banter, I reminded her that, unfortunately, there was a serious side to this whole business. We both agreed that we must now wait to hear further before contacting Vincent. What pleased me greatly was her news that she could come to London at the end of the next week. She would confirm the time of her arrival at the airport once she had purchased her ticket. Our conversation ended with suggestions of what we might do, as I would have to regard her as a tourist, and organise some pleasant trips around the city.

Over the course of the next few days I heard back from Monsieur Durand. He had put out some 'feelers', which had resulted in him being made aware that there was indeed an opportunity to purchase some adjoining pasture land, which also had the benefit of a number of outbuildings and a small, rather neglected farmhouse with barn attached, that he pronounced, 'suitable for improvement'.

This holding was owned by an elderly farmer, now becoming too frail to manage those tasks that he had carried out daily for past decades. Unmarried, and having no children or immediate family, he had decided finally that he would sell, and find something better suited to his final years. Monsieur Durand was quick to point out that the farmer had not decided how soon this was likely to happen, and this information had been given to him by one of his contacts, the farm not as yet being offered for sale.

I asked him for further details, particularly the acreage of the pasture land, some more details about the buildings, and of course, the likely price to be asked.

'I can obtain most of this information for you, Monsieur, but I have the feeling that he does not know yet what price to ask. He has lived there all his life, his father before him, so he will have to seek advice. Of that I'm sure.'

'Is this advice likely to come from your contact?' I asked, not being sure how such matters were normally conducted in rural France.

'That is probable,' he replied, before adding, 'I have indicated that I may have a client who would be interested – at the right price, of course,' he added.

'Please keep me informed, Monsieur Durand. Thank you for your efforts, and in the meantime I will speak to my friend.' I was certainly pleased that he had found something so quickly, as I felt sure that farms did not come on the market very often.

My call to Céleste that evening confirmed that she was aware of the farm, but certainly not that it may soon be offered for sale. She knew the farmer, and agreed that he would by now be quite elderly, remembering also that he lived quite alone.

'I believe that the land was in good heart, when it was farmed in earlier years,' she enthused, 'but as I recall the farm has been rather neglected for a while – decades, even.'

Talking more, we decided that this could be a suitable extension to her father's farm, although she felt that the cost may be prohibitive.

'Monsieur Durand has suggested a possible figure to me, which I consider to be acceptable,' I replied. 'He is likely to be contacted as soon as the farm is put up for sale, so I should be well placed to agree a purchase.'

We then continued our conversation and agreed that if a purchase could be made, Céleste would have to speak to her father and some form of agreement made. She was able to confirm that her mother had now spoken to Lucas's parents, who had expressed the view that he would welcome the opportunity to work on the farm. It seemed that our plans were now taking shape.

'I'm pleased that I'll be able to visit London next week, Jean, following my meeting with Alice the publisher in Lyon. I'm so looking forward to seeing you again. A bientôt.'

The expression in her voice again showed that the depression of the previous days was now lifting.

CHAPTER TWENTY-EIGHT
A Romantic Visit

We had arranged to meet at the airport terminal at two o'clock. I had arrived a little earlier, allowing myself adequate time to drive through the busy London traffic. I was able to park the MG close to the arrivals lounge, and ordered a coffee as I waited anxiously for her arrival. She had flown direct from Geneva, Gaston having driven her to the airport from Les Cyclamens.

Twenty minutes later I saw her come through from passport control into the lounge, suitcase in hand. Looking around, she finally saw me coming to greet her, a broad smile now lighting her face. As I approached she put down the case, and we embraced affectionately, oblivious of the other passengers who milled around us, as they waited to be reunited with family and friends.

After a few murmured greetings, and further embraces, I picked up the case and we went outside to the waiting car.

'A chauffeur for each journey,' she commented, her smile indicating the intense pleasure she was feeling, having now arrived, and being with me again.

'A smaller car here in England,' I replied with a smile, as we reached the car. Her delight was obvious at seeing the MG, its low sports body being an unusual sight in France.

I drove back to the mews, and her exclamation on arriving at the cottage indicated her obvious delight at the scene before her: a number of adjoining cottages with gaily coloured displays in window boxes and containers of ornately moulded terracotta and lead. I parked the car outside, leaving it on the cobbled mews, and walked round to open the passenger door, helping her out. Suitcase in hand, I opened the front door and we entered the hallway.

'Would you like a tour of my humble abode,' I quipped, 'or would you prefer to freshen up first?'

'Oh no, Jean, I would like to see the house first, please,' she answered. 'It is not at all like the house in Evian.'

'That's true,' I agreed. 'We call this a bijou residence, I suppose. Ideal for one, or possibly two people, but no more.'

'I like the thought of just two people here,' she almost purred in a most seductive way.

'Well, there are two of us here now,' I answered, flustered into a vague reply. 'Let me show you around.'

We went through to the kitchen, and I opened the top half of the stable door, which brought more exclamations of pleasure from her on seeing the small courtyard, now in its full springtime glory. Pausing for a while, we then took the staircase upstairs to the living room.

'Why, it is all so charming!' she exclaimed, admiring the newly decorated room with its mixture of assorted furnishings displaying my bachelor taste.

'The bedrooms and bathroom lead off here,' I indicated, pointing to a door that led to a narrow passage.

She opened the door, and again marvelled at how much had been squeezed into such a relatively small space.

'Shall I bring my suitcase up, Jean?' she asked, with a mischievous smile on her face, as she looked in the larger bedroom, fully aware of the unsettling effect this was having on me.

She had hinted at her intentions on that last Sunday we spent together in Evian, but at last, being finally alone, this was all now becoming a reality. I must confess that I still felt a little unsure about the situation, though the thought of our lovemaking was my greatest wish. Certainly, I had previously enjoyed romantic interludes, but, for various reasons of incompatibility, these had never endured. But I had already made an earlier decision to hold back in my wooing of Céleste. My fear in this was that by being too impulsive she might regard me as a shallow suitor, seeking only personal gratification, and thus the spell between us might be irreparably broken.

But her feelings, though tinged with humour, were now being made clear to me.

'Yes, I'll put your case in the guest bedroom. You can use it as a dressing room if you like.' I replied almost flippantly, and leaving the question of sleeping arrangements open. 'We can decide where to sleep later, perhaps?'

'Oh, I think we both know where that will be,' came her response, a smile lighting her face again.

Our little game over for the moment, we both agreed that a meal would be welcome, and I suggested that we drive over to the King's Road area of Chelsea and find a restaurant. She took this opportunity to run a bath and freshen up after her journey, while I took her suitcase up to the guest bedroom.

I called through the door to her that I would make some tea before we set off, and went down to the kitchen to prepare this. She came down in a few minutes, taking an interest in everything on display, chatting incessantly about the journey, and her delight at us being together again. My enquiries after Gaston and Florette evinced the pleasure she felt in staying with them both, and how a friendship had already developed in the household in such a short time. The house had been more than a refuge, she said, joking that she was now becoming accustomed to having a housekeeper, something she had never remotely considered before.

This of course led to further discussion about the situation with her father, which I attempted to cut short by confirming that I had not yet heard from Monsieur Durand, so we must wait and see what transpired. At the same time I reminded her that she could stay in Evian for as long as she wished. This reference to her father left her a little subdued, so I proposed that we try and forget about these troubles for the present, and instead she must enjoy her time in London.

I poured out the tea, which we drank, as I asked her about the translation work, which she confirmed she had now started. She would do some more work whilst in London if time permitted, as I must surely have to spend some time at my office during the week. Gaston had driven her to Lyon, as the train services were now affected by the ongoing strikes in France, and he had taken this opportunity to visit some of his family while she had her meeting with Alice, the publisher. I was happy that my old friend was looking after her, though a little sad that I couldn't have been able to drive her there myself.

Having caught up with recent events we were now ready to find a suitable restaurant. Driving from Fulham we soon found ourselves in King's Road, Céleste showing some excitement as we passed the many clothing emporiums displaying their colourful creations. Late shoppers were still evident as we passed them by, miniskirts showing an expanse of leg, a rare sight in provincial France. This brought comments of surprise from my passenger, who asked how I could concentrate on driving, surrounded by such visions. I laughed at this, saying that one became used to it, seeing it every day.

Finding an empty parking space we both got out of the car, and I paid the meter before we walked along the road to find a suitable restaurant. A waiter showed us to a table, handing us both a menu, and enquiring if we would like to order drinks. As I was driving we decided to share a carafe of wine with the meal. The restaurant was relatively small with the tables arranged in small cubicles, the decor and layout making some attempt at giving the impression of an old-fashioned bistro. Despite the clientele being chiefly tourists, the food served had always been to a good standard, I had found, on previous visits.

As we waited for our meal Céleste questioned me further about the recent offer of a consultancy in France. She was, I guessed, interested to know if I would live in Evian should I take up the position. While it was perhaps too early to be certain I said that this was quite likely, for I already had the house there, and the final location of an office did not seem to be of paramount importance, as we were not going to be reliant on passing trade.

'But, what will happen to your cottage here in London, Jean?' she asked.

'If I can afford to I'd like to keep it, as I'll need to come to London occasionally for meetings with the partners in the firm,' I replied. 'It's quite small, as you've seen, and hopefully will not prove to be a great expense in future.'

'Have you made any decision about Florette and Gaston if you decide to move to the Alps? I only ask out of interest for their future,' she added, in case I misunderstood the reason for her asking.

'Well that depends on a number of things, I suppose, and it will have to be discussed. They have both been well provided for in my late uncle's will, of course, so would be able to leave if they wished, but I'm not sure that they would choose to do that. Fortunately, for the next few months they are happy to stay and look after the house for me, but as for the future . . . I really don't know.'

'Yes, they both seem so settled there, and I find it hard to imagine the house without them.'

We both seemed to be in agreement on this, but the waiter now returned to the table with our meals, preventing further any immediate discourse on the subject.

We passed a pleasant hour enjoying the meal, followed by a dessert and coffees. Céleste hadn't realised how hungry she had been earlier, but we were by now quite replete.

'Thank you for a lovely meal,' she said, as we left the restaurant, and reaching for my hand.

'Yes, restaurant meals in England are improving. That is, if you know where to eat,' I replied, before suggesting that we take a walk and look in some of the shop windows, before returning to the cottage.

This she found most entertaining, the fashions displayed in some of the boutiques appearing quite outré to her provincial taste, and prompting such questions as surely they could not be suitable for the office. I suggested, in turn, that they might be better suited to the circus ring, and we walked on a little further, both giggling like schoolkids. I felt so fortunate to have her company again so soon.

I drove back to the cottage, opening the garage doors and parking the car, before we both went indoors. I suggested that we could listen to some music on the hi-fi system, and asked her to choose a record, while I took a bottle of champagne out of the fridge.

I answered her questioning look. 'It's a special occasion, your first night in London.'

'Our first night alone . . .' she replied, to which I nodded, and, taking the bottle and two glasses, I followed her upstairs to the living room.

My modest collection of records seemed to impress her, occupying as it did, two shelves above the hi-fi, comprising an eclectic mix of jazz, rhythm & blues and pop, together with some much-loved classical works. She finally made her choice, a Françoise Hardy album, which we both agreed would be suitable easy listening. I put it on the turntable, the volume set to low, then poured the champagne, before joining her, already seated comfortably in a laid-back posture on the sofa.

We toasted each other, expressing our happiness to be back together again. Inevitably, we moved closer together, our lips tenderly re-united, our passion intensifying, as the music faded insignificantly into the background. The glasses by now had been put to the side table, our embrace ever more resembling a wrestler's clinch, as our bodies became entwined.

I whispered softly to her, suggesting we may be more comfortable in the bedroom, and we made our way there slowly, still locked in a passionate embrace. The culmination of our feelings for one another after our recent parting now being expressed so openly. Finally, the sublimation of our sexual yearning for each other now at last dismissed, we were overtaken by a consummate desire that could only be sated in an ecstatic melting of limbs. Caressing each other, we came together with hungry urgency, a love that inflamed both body and soul.

CHAPTER TWENTY-NINE
A Proposal

We remained in bed until late Saturday morning, wrapped in each other's arms, little being said, our thoughts still overwhelmed by the intimacy of the night.

Smiling now, Céleste enquired, 'Ah, mon amour, such a wonderful night! Can I perhaps make us a coffee now?'

'Don't be too long, my darling,' I murmured drowsily as she rose from the bed; the slight hollow where she had lain, now impregnated with the scent of her eau de parfum, radiated a vestige of her body's warmth. A sweet warmth in which I now languorously luxuriated. I could only wonder at my good fortune in having found someone who had so totally transformed my life. Within a few minutes, she had returned, loosely enveloped in a pale-blue dressing gown and carrying a tray with the coffee and a few biscuits.

She sat on the bed, at my side, and offered me a mug. We drank slowly, the caffeine having the desired effect, my mind now fully awakened.

'I like to play at housekeeper,' she murmured, 'and your kitchen is so charming. It is so different to the house in France, where Florette always does everything.'

'So would you like to be my housekeeper?' I enquired, my tone becoming a little more serious.

'Oh, I think I could look after you very well, mon amour,'

she replied, a quizzical look now apparent on her face.

'Being my housekeeper, though delightful, would not be enough for me, my darling. What I desire most of all is that you become my wife.' I paused for a moment, in the hope that it might add a further dimension to my question. 'Will you marry me, Céleste?' I asked, my mouth becoming dry at the tension I was now experiencing.

'You are serious, Jean?' her tone indicating some disbelief at what she was hearing.

'I have never been so serious in my life. I feel so sure we should be together always,' I said, taking her hand in mine. 'I have felt this almost from the first moment we met.'

'I have strong feelings for you also, but marriage is such a big step to take.'

'Not if we both feel sure of our love. I have no doubt of mine at all. I have tried to conceal the full extent of my love from you a little, with all the problems you've had recently. But I think they can now be resolved, so I'm letting you know how strong my feelings really are.'

'Two proposals in one month, what can a poor girl do?' she replied, the hint of a mischievous smile apparent on her face.

'I hope you say yes to mine,' I earnestly begged her.

'I do say yes to you, Jean. We have both known for some time that we don't want to be apart. I think we will be very happy together.' Her face was by now wreathed in a smile, indicating the happiness she now felt.

'I'm so pleased, you have made me so happy, my darling girl,' I replied, drawing her to me in a passionate embrace.

We spent the next hour, still lying in bed, avidly discussing our plans for the future. I explained to her that it was my wish to seek her parents' consent before we became formally engaged.

This would necessitate Céleste being reconciled again with her father, which I felt maybe no small task. Hopefully, I added, we now seemed to be making some progress in this.

I raised the question of an engagement ring, saying that the final choice would be hers to make. My mother, I explained, had left her jewellery to me, as I was her only child, and had indicated in her will the desire that it would one day pass to my wife. I could show her the engagement ring now, and I would be delighted if she accepted it, but would understand if it was not to her taste, in which case she could choose another.

I leant over, and opened a small drawer in my dressing table, and offered her the small red leather box containing the ring.

'I am no expert myself,' I ventured. 'Mother always said it is a classic design, and it has some provenance. It's a single diamond set in platinum, and she always kept it, when not worn, in the original Cartier box.'

This prompted an intake of breath from Céleste as she opened the box, declaring that she would not dream of leaving so valuable an article in a bedroom drawer.

'It's so beautiful, Jean, but must be so valuable!' she exclaimed. 'Would your mother approve of me having her ring?'

'I know she would, and I'm only sorry that you never had the chance to meet her.'

'Gaston showed me her photograph. She was very beautiful.'

'And so are you, my darling girl,' I murmured.

I took out the ring, and carefully tried it on her finger. We both agreed that it would require resizing to fit her perfectly, but she was clearly enamoured, expressing her delight at receiving such a magnificent ring.

We could visit a jeweller this afternoon, I suggested, and make arrangements for the alteration to be carried out. I could then keep the ring in readiness, and wait until I received the consent from her father. She made light of this, arguing that it was not the father I was marrying, but finally conceded that, of course, she wished for his blessing.

I also suggested that we had best keep the engagement a secret from our friends in France, for the moment, as I would not like her parents to hear from others before we had spoken to them. Céleste agreed, although she added that she did not normally like secrets, as she preferred to be always quite open with everyone.

This resonated greatly with me, for I still held the dark secret of the lake, recounted by Gaston. This was the secret which had initially led me to our first meeting. I resolved now that I would divulge this to her later, for I was in agreement with her. I did not wish there to be secrets between us.

I also pointed out, much as I now hated the thought, that we should ensure we retained separate sleeping arrangements in Evian. I mentioned that Florette, in particular, being deeply religious, would be troubled, and probably think less of us if we shared the same bed before marriage, as might her parents. She understood my concern, adding that she was pleased we did not face this difficulty in London. I could only agree with this, wondering still at my good fortune in being able to share my bed here with her.

We talked further, and I raised the subject of my own father, of whom I had spoken previously. Céleste's stay in London provided an opportunity for both of us to visit him, and I would be proud to show off my beautiful fiancée. We both agreed that I should try and arrange for us to see him tomorrow, which, being a Sunday, usually found him at home with his family.

Now, happy in the afterglow of our passionate night, and

while still discussing further our plans for the future, we finally stirred ourselves sufficiently to get dressed and face the remainder of the day.

After a light brunch, which we took in the kitchen, Céleste again happily playing her role as housekeeper, I made a call to my father.

Finding him at home, and after hearing the latest news from his family, I enquired if I could call on him tomorrow. He seemed pleased to hear from me, and confirmed that the family would be at home in the afternoon. To prepare him for tomorrow I decided to tell him that Céleste would be coming with me, and that I had some news to share with him.

Clearly now intrigued by my talk of news, he suggested we came at three o'clock, and from the expression in his voice he clearly looked forward to meeting my friend.

Saturday afternoon was spent visiting Cartier's in Bond Street, to discuss the alterations to the ring. Céleste was initially rather bemused by the number of stores displaying luxury goods of all descriptions in such a relatively confined area, and I explained that we were in one of London's major shopping districts, bounded by Oxford Street, Piccadilly and Regent Street.

Upon entering the Cartier store we were initially bedazzled by the displays on show, not failing to note the well-heeled customers, being served by assiduously attentive staff. We in turn were served by a pleasant older gentleman, who was evidently a knowledgeable jeweller. Upon inspection of the ring he commended us on both its quality and condition, pronouncing it to be a desirable classic design. After some time spent checking the size Céleste would require, he confirmed that he would arrange with the workshop to have the alterations carried out, and advise me when the ring was ready for collection.

Leaving the store, our business attended to, we strolled along Bond Street towards Piccadilly, both of us interested to look at the merchandise displayed in the shop windows. It was obvious, from the comments she made, that Céleste was not one of those women who spent their days compulsively going from store to store, in search of garments which would perhaps be worn only once, then forgotten, only to spend their remaining days at the back of a wardrobe.

'It is all so much like the chic shops in Paris,' she observed, and wondered aloud if the shops were there only for the rich tourists, who frequented the luxury hotels to be found in this part of London.

'There are also the rich residents in cities such as London and Paris, who will give them their custom,' I replied, looking at the young woman by my side. She was dressed in the dark blue outfit that she had worn once before when we had dined with Michael and Yvette, and it was set off today with a contrasting silk scarf. This only served to remind me that she had no need of such fripperies, her taste in clothes always so chic.

Arriving now in Piccadilly, we crossed the road, and proceeded towards Fortnum & Mason, the renowned department store. On entering through a set of double doors we were greeted by the sight of staff dressed as butlers, tending to the needs of their customers, the majority of whom appeared to be tourists. Céleste, after careful examination of the goods offered on the numerous shelved displays, finally made her choice and selected gift boxes for her mother, Florette, and the two children she was to meet tomorrow.

Our expedition having now been completed for today, we made our way back through the late afternoon traffic to Fulham.

CHAPTER THIRTY
A Purchase in Prospect

The telephone in the hall was ringing as we opened the door, and, upon picking up the receiver, I was surprised when the operator put me through to Monsieur Durand.

In his business-like manner he explained the reason for his call. His contact had spoken to him earlier and had confirmed that the farmer, of whom we had previously spoken, had finally decided to sell up, as his poor health was now becoming too much of a burden. His days as a farmer must now end. This prompted me to ask whether a firm price had been discussed. He confirmed that in the event of a quick sale the farmer would be prepared to accept a figure which I mentally calculated to be well within my proposed budget.

'How soon does he need an answer?' I asked, not being sure of the way in which such sales were normally conducted.

'If you are able to proceed immediately, Monsieur Dawson, it could avoid much time, together with saving various expenses, such as advertising and preparing auction particulars, as this would be the route normally taken in the sale of such farms. A fair offer made today could well be accepted, for I am showing him two apartments on Monday, and I feel sure that a suitable agreement can be reached.'

Confirming that I was happy to proceed in principle, and asking that he try to agree the best price possible, I suggested that we could speak again, later on Monday, when perhaps we could finalise matters.

Céleste, having overheard one side of this conversation, came out of the kitchen, her expression indicating a concern to know more.

'It appears that the farmer now wishes to sell, and quickly,' I told her. Then seeking further her opinion, added, 'Do you feel sure that this will prove a good buy in order to carry out our plan? You have far more experience of agriculture than me. I have really only had Monsieur Durand's advice to rely on, but I do believe he is trustworthy. Perhaps you should speak to your mother again, and say that a deal is now on the table, so a meeting could be arranged soon with your parents to discuss how we are to proceed.'

'Jean, I think this is wonderful news, if you are sure that you can buy at a price you feel is affordable. The land was always productive in the past, I remember, though it has been rather neglected in recent years, due to the farmer's poor health. But I am sure that a younger farmer can improve the situation, and have the land in good heart again. Of course my father would know exactly what would be required, and with the help of Lucas they would quite soon restore this into a very workable farm, I'm sure.'

After Céleste had spoken to her mother on the telephone she was able to confirm that a meeting could perhaps be arranged in a fortnight's time, if I was free to travel then. Her father had already begun to regret the estrangement from his daughter, he had confided to his wife, and was now becoming reconciled to the fact that she would never marry Guillaume.

'Maman is sure that Papa now very much regrets our argument, and is missing me.' The tears in her eyes were testament to her feelings. I put my arm around her shoulder in an attempt to console her.

'Within a fortnight I hope that we will have instructed the notaire, and the preliminary sales contract could be ready to sign,' I offered, by way of some comfort. 'So that will be a good time to arrange a meeting with your father.'

Having given the matter some thought I now suggested that we should buy the farm in our joint names, as this would no doubt prove more acceptable to her father. The question of renting the farm would be open to negotiation, of course, but I felt that as we would be proposing to charge a low rent initially, agreement should, hopefully, be possible. The intention, after all, was that Lucas, when he became of age, would eventually become the tenant, perhaps buying the farm at some future date, thus ensuring his livelihood in years to come.

'There is so much to take in, Jean. Are you sure that you are prepared to buy this with me as joint owner? After all, I have no money to invest.'

'We are soon to marry, so this is all quite academic anyway, and I'm certain that your father would be happier to know that your name would be on any contract.' I replied.

We continued discussing the matter further, both agreeing that the unexpected availability of the farm could not have come at a better time, both of us now looking forward, although with some trepidation, to our next meeting with her parents. Finally, now realising the time, I suggested that we should be celebrating our engagement this evening, so shouldn't I make a reservation at a restaurant?

'That would be lovely, of course, Jean, but I would like to cook a meal for you. I would rather we were alone together this evening, as we have had so much excitement for one day.

I have already seen that you have plenty of ingredients in your kitchen.'

'If you're sure, my darling, I can think of nothing better. There'll be plenty of time for celebrations once we've given the news to our friends and family. I'll open a bottle of champagne as an aperitif before we dine,' I said, opening the fridge and bringing out the bottle I'd put in earlier.

I offered her a glass, then raised mine, saying, 'No long speeches from me today, but a toast to the girl who has made me the happiest of men.'

'To my dear fiancé,' she replied, her own happiness in our newly found relationship quite apparent in her smile.

Finishing our drinks she suggested that I might go upstairs to the living room, as she didn't want an audience while she cooked. 'I'm not used to your kitchen,' she explained, 'so I'm bound to get muddled, but hopefully I'll soon learn where everything is.'

'I understand. It must be the same for all new housekeepers,' I joked. 'I'll go up and listen to some music, while you work away down here.'

She laughed at this, saying that she would call me when the meal was ready to be served.

I switched on the hi-fi, being in a reflective mood, having decided that I would be sharing the secret of her late aunt's demise with Céleste later this evening. I chose a favourite recording of Elgar's Cello Concerto, feeling that the contemplative, and at times anguished music, written by the composer in the aftermath of the Great War, best suited my present mood.

An hour or so later Céleste called me down to the kitchen, imbued with the tang of chicken fricassée deliciously redolent with herbs and wine. I was pleasantly surprised at what she had achieved with the relatively meagre ingredients she had at her disposal, my taste buds delighting in the meal.

'I adapted one of Maman's recipes,' she explained, as we ate, almost by way of an apology.

'But it is truly quite magnificent,' I retorted, my empty plate finally providing further confirmation of this.

Having finished the meal we went upstairs, and, both seated on the sofa, were lost in our thoughts for a while. I knew that I had to divulge the secret that had, in a circuitous way, led to our first meeting. Céleste had made clear to me her dislike of secrets only this morning, and I felt that things left unsaid now might be put off indefinitely, which to my mind I now regarded as sinful.

CHAPTER THIRTY-ONE
A Secret Revealed

'Céleste,' I began, cautiously, 'do you ever wonder why I came to visit your family on that first occasion?'

She looked at me, her eyes expressing uncertainty about what I was going to say. 'I thought that Gaston had brought you to meet some friends,' she suggested, warily.

'That's true, but we had come at my request, after he had told me about your late aunt, Célestine.'

'She was drowned in a boating accident. That's what my mother has always told me.' Her hesitant reply now indicated that she feared she was about to hear something unpalatable.

'I'm so sorry, but I feel I must tell you this tale. It is particularly difficult for me, when today should be a time of happiness for us both, but I don't want there to be any secrets between us.' I began, ready now to divulge the sad truth.

'Yes, Jean, but isn't my mother the one who should really be told, as Célestine was her sister? To me she has always been a shadowy figure from past family history.'

'Yes, I understand that, but this story shows how both our families have been linked together in the past. So are you happy for me to continue?' I asked, feeling for her now, her head lowered in anticipation of some dreadful revelation.

She nodded, clearly unsettled by what I was about to reveal.

I tried to recount the story as sympathetically as I possibly could, explaining Gaston's role at the lake, then Felix's disclosure about the letter, culminating in their pact to keep the awful truth a secret. A dark secret, and one that they had both kept for fifty years.

I finished by explaining, 'I believe my uncle Felix never really recovered from this tragedy, and I can only suppose that is the reason for his never marrying.'

Céleste had clearly been deeply moved by my tale, and silently gave this revelation much careful thought. 'Jean, even today unwanted pregnancies are still regarded in many quarters as shameful. I can only begin to imagine how my poor aunt must have felt, while bearing this perceived guilt alone, and made far worse by the thought of an unwanted "Boche baby" being born during the Great War.'

She looked at me, tears in her eyes now, shaking with emotion, her sadness palpable, as the full horror of the tale became apparent to her. She sat, silent for a few moments, her mind obviously filled with unwanted images, before she exclaimed, 'How can I possibly tell my darling mother this? I fear it will break her heart. She has borne the loss of her older sister for so many years. The sister, who at that time had acted as a surrogate mother. Now, I must be the one to tell her that this was, after all, no accident, but a suicide.' She spoke again, her voice now subdued. 'But to know that the suicide was due to the ignorant imaginings of a naive young woman, who died so needlessly. Jean, this is more than I can even begin to comprehend. It will surely destroy my mother to be told the truth.' She looked at me, her face visibly whitened. 'I don't know if I am strong enough to tell Maman that her sister killed herself for nothing.'

I leaned over in an effort to comfort her, quietly suggesting that we would find a suitable time later for her to tell her mother the sad tale. 'As for Gaston, he will understand, once he has learnt of our engagement, and our wish to keep no secrets from each other. I will speak to him when we both return. I felt that he found the recent sharing of the secret with me quite cathartic. I can only begin to wonder at the strain he has endured, having known both your mother and grandmother for all these years, while sworn to secrecy to never divulge the truth.'

'What a sad chapter this has been in the history of both our families,' she continued, attempting now to recover her demeanour a little.

'When we are both next in Evian I will show you the photograph. The resemblance to you is quite startling, so I can fully understand Felix's feeling towards her' I suggested, warily, not wishing to add more to her pain.

'Yes, I would like to see the photograph. But, of course, my mother could also have been mistaken for me, if you saw photos of her as a young woman, so I suppose it is not so unusual. Perhaps we should just call it the Aubert inheritance.' She smiled at this, and I was pleased that she was now beginning to recover from her earlier distress.

CHAPTER THIRTY-TWO
Meeting My Family

The revelations had, fortunately, not dampened our ardour for each other; both of us were engulfed in the intensity of the most pleasurable lovemaking again that night.

Having woken late on Sunday morning, neither of us wanting to break the spell between us as we lay in each other's arms, we finally stirred ourselves and took a late brunch. Céleste was keen to question me further about my relationship with my father, who we were due to meet that afternoon. She recalled that I had previously told her about my parents' divorce that had taken place some years previously, remembering also that having remarried, my father now had a new young family.

'Yes, our contact has gradually lessened over the years, although we still keep in touch. I'm sure he'll be pleased to see us both, and certainly sounded intrigued when he heard about you. I'm sure that I told you about his affair with Estelle, who is now his second wife, being given as the cause of the divorce, although over previous years there had been a number of other liaisons. But as she was expecting his child, this time the affair couldn't be overlooked.' I explained, recollecting the sadness that I had particularly felt at this time for my mother.

'My parents met in 1936,' I explained. 'My father, Daniel, was at that time based at the Paris headquarters of an international bank. Eugenie, my mother, was enjoying a somewhat hedonistic lifestyle, having previously studied Fine Art at one of the leading Art Schools in the city. She told me later that she was at that time residing in a bijou apartment, situated in La Rive Gauche, the Latin Quarter so beloved of artists and intellectuals.'

'So, did they marry soon after that first meeting, Jean?' enquired Céleste, perhaps wondering if their initial romance could in any way be compared to ours.

'Not for some months, although they became quite inseparable; she accompanied him as his partner on numerous occasions, dining out, making visits to the theatre or attending private viewings of artist's work, all as a result of his role at the bank which required him to entertain important clients. She clearly enjoyed this life, and all in the company of a man that she soon came to adore. Finally, with talk of marriage being proposed, a visit was arranged in order for him to meet her family at their home in Evian. They at once accepted this Englishman who appeared so charming, with his impeccable manners and fluency in French, and within the year my parents were married. I was born a year later in 1938, in Paris, but was destined to be an only child.'

'When did the family move to England, Jean?'

'That was in late 1938, shortly before the outbreak of the war. It became clear that France may yet again be involved in fighting with its hostile neighbour on the border, so my father took the wise precaution of accepting a position that had become available, due to retirement, with his bank in London. Thus he avoided by a few months the invasion and fall of France that would have ended with his incarceration as an enemy alien.'

'Yet you still speak French fluently, Jean, despite having lived in England for most of your life' commented Céleste.

'Yes my mother always insisted that we spoke French

whenever possible at our home in Chelsea, in an attempt to retain a French identity for the family, and going so far as to employ a French nanny. I still remember how I impressed my French tutor, Madame Leroy, when I first attended my local prep school.'

The afternoon found us in Carlyle Square, Chelsea. The period houses, their facades contrasting in white painted stucco and London yellow stock bricks, overlooked a central garden, its neatly manicured lawns planted with specimen trees and shrubs and enclosed by iron railings. It was typical of so many other squares in London, though tended to a higher standard than some. Although little more than a stone's throw from the bustle of the King's Road, the square exuded a sense of peace and tranquillity, suggestive more of an earlier century than the present day.

It was with a little trepidation that I knocked on the entrance door, feeling unsure of the reception we were about to receive. Apart from recent telephone conversations I had not visited my father and his family for some time. Although our relationship could not be described as frosty, I had in my most recent visits sensed an air of formality between us, such as was normally reserved for more distant relatives.

The door was opened by my father, who, after greeting us both, showed us through to an imposing drawing room, comfortably furnished with sofas and chairs of a classical style upholstered in pale green silk, grouped around a marble fireplace adorned with a gilded over-mantle mirror. Walls displayed a carefully chosen selection of watercolours, and the carpeted floor overlaid with fine Persian rugs, completed a picture of restrained affluence, that I supposed displayed the influence of Estelle in matters of interior design.

Standing before us, it was clear that he still retained the

vigour of the younger man that I had known so well in my earliest years, the grey streaks in his well groomed hair the only visible indicators of the passage of time since then. He still retained his charming persona, his eyes expressing interest in his interlocutor as he asked Céleste how she found London, and whether she was staying for long.

He bid us to sit down, explaining that the family were downstairs at present, and would be joining us shortly. He made a point of asking Céleste to call him Daniel, to put her more at ease, and it was clear that he was keen to know more about her, complimenting her on her mastery of English as she replied to his questions. On enquiring about her family, he showed some delight on being told that her family owned a farm in a rural commune in the mountains above Evian, and commented on the pleasant times he had spent there. Upon wondering aloud how we had met, I mentioned that the family had been known to my uncle, and Gaston had made the introduction.

This prompted further questions about Gaston and Florette, and he seemed pleased to hear that they were both still very much in evidence at the house. Mention of the house prompted him to say again how sorry he had been to hear of Felix's rather sudden death, and knowing something of my new-found circumstances, wondered if I might be tempted to move over to France at some point.

'It's something that I'm considering, certainly.' I replied, not wishing to discuss at present the offer that I had recently received from the firm.

'Well, at least you are fortunate in having dual nationality,' he replied, and turning to Céleste explained, 'Jean was born in Paris, so his birth was registered in France.'

'Yes, he has told me,' she replied, asking further, 'Did you live in France for long, Daniel?'

'For a few years before the war I was based at my bank's branch in Paris, where I met Jean's mother. After we were married it is quite possible that I might have stayed there longer, but the threat of war convinced me that the family should return to London. But I will say that I certainly enjoyed my time in France, and am still quite fluent in the language.'

At this juncture I felt that it would be appropriate to share the news of our engagement before we were joined by all the family. Holding Céleste's hand as we sat together on the sofa, I began.

'As I told you, Pa, I have some news to share with you,' now suddenly feeling surprisingly nervous. 'Céleste has consented to become my wife, and for reasons that I will explain shortly to you, we are now informally engaged.'

His smile, as it spread across his face, expressed his feelings at my announcement, and he stood up, coming over to shake my hand, and stooping to kiss Céleste, he offered us his warmest congratulations.

'I'm so pleased my dear boy, and may I say that you make a lovely couple. This calls for a celebration, of course. I'll go and fetch a bottle of champagne, and ask Estelle to join us.'

'Thanks, Pa, but first I need to explain why we are keeping our engagement quiet for the moment. Unfortunately, Céleste's father had hopes that she was to marry the son of an adjoining farmer, who she has rejected, which leaves matters unclear at present in France.'

'And am I right in thinking that land is at the heart of this?' Daniel queried, his incisive understanding of the French farmer so well-honed after many years of dealing with such matters at the bank.

'Yes, but we have found a solution, we think, which we must put to him before I ask for his consent to the hand of his daughter. I'm hopeful that everything will be resolved on my next visit to Evian, so we won't be telling Gaston or Florette until then.'

'But you are both sure that you will marry regardless of this problem, I assume?'

'Oh yes, we are quite certain of that,' exclaimed Céleste, squeezing my hand in hers.

'Then that is all that really matters,' came Daniel's response, and, turning to the door, said, 'I'll fetch Estelle, and the children. I won't be long.'

We sat down again, Céleste commenting, 'Your father is very charming, I think.'

At this I smiled inwardly, remembering his reputation of old as a ladies' man.

A few minutes later Daniel re-appeared, a bottle of champagne in his hand, Estelle and the two children at his side, excited no doubt to meet the new visitor.

Putting down the bottle, he effected introductions as we proffered our gifts for the children and flowers for Estelle, who after thanking us was earnestly in conversation with Céleste, prompted by an obvious sense of mutual liking. The children, Caroline and her younger brother Geoffrey, were keen to show off their 'schoolboy' French to this new visitor, who kindly responded to their attempts in her native tongue, her replies spoken slowly, at a pace equal to their own.

Meanwhile Daniel had uncorked the bottle, and filled glasses were handed around. He then proposed a toast, wishing us both much happiness, which was gladly acknowledged.

Estelle asked if we had yet set a date for the wedding, being unaware as yet of the situation in France, so I gave a non-committal response indicating that it would probably be later in the year, nothing having been decided yet. I assumed that my father would let Estelle know a little more of our problem after we had left.

To the delight of the children Céleste joined them on being invited to a tour of the house, while Estelle said she would take this opportunity to go and prepare tea. This left me alone with my father, who immediately offered to help in any way that he could to resolve the problem in France. I explained the situation to him in a little more detail and assured him again that we had found a solution, and had enlisted the help of both my notaire and agent in the matter. This seemed to satisfy his concern, adding that he felt certain that I wouldn't enter into any transaction lightly, and without due consideration. I went on to say that the marriage would be in France and, of course he and Estelle, together with the children would be invited.

'Céleste is a beautiful young woman with such a kindly, intelligent nature,' he observed. 'Your mutual happiness is clear to see, and I think you are a most fortunate young man.' Saying this he put his arms round my shoulder in an embrace, something he had not done for many years, and which I found quite moving. He asked whether I intended to keep the house in Evian and I could only reply that for the present I certainly would, but no final decision had yet been made as to the future.

We were now interrupted by the return of two rather excitable children, Céleste in their wake, the tour of the house having clearly proved a success.

'Is it true Céleste will become our sister when she marries Jean, Daddy?' asked Caroline, her eyes shining with fondness for her new-found friend.

'Well, she will certainly be your sister-in-law, which is much the same, I suppose.' Daniel responded, smiling, much to her obvious delight.

Then, on hearing Estelle calling that tea was now ready, we all trooped downstairs, Caroline and Geoffrey both hand in hand with Céleste.

Eventually, after a further pleasant hour spent discussing the latest gossip as we ate our tea, it was time for us to return to the cottage. Estelle had arranged to meet up with Céleste on Tuesday, while I would be at the office, and had promised to be her guide to London for the day. So we said our goodbyes, with promises to all meet again soon. I certainly felt pleased that relations with my father had thawed since our previous meeting, and could only feel that the presence of my fiancée had played a significant role in this.

CHAPTER THIRTY-THREE
Haute-Savoie Beckons

I spent some time on Monday speaking again with Monsieur Durand, who had been successful in being able to finalise details of the farm purchase on my behalf. It had been agreed that Jacques Martin would act as the notaire, he in turn having confirmed that he would try and arrange for a preliminary contract to be ready for signature by the end of the following week.

The rest of the week passed quickly enough, my time being taken up at the office during the day. Céleste was now busily involved carrying out her translation work, interspersed with an occasional outing. At these times she accompanied Estelle on what she described as 'educational visits' to a number of the many art galleries and museums that abounded throughout the capital.

Our evenings were spent quietly together. Sometimes we simply stayed at home in the cottage, at other times visiting a local restaurant or pub. We took these opportunities to discuss in further detail the plans for my eventual move to France, after which time we would finally set a date for our wedding. L'église St André, by the lake, was our choice for the wedding ceremony – Florette was so pleased! Céleste was quite adamant that her mother would expect the reception to be celebrated at the farm, as this had always been a family tradition.

Céleste regularly kept in touch with her mother at this time, and understood that her father now realised fully how hurtful his harsh words had been to his daughter. 'Maman thinks that if I return in the next few days, she is sure that Papa is ready to apologise to me. They will both then wish me to return home to the farm, I'm sure, which I'll be happy to do, though I will miss my pretty room in Evian.'

'But we'll both be living there once we're married, my darling, and then we'll be together, finally,' I asserted. 'In the meantime I'll make the arrangements to return to Les Cyclamens, in order that you can see your father. I suggest we fly to Geneva next Thursday, and we can meet up with your parents the following day.'

Over the course of the next few days I booked our flights, and let Gaston know of our plan. It was agreed that he would meet us at the airport, and drive us back home. He updated me on the present situation in France. The widespread strikes were continuing, factories and major stores occupied by the workers, rubbish lay uncollected in the streets. Petrol was no longer generally available, but he had ensured that the Citroën was kept fuelled. 'There are rumours that De Gaulle has fled France, M'sieur Jean,' he continued. 'The country is deeply divided. Yesterday it was the turn of the Gaullist supporters to march in Paris to show their solidarity with the embattled President. There is no sign of any return to normality yet, but life carries on for us here in Evian. I will meet you both as arranged next week with the car. A bientôt, M'sieur Jean.'

Céleste and I were both conscious that our time together in London was coming to a close, so I endeavoured to arrange a theatre outing and dinner with my father and Estelle, before we left for France. They had both already come to regard my fiancée as a good friend. It seemed to me that Céleste had acted as the glue that now bound us all closer together, and I began to appreciate Estelle for the first time as the intelligent, caring young woman that she truly was, rather than 'that creature', as she had always been referred to by my mother.

Our return to France now imminent, with best wishes for our journey from my father and Estelle, we packed our suitcases, and prepared ourselves for the reception that might await us at the farm.

Thursday had arrived too soon, bringing our romantic interlude á deux to a close, and before long we found ourselves aboard our flight bound for Geneva. The weather was clear, with bright sunshine soon highlighting the majestic Alps, the peaks as ever snow-covered below us. The aircraft turned, as it made its final approach for landing, affording a panoramic view of the lake, shimmering in the morning sun.

Gaston was waiting for us in the Arrivals Lounge, a broad smile breaking out on his grizzled face the moment he saw us enter. After warmly greeting us, he insisted on taking Céleste's suitcase, and led us out to the waiting car.

This drive was certainly less fraught than the previous occasion, which had seen Céleste break down, and confide to Gaston about the savage row with her father. Nonetheless, the memory of this was still fresh in her mind, but not mentioned, although referred to in a roundabout way when we spoke to him of the visit we had planned to the farm tomorrow.

Gaston had clearly been kept abreast of local developments by Amélie, for he was aware that Lucas, the grandson, had now agreed to assist with the farm. Our intended purchase of the adjoining farm, however, was not known to him at present. I had insisted that Amélie told no one, other than her husband, for fear that it might become common knowledge and arouse the interest of other farmers.

As we had both previously agreed, our engagement was not yet to be made known until I had received Vincent Bonnaire's consent, so for the moment we had to keep our own counsel in the matter, despite our eagerness to share this news with our old friend. Tomorrow, despite some trepidation felt by both of us, couldn't arrive soon enough.

Florette welcomed us both on arrival at the house, and being aware that Céleste would be staying for the night, confirmed that her room had been prepared in readiness. She would prepare tea, and bring it through to the salon when we were ready, perhaps after we had unpacked, and settled in first.

'Will you be dining at home tonight, Monsieur Jean?' she asked. 'I ordered a gigot of lamb in earlier from the butcher.'

'Marvellous!' I exclaimed, continuing, 'Perhaps we can all eat together this evening.' To this everyone was in agreement.

A short while later I was joined in the salon by Gaston. Céleste would join us later, having decided to take a bath after the journey.

It is so good to see you both back here, M'sieur Jean,' commented Gaston. 'I do believe Mademoiselle has become quite settled here, since her recent stay.'

'But she expects to return to the farm, if the meeting goes well tomorrow with her father.' I replied, at the same time wishing that I could let him know that she would soon be returning as my wife. Then, remembering the help he had given when Céleste had stayed at the house, I thanked him again.

'M'sieur Jean, I was only too pleased to be of service,' he replied. 'This business was very bad for the poor girl, but hopefully she will now be re-united with her father again. Of course, as you already know, her mother has been very supportive.'

'Yes, I realised when they dined with us that she was trying to warn me of the attention that was being paid by the farmer's son, and perhaps I dismissed the matter too lightly. But fortunately that episode seems to have been resolved.'

'Céleste is such a beautiful young woman,' said Gaston, a smile on his face, no doubt trying to prompt further reaction from me.

'Of course, I agree with that sentiment.' I replied. Then, attempting to change the subject, I told him about my acquisition of the adjoining farm, asking him to keep this knowledge to himself for the present.

He was able to grasp the rationale behind what I told him quickly, being well aware of the legal implications of inheritance in France. 'But this will surely involve you in great expense, M'sieur Jean?' he asked, curious to know more.

'It will hopefully satisfy Vincent, and of course Lucas, as to the long term future,' I explained carefully. 'I don't want there to be any question of Guillaume's family attempting to sway Vincent again with promises of further land,' I continued.

'I can't think many would be prepared to go to such lengths,' was his questioning reply.

'But it does make sense as a business proposition,' I answered, receiving only a knowing smile and a nod in response from him. Clearly he could sense that more than business was involved in this transaction.

We were shortly joined by Céleste, who regaled both Gaston and Florette, during tea, and later dinner, with her exploits in London.

Gaston was keen to tell us both of the latest twists and turns of the recent events in France. De Gaulle had disappeared at the end of May, apparently going to Baden-Baden to ensure the support of the army, before returning to France the next day, when eight hundred thousand of his supporters staged a march in Paris.

'Today it has been announced that they have called for a General Election on 23 June, so we will have to wait and see how the country reacts. But the strikes are beginning to falter it seems, so perhaps things will before long return to normal,' he explained. 'I see that your friend Monsieur Phillips has been very busy writing articles for a number of journals since we last met him at Evian.'

I agreed that I must contact him again, but did not explain that I was waiting to receive Vincent's permission to marry his daughter before I made news of our engagement official.

The evening passed pleasantly for us all, despite any misgivings Céleste or I were feeling about the meeting at the farm tomorrow.

CHAPTER THIRTY-FOUR
A Happy Reconciliation

The following morning, after a leisurely breakfast, Céleste and I attended the offices of Jacques Martin to discuss the contract relating to the purchase of the farm. We were greeted warmly by Clarisse, who, on being introduced to Céleste, was clearly intrigued, and left guessing as to my relationship with this young woman who was to be my joint signatory on the document. She informed Jacques that we had arrived, and he came out of his office to meet us, making some attempt not to show a modicum of agreeable surprise, welcoming my companion as he took her hand, with a well practiced 'Enchanté mademoiselle, enchanté.'

He ushered us through to his private office, after asking Clarisse to bring in coffee, as we would be engaged with our business for some time. After some general conversation he turned to the matter in hand. He confirmed that Monsieur Berger, the farmer, was now in the process of buying an apartment, the indications being that he would like to complete the business within the next month. As the financial arrangements for our purchase were in place, it only remained for us to sign the document when ready.

Having discussed earlier my plans for the future of the farm, he confirmed that he could prepare a suitable legal agreement that would encompass my requirements.

'I note that you share the same surname as Vincent

Bonnaire, the prospective tenant, Mademoiselle. Are you related?' Jacques enquired, turning to Céleste.

'Yes, he is my father,' she replied, looking towards me, but adding nothing further.

A knowing look from Jacques indicated that he now had a better understanding of my relationship with the Bonnaire family.

Our business concluded for the present, we returned to the house, where Florette had prepared a light lunch, at our request. Our appetites were somewhat affected by a feeling of anxiety over meeting with her parents in the afternoon.

Over lunch we discussed how we would address the question of the farm, both agreeing that Céleste should initially raise this subject when she was alone with her father, Vincent. But only, I stressed, if their conversation had first led to the hoped-for reconciliation. I could sense the trepidation she was feeling about this meeting with her father, and did not wish to add further to her unease.

Meanwhile, I continued, I would be speaking with Amélie, and announce my wish to marry her daughter. I also intended to discuss with her the future plans for Lucas, the nephew, and our purchase of Monsieur Berger's farm. We went over everything once more as I drove the Citroën up towards the farm.

The door was opened upon our arrival by her parents, both standing together, which I took to be a good sign. Amélie greeted us both warmly with a fond embrace, obviously pleased to see her daughter back home again. Vincent was more circumspect, though nonetheless he embraced his daughter, and then shook my hand. It was Amélie who spoke first, suggesting that her husband and daughter may wish to go into the study, to talk alone, while she would take me through to the kitchen. We could all join together later in the salon.

Agreeing to this, I followed Amélie, and we both seated ourselves at the neatly scrubbed table, bedecked as usual with a vase of freshly collected blooms from the garden.

'I am so pleased to see you again, Jean,' she began, before continuing, 'I must thank you for allowing Céleste to stay in Evian. It has been a most troubling time for everybody.' She gave a sigh, and despite her apparently bright demeanour, I sensed that these past weeks had taken their toll. I could only begin to imagine the atmosphere in the house during this time.

'I understand your concern, of course. This has been such a difficult time for Céleste too, and I do hope she can be reconciled again with her father today.' I replied. 'They always seemed to be so close before this disagreement arose.'

'But I'm afraid that they are too similar in many ways,' Amelie continued, 'they can both be stubborn if they believe their point of view is the correct one.'

'Yes, I haven't failed to notice that your daughter certainly knows her own mind.' I remarked, with a smile on my face.

'That's true,' she agreed, 'she's certainly no shrinking violet when there is a point to be made, which I have always felt could be a problem if she was to meet someone with a similar disposition. Don't you agree, Jean?'

'I can see that would be the recipe for a volatile relationship, but fortunately I'm more of a pragmatist.' I responded, hoping that I could now introduce the subject of marriage into the conversation.

Aware of a tightness in my throat, in an earnest voice I confided, 'Amélie, I think you have already guessed that it is my dearest wish to marry your daughter. I am pleased to say that she has agreed to become my wife. But, of course, I would like to receive her father's consent first, before announcing our engagement, particularly in light of the recent difficulties.'

'Oh Jean, I am so happy for you both!' she exclaimed, taking my hand in hers, a look of genuine pleasure on her face. 'I have sensed for some time that you were both destined to be together. Céleste was always so excited whenever she mentioned you, between your recent visits here.' Then, giving the matter some thought, and looking more serious, added, 'But where will you live?'

'I shall be moving permanently to Evian, before long, to work as a consultant in France for my English law firm,' I was quick to reply, knowing that this would add to her feeling of happiness.

Her delight at this news was unreserved; the knowledge that her daughter and son-in-law would be living locally was clearly joyous news, and she embraced me lovingly.

'I will speak to your husband, if I may, once Céleste has finished,' I said, recovering my own emotions a little, after her display of obvious pleasure. 'In the meantime I can let you know what progress we have made with the Berger farm. My notaire has a contract ready to be signed, once your husband has agreed to our plan.'

'Lucas is very excited about coming to work with his grandfather, and, as you have indicated, the Berger farm may one day be his. Vincent will now be able to carry out his plans for expansion, and so the future will be assured. As you know, Jean, his plans for the future of the farm, and collusion from a neighbouring family, was behind the terrible argument he had with Céleste.'

I nodded at this, knowing the story only too well.

Clearly there would be much more discussion once the purchase of the Berger farm had been made known to Vincent by his daughter. Hearing no sign of raised voices in the background I assumed that this bode well for the sought-after reconciliation.

Shortly, as we heard them approaching, we looked up to see Céleste and her father, both now arm in arm, and looking much more at ease. She came over to me, her face lit by a smile, and quietly whispered that she had told her father about the farm, to which he had been most responsive. It appeared he had already guessed that we were intending to marry, no doubt following recent conversations with his wife.

Standing up, I now asked him if we could speak alone for a while, and he graciously suggested that we go into his study, while we left mother and daughter to share the happy outcome of their earlier conversations.

Vincent offered me a seat before confirming that the disagreement with his daughter had now been resolved. 'I had been blinded by my own wishes,' he confessed, 'and failed to comprehend how my daughter would stand in all this. But the sadness I have felt during these last few weeks finally cleared my mind, and I realise now that I had been almost tricked into putting the promise of land from my neighbours before my daughter's happiness.' He paused for a moment, before continuing. 'Céleste has told me that she is happy to return home again, which will delight both her mother and me.'

'I'm so pleased you've settled your differences,' I replied, happy that they were once more reunited. 'I believe she has spoken to you already about the Berger farm.'

'She has explained this briefly to me, and my understanding is that I will be offered a lease.'

'Céleste tells me that this farm would provide both you, and your grandson Lucas, with the possibilities that you seek, and of course the details we can agree later.'

'You have considered this matter carefully,' responded Vincent, 'and I agree that this offers Lucas an option that many young men would willingly accept.' He paused momentarily, before continuing. 'Surely this must be costing you a great deal of money. Are you really prepared to do this for your friendship with my daughter?' He asked, looking at me, a curious expression on his face.

'Monsieur Bonnaire, I hope that you have already seen the fondness we have for each other, and I must say it is now my dearest wish that she becomes my wife.' I hesitated momentarily, as he absorbed what I had said, before continuing, 'I would ask you, most humbly, to give your consent to this marriage. I will love and cherish her for as long as I live.'

This brought a hint of tearfulness to Vincent's eyes, for despite the recent troubles he had always loved his daughter. Being the youngest child, she had always held a special place in his heart. 'What can I say, Jean. I know my daughter well enough to be certain that she will do as she wishes, even if her parents disagreed. But I can see that you both have great feelings for one another, and can only wish you both as strong a marriage as I have with my own wife. I am very happy to give my consent. But, please, let us do away with formalities. You must address me as Vincent.' Saying this he got up from his chair, shaking my hand, before he embraced me.

'Now, let us join the others, I'm sure they will be anxiously waiting.' Vincent added, with a smile now on his face.

We joined them in the salon, our expressions showing that all had been agreed, much to the delight of everyone.

'This calls for a celebration,' exclaimed Vincent. 'I will fetch a bottle of champagne, so that we can propose a toast to the happy couple.'

While he was out of the room Amélie embraced me again, excitedly saying that there hadn't been a wedding at the farm for ten years, not since her daughter Chloé was married.

After an eloquent speech made by Vincent, in which he welcomed me to the family, to murmurs of approval, we drained our glasses.

Amélie and Céleste brought in the tea they had prepared from the kitchen. We ate, while at the same time discussing future plans for the wedding, my intended move to France, as well as Vincent's ideas for the newly acquired farm.

Finally it was time for us to set off to collect Céleste's belongings, which she would be taking with her on her return home later that evening.

CHAPTER THIRTY-FIVE
Return to Evian

Now delighted that her parents had consented to our marriage, I suggested we should celebrate privately, before returning to the house. We decided to call at the hotel by the lake where we had previously dined, and were greeted by the maître d'. Upon hearing my request for champagne, and guessing at a special occasion, he thoughtfully showed us to a secluded table in the bar.

Our glasses charged, I now proposed a toast to our future happiness. Drawing out the Cartier case from my pocket, and holding Céleste's left hand, continued, 'Darling, you have made me so happy by accepting me as your husband,' as I slipped the ring on her finger.

She held up her hand, displaying the ring to me, which now fitted perfectly. Leaning over she kissed me, murmuring, 'I am also very happy that we don't have to keep our engagement a secret any longer, Jean – I want everyone to share in our happiness.'

'So shall we return to the house now so that Florette and Gaston can share in our happiness,' I ventured.

'Oh yes, I can't wait to let them both know. They've been so kind and helpful to me.'

We left the hotel together, arm in arm, about to cross the road to the car parked by the lake, when Céleste hesitated, laughingly saying 'Jean, in all this excitement, I've left my handbag under the seat. You go on, while I quickly fetch it.'

Unlocking the car I looked over to see her coming towards me from the hotel, a smile on her face as she now held the bag aloft in her hand.

Then I froze, as I suddenly became aware of a dark Peugeot saloon hurtling towards her, seemingly out of nowhere, as she crossed the road. My shouted warning came too late as the car struck her a glancing blow, before speeding off out of sight.

Panic-stricken I rushed over to her apparently lifeless body, holding her in my arms, only vaguely aware of shouted instructions to call an ambulance coming somewhere from the small crowd that was now gathering.

Other onlookers hastened to direct traffic around the two figures now locked in a silent embrace in the middle of the road; the still, brooding waters of the lake ever present in the background.

THE END

Historical Note

One of the effects of the Great War had been the displacement of large numbers of the civilian population in areas where fighting occurred. Areas occupied by the enemy were to the north and east of France in the Pas de Calais and along the Belgian border; in all a total of ten departements were either fully or partially occupied during the course of the war.

In the early months of the war this had resulted in many panic-stricken refugees fleeing the onslaught of their own accord, leaving their homes in the combat zones by whatever means possible, often with little or no possessions or money. Others were forced into exile on the orders of the French government, in an attempt to clear areas affected by the conflict, and special trains were arranged to remove them to safety.

Bilateral agreements, signed between the warring countries bordering Switzerland, allowed for civilians that could not be mobilised in the war effort to return to their country of origin, through the Office for the Repatriation of Civilian Prisoners, founded in September 1914, and set up in Bern. This would normally include women, children to the age of seventeen, and men who were either sick, infirm or above the age of sixty. Whilst the process of repatriation may seem to be founded on humanitarian principles, the movement of people out of occupied areas very much depended upon German strategic and economic imperatives.

Initially, those repatriated were French citizens who either found themselves in Germany at the outbreak of the war, or had been transported over the German border following the occupation of their area in the early stages of the war. By early 1915, however, repatriation began by rail directly from the invaded departements of France, and with the numbers greatly increasing, Geneva became the Swiss hub, with the refugees finally arriving by tram in the French town of Annemasse, close to the border, where the French Repatriation Service was initially set up.

Here the Repatriation Service carried out its role of receiving and registering the French repatriates, providing temporary accommodation and healthcare, before sending them on to other departements, effectively becoming a short-stay staging post. As each group arrived in Annemasse by tram it was intended to process them within a few hours, arranging an onward journey by train from the nearby stations of Thonon and Evian. The lucky few, having been claimed by family members from unoccupied France, were allowed to make their own travel arrangements, while others in need of medical care were directed to the nearest hospitals.

The system introduced in Annemasse began to reach saturation point, and this became clear, as numbers being processed continued to increase. A large numbers of complaints were being made that not enough time was being devoted, by the now overwhelmed service, to establish places of origin, locate family members or provide adequate hospitality.

By late 1916 it was decided that Evian, with its superior hotel and medical facilities, thanks to its spa and tourism trade, would become the new reception centre, replacing Annemasse. Trains would now bypass Geneva, heading instead eastwards on the northern lakeshore, arriving at St Gingolph on the French border and then onwards to Evian.

A planned break in the arrival of convoys between Christmas 1916 and mid-January 1917 allowed for the transfer of services to the spa town, and arrivals would be welcomed at the recently built casino, now a major landmark in the town, with its large domed cupola, and situated overlooking Lake Geneva (Lac Leman). This provided the space to accommodate an enlarged service, which, together with a number of charitable organisations, could cater for the needs of the ever increasing numbers in the convoys. There were now two trains arriving each day: one in the morning, the other in the early evening, bringing between 600 and 650 people at a time.

Over the course of the war some half a million people were repatriated through Haute Savoie, the majority in the years 1917–18 when the Repatriation Service was based in Evian.